Dancing In Sin

Sins and Obsession Duet

The Marchetti Family
Book 1

kelly Kelsey

Copyright © 2024 By Kelly Kelsey

All rights reserved.

No part of this book may be reproduced in any form or by any electronic or mechanical means, including information storage and retrieval systems, without written permission from the author, except for the use of brief quotations in a book review.

This is a work of fiction. Names, characters, places, and incidents are either the product of the author's imagination or are used fictitiously. Any resemblance to actual persons, living or dead, events, or locales is entirely coincidental.

Cover design by Crowe Abbey Covers

Editing by Ce-ce Cox of Outside Eyes Editing and Proofreading

Proofreading by Mich

❦ Created with Vellum

If you are looking for a nice, hearts and flowers type of Hero, then this is not the book for you. Now if red is your favorite color, then you are in the right place. Nico Marchetti is every shade of red, over the top, morally gray and alpha in all the best ways. So, buckle up and make sure you have a spare pair of panties because Nico awaits you in all his deliciousness and red flag glory....

Trigger Warnings

Somnophilia
Dubious Consent
Violence (Not toward the heroine)
Controlling Behavior
Mine, Mine, Mine
Red Flags Everywhere
Morally Grey Alpha Male

Playlist

- Morally Grey - April Jai
- Middle of the Night - Elley Duhe
- Love in Ruins - Gyffin, Sinead Harnett, Luxlyfe
- Sound off the Sirens - Sam Tinnesz
- Wrong -- Max Schneider (feat. Lil Uzi Vert)
- Gasoline - Halsey
- Adrenaline Rush -- (feat. MORGAN) Sigma, MORGAN
- Supermassive Black Hole – Muse
- She Drives Me Crazy – Fine Young Cannibals
- Many of Horror – Biffy Clyro
- Closer - Nine Inch Nails
- Radioactive - Imagine Dragons

Chapter 1

Nico

My black loafers pound on the tile floor as I make my way to my office. Dante Vitale, my best friend since we were children and a capo of mine, follows close behind. The loud bass of the music vibrates off the walls, through to my chest as the noise pounds in my ears. We are at The Executive Club, my high-class gentleman's establishment. I haven't been here for a while, too caught up in business with the Marchetti *famiglia*. *My* family.

My papà is Lorenzo Marchetti, Don of the most powerful organized crime family ruling New York and Capi Di Tutti Capi of the Cosa Nostra. I have been primed since the day I was born to follow in my papà's footsteps and will eventually fulfill my legacy, my birthright, when the day comes for him to eventually step down. For now, I am his second in command, his underboss, learning everything there is to know and helping him rule the *famiglia* and our city with an iron fist.

"Leo informed me that we had some new girls start a couple weeks ago," Dante says from behind me. Leo is the manager here at The Executive Club. Like most of my inner circle and friends, he is someone I have known since childhood. I know that he is someone I can trust to run the place, which is why I gave him the position in the first place.

"Have him bring their files to the office, so we can look over them," I grunt. It's something Dante and I always do. Personally go over every new girl's file and vet them. It's for our employee's safety more than anything, but it's also to make sure the people I have work here don't have any affiliation with or are spies planted by our enemies. We don't want that. We like to know who we are bringing into our clubs.

"Already asked for them," he responds drily, a hint of insult in his voice that I even asked him.

Pushing through the door to my office, I round my desk and take a seat. My gaze shifts to the blackout window that overlooks the whole club. I can see everything that happens down there, but nobody can see what goes on up here. Exactly how I like it.

"Drink?" Dante asks as he pours his glass of whiskey from my bar cart.

"Macallan." I drawl as I start up my laptop.

Logging into the system, I pull up my emails and start to go through them. It's mainly boring shit. Figures. Consignments. Outgoings. Profits. All stuff I hate to look at but know I need to, to keep the place running smoothly. Though I trust Leo, I like to see for myself what's going on with my businesses.

Dante places my drink on a coaster before dropping down in the seat opposite me. I focus back on my laptop, only for my head to snap up when a heavy knock raps at the door. "Come in," I say, knowing full well that it will be my manager. The door pushes open almost immediately and Leo steps inside, confirming my thoughts.

"I have the files for you," he says, holding up what looks to be several manilla folders.

"Thanks. Take a seat." I motion to the empty chair beside Dante.

Doing as I asked, he drops the files on the desk and sits. "We have four new starters. I did the necessary checks, and they all came back fine." He gets straight to it, telling me exactly what I want to know. Leo clears his throat. "One of the girls. I couldn't find any background information on her. In fact, she is kind of a ghost..." I glare at him, and he trails off. "Look Nico, she was desperate for a job. Told me that she lost all her family, and she was all alone in this world. I didn't outright ask her, but I dropped hints about your enemies, etcetera, etcetera, and she was confused when I started spouting shit. She didn't have a clue what I was talking about. So, I passed her."

"It doesn't work like that, and you know it." I bite out.

"I know. I know. But she has this whole innocent thing going on and the clients love her." He sighs. "Honestly, I think I'm quite good at reading people and she isn't a spy Nico. I know that much."

"That's for me to decide," I growl, my skin heating with anger. Leo knows better than this.

He holds his hands up in surrender, trying to placate me. He knows he fucked up though, the next words out of his mouth confirm as much. "Okay, man. You're right. I messed up by going against our usual protocol. But my gut told me she was fine. Meet her for yourself. I think you will agree." He rushes the words out, trying to save his ass.

"Your gut won't save you if the Russians fire up the place." My jaw is clenched, my body tense with rage. Leo feels it, the darkness surrounding me, and swallows. Good. Had it been anyone else, I would have fired their ass by now, taken them to the basement, and inflicted untold pain on them. Being a friend gives him a little grace. Not much. But it's why he is still sitting here.

"Is she working tonight?" Dante asks, trying to break the tension.

Leo glances at him, scrubbing a palm down his face. "Yeah. She has been here for two weeks and is on the roster every night. I asked if she wanted at least one night off but she said she needed the money. And like I said, our clients love her. She is our most popular girl. Men are coming from all over the city just to watch her dance. Our profits are up by at least fifty percent since she started." He rambles on, trying to downplay his fuck up.

"Bring her to me," I demand, my tone leaving no room for argument.

Leo nods, pushing out of his chair. "I will go get her." Rushing toward the door like his ass is on fire, he disappears in the next second.

I shake my head, blowing out a breath. "I swear he is getting softer the older he gets. Hiring girls because he feels sorry for them and without using the proper protocol? I might need to rethink his position here."

Dante snorts. "He is twenty-eight, the same as us. You don't see us getting soft. I also don't think there is more to it than what he told us. My guess is his dick got hard for the girl and that ruled his decision."

I mull over Dante's words for a minute, shaking my head when I come to the same conclusion. "You're right. But Leo was spared some of the stuff we went through. He isn't in this life like we are. He fucked up this time, but he is our friend. I trust that he wouldn't compromise this place by making a rash decision just because he took a liking to a piece of pussy, no matter how much he liked her."

"You know as well as I do, that he wants to fuck whoever this girl is and that's the only reason he hired her without doing a thorough vetting." Dante laughs.

I shrug nonchalantly but my curiosity is officially piqued.

"Maybe. Guess we will see what's so special about her when he brings her up here."

"Guess we will." He shakes his head, amusement flashing in his eyes. "He knows he can't fuck the dancers, so it was pointless hiring her if that's what he wants. He knows full well there is a no fraternizing policy. He fucking manages this place." He grunts.

Steepling my fingers in front of my chin, I wait for Leo to return. I am officially intrigued as to why my manager made an exception for this girl. It's not like all of our dancers aren't beautiful because they are. We only hire beautiful women because The Executive Club is high-end. All our clients are rich - you have to be with what it costs to have membership here. My club is the perfect place if you are looking for discretion, which is why the client list is prestigious. A mixture of politicians, movie stars, Wall Street traders, and business owners frequent here most nights, which is also helpful if I ever need to call in a favor. I have so much shit on most of these guys, they are all just waiting to do my bidding should I ask.

Any man with money and looking for a good time, you can guarantee they are a member of The Executive Club. Which is why the caliber of girls that work here is high. A couple of them are even catwalk models who are looking to earn extra cash. And they do because they are fucking gorgeous. The men love them, and they pay them the big bucks. Sometimes more than they would ever earn on a modeling job. This leads me to my next thought and the reason my curiosity is getting the better of me. What is it about this new girl that has all my members losing their damn minds and my manager acting so recklessly?

A knock on the door drags me from my thoughts. I know it's Leo, so I call for him to enter. He steps inside my office. For a second, I think he is alone until I see a bare pair of legs shifting behind him. The *girl*. My head cocks to the side, as I try to get a good look at her, but it's no use because Leo is shielding her with his big body. I frown at the protective stance of my friend, at the tension currently radiating from his body. My jaw clenches. I am over whatever claim he thinks he has on her. Narrowing my eyes, I jerk my head, silently asking him to get a move on. Sighing, he reaches back, taking her hand in his. My nostrils flare in anger as something like possession surges through my body. *What the fuck?* I don't know why, nor do I understand it, but it's there all the same and I haven't even laid eyes on the fucking woman. I have never, not once in my life, felt possessive over pussy. But right now, I am trying to hold myself back from killing my friend just because he is holding her hand.

Inhaling a breath, I try to calm my racing thoughts and my pounding heart. Running a finger across my bottom lip, I watch my friend with maddening interest, studying him for any sign of what he is thinking, but his blank face gives nothing away. When I feel controlled enough to speak, I say. "Well?"

Leo tenses but having known me long enough by now, he knows what I want with that one word and if he knows what's good for him, he will not disobey me. His eyes squeeze shut for a brief second and then without saying anything he pulls the girl in front of him. My gaze rakes over her and when it lands on her face the damn air is knocked from my lungs.

Fuck. Me.

Now I see exactly the reason why she is so popular with our customers, and why Leo didn't vet her properly. I don't think there is a word to describe this girl. Stunning or beautiful don't do her justice. She is just more than both those words. So much more.

My eyes roam over every inch of the scared-looking petite girl, studying her, and taking all her beauty in and committing it to memory. Fresh, innocent face with only a lick of mascara and

Dancing In Sin

something glossy on her pouty lips. Lips that were made to suck cock. *My cock.* I shake the thought away so I can carry on my perusal, and I am happy with what else I find. Big sapphire blue eyes. Perfect round breasts and a waist so tiny, I could circle it with one of my large hands. Long, tan legs that look like they go on for miles. And the pièce de résistance and a fetish of mine. Blonde hair so long that it nearly touches her heart-shaped ass which I get a little glimpse of from the way she stands.

Yeah, I can *definitely* see why Leo made an exception. Still, it doesn't excuse his irresponsible behavior. He shouldn't have just allowed her to work here without the necessary checks. And I can't be seen to let him get away with it, no matter how beautiful she is. I know I said there were no words to describe her beauty, but she is probably the most exquisite thing I have ever seen – and that's saying something considering I am surrounded by gorgeous women. I have to blink a couple of times to make sure she is in fact real and I'm not just seeing things.

But she is real. So very real and so fucking beautiful that it almost hurts to look at her. She stares at me with those big, blue, hypnotic eyes. She looks so innocent. So damn sweet. My cock hardens in my pants, and I shift to allow it some room. Not wanting to give away the effect she is having on me, I narrow my eyes. Jerking my head to the empty seat, I bark out. "Sit."

She jumps at the bite in my words, before scrambling to the chair and sitting, like a good little girl. Hmm. Submissive. The things I could do to her. Teach her... I shake my head. Nope. Not going there. I have never fucked a woman that works for me and I'm not about to start now. She will not be the exception, even if she is the most beautiful thing I have ever seen. *But what if she didn't work for you?* The devil on my shoulder asks. I block out the words and focus on the girl in front of me.

"What's your name?" I don't miss the way she stiffens, her

whole body going rigid with that one question. My eyes narrow at her reaction but she quickly recovers, her face going completely blank. I search her face, for any sign of anxiety or discomfort but when I find none, I almost begin to think I read her wrong. Questions circle in my head, but they are soon forgotten when the most angelic voice I have ever heard breaks the silence in the room.

"Ocean. My name is Ocean."

Chapter 2

Ocean

My whole body trembles under his cold blue gaze. He scrutinizes me in a way that makes me both come alive, and want to shrink into myself. I don't know whether he believes me when I tell him my name, but it's all he is getting, no matter how much he scares me. My fake ID says Ocean Embers, and that is who I am. I was reborn the day I left my old life and that was the day I became Ocean.

A friend from back home put me in touch with someone who could make me a really good fake ID. She wasn't lying. It is so good that no one would question that it's not real – well no one but maybe this guy. One look at him and I can tell that he is not to be messed with. He exudes power. Money... All the things I am running from. And I know without a doubt that he has the resources to find out my truth and, unlike Leo, I don't think I will be able to use my looks or innocence to my advantage with this guy. He will see right through that, which is why I need to put my mask in place and keep calm. Though my heart pounds erratically in my chest, I know that if I don't keep my cool right now, then it will give him more of a reason to look into me. I can't have that.

I have only been at The Executive Club for a couple of weeks and to be honest I thought everything was settled with me working here. Leo never mentioned any other guy wanting to interview me, so I kinda let my guard down and relaxed into my surroundings. That was my first mistake. I should know better by now. Know never to be careless or get comfortable. In the blink of an eye, things can change. I know that better than anyone.

Though I overheard some of the other girls talking about the mysterious owner, I never took much notice because, in the weeks that I have been here, I never saw him. But right now, at this moment, with his cold, detached eyes on me, I wish I had taken more interest in what they were saying. My gaze rakes over his face slowly, my pulse kicking up to an unnatural rhythm. There is something about him. He screams danger, and though he tries to hide it, I see the darkness lurking beneath the perfect features of his face. A face so handsome, he could easily lure you in and make you forget the danger. From that assumption alone, I should be getting as far away from him and this place as I can. But I can't. I need money and I make more of it here than I ever even dreamed of making when I came to New York. I know full well I wouldn't be earning the same anywhere else. The Executive is high end, and it shows with the thousands of dollars I take home every night.

"Ocean," he repeats my name, almost like he is tasting it on his tongue.

I swallow around the dryness in my throat and nod. "Did I do something wrong?"

His eyes narrow in on me as if he is trying to see straight through to my brain and all the thoughts currently running through me. "I don't know. Did you?" His words are taunting, and I know it's his way of trying to get a reaction out of me. I

Dancing In Sin

want to cower and hide but I stand tall, not letting him see my fear.

My brows jump, feigning confusion and I shake my head. "I-I-I don't think so." I stutter, committing myself to the scared girl act. Don't get me wrong, I am scared, but I can't show it right now.

"How old are you, Ocean?" he continues, as if I didn't even speak.

I swallow, glancing at the man beside me. He is hot and though he screams bad boy, he doesn't intimidate me like the man in front of me. His eyes narrow in on me, searching my face but before he can see something I don't want him to, I look at Leo who is now at my right side. Leo, with his kind eyes and soft, encouraging smile.

"Twenty-one." I finally say, turning back to the man who sits like a king at the desk. It's a lie but it's what's on my ID. I knew the only jobs I could possibly get in this city were as a waitress or a dancer. The latter pays more. But you have to be twenty-one, so that's the age I asked for.

He runs his thumb across his full bottom lip as narrowed, inquisitive, albeit suspicious, eyes watch me. A pulse starts between my legs. There is no doubt that this man is attractive, and he definitely knows it. With his pale blue eyes, dark hair, and bad-boy aura he is one hundred percent my type. Which is why I need to stay away from him.

"Twenty-one." He repeats my answer again as if he is a damn parrot.

Anger bubbles up in me. Wanting to get out of this room, which feels like it has no air, over this interrogation and feeling a little brave, I grit out. "Yes. Now may I leave? I'm due on stage," I glance at my watch, "in twenty minutes and I need to get ready."

His eyes spark and I have no doubt it's at the tone of my

voice. I bet this man has never had anyone talk back to him or show him attitude. He smirks. "No. You may not. Leo will get you covered." He throws a pointed look at Leo who scrambles out of his seat and disappears to do his bidding. *Traitor.* He told me he would be by my side the whole time and now he runs away with his tail between his legs, leaving me to deal with this man alone. I shift uncomfortably now that my ally has gone. Leo has been a friend of sorts since I started here, and I felt safe with him – well, as safe as a girl like me could – but now I just feel let down. Logically, I know it's stupid of me to feel this way, but I can't help but feel disappointed that he didn't at least fight to stay here with me. Now he is gone and I'm here with two strangers, I feel like I'm prey that just got caught in the predator's lair. By the smirk on the asshole's face, he knows it too.

Leaning back in his chair, his gaze never leaves me. I squirm under his intense scrutiny though my face looks unfazed. "Now *Ocean,* tell me. Why my club? Why did you want to work here specifically?"

I stare at him, wishing he would stop asking me questions right now, but something tells me I won't leave this office until I give him something. So, I give him the only thing I can. The truth. Well as much of the truth as I can without actually giving him anything.

"Because your club pays better than any of the others I interviewed at. I need to make money. I can do that here. Not that it's any of your business, but I also looked for waitressing jobs. Again, the pay was poor. I would have had to work more than a week to earn what I can in one night dancing here. I am a dancer. Have been since I was a child. Ballet to be precise. But I can acclimatize to most forms of dance. My parents died in a car crash nearly a year ago. I was left with nothing. I have no other family, so I had no other choice but to find work if I wanted to keep a roof over my head and food in my stomach." I finish, glancing away from him and his penetrating gaze. I don't want him to see the lies in my eyes.

"Hmm," he hums, making my attention shift back to him. "Okay, *Ocean*," the way he says my name, mocking but sensual, has wetness seeping into my panties. He smirks as if he knows the effect he has on me. "That's all. You can get back to work."

I jump out of my chair so quickly that I tumble forward and have to steady myself on his desk to stop myself from falling. "Thank you..." I trail off because I don't know his name.

"Mr. Marchetti." He drawls. "But you can call me Nico."

I nod, shooting him a cautious smile. "Thank you, Nico."

Before he can say anything else I practically run to the door, pulling it open in the next second. Stepping outside, I blow out the breath I was holding, only for my ears to prick when I hear a deep voice drawl. "Bad idea, Nico. You know it. I know it."

There is a huffed laugh and then I hear Nico's deep rumble. "Hmm. Maybe. But I always liked living life on the edge."

Deep laughter sounds and before I can hear anymore or try to analyze what any of their conversation even means, I make my way back to the changing room.

***

A couple of hours later, I am pushing the key into the door of the small room with a private bathroom, that I rent in an all-female hostel, shoving it open and stepping inside. Though it's a tiny space, it's cheap and only around four blocks from the club.

Blowing out a breath, I close and lock the door, then make my way over to my bed. I showered at the club, knowing I would be too exhausted to do it when I got home.

Dropping my bag down on the floor, I climb on the single bed and lie down. Staring at the ceiling, my thoughts go to the night and my time in Nico Marchetti's office. The intensity of him. The way he watched me. I shiver just thinking about it. Exhaling, I shake all thoughts of him from my head. I need to stay away from men like him. Not only does he exude danger, but he is also way too old for me. I don't know his exact age, but I would put him in his late twenties, or early thirties. I snort to myself at the fact that I even think that's the biggest issue here. His age is the least of my worries. I can't be getting involved with anyone, let alone him. I need to focus on my game plan and do what I came here to do. And that is making enough money to eventually get my own place. Something that I can call mine. Small and cute. Maybe in a small town. Somewhere that I can never be found by my father.

I shiver just thinking of that word and push all thoughts of *Daddy dearest* to the back of my head before I can even allow them to form.

I have managed this far without being caught. And I don't have any intention of him ever finding me.

As long as I lay low, and keep doing what I am doing, I should be fine.

I can't or won't accept any other outcome.

Because if he ever finds me...

My life will be over.

Chapter 3

Nico

A week has passed since the night I called Ocean into my office. And in that time, I have been to The Executive Club a grand total of... every damn fucking night.

Though I pretend that I am here to work, I have never been in the club this much and it hasn't escaped Dante's or Leo's notice – even though they would never say anything to me about my sudden obsessive interest in this place.

No matter what other shit I have going on, I always make an excuse to be here. It's infuriating to say the least. Because I know that no matter how much I try to lie to myself, my being here has nothing to do with running this club and everything to do with the enticing, petite, blonde-haired, blue-eyed girl. I groan inwardly. Those eyes... Just like her name, they are as blue as the Ocean. So unique in their color that I have never seen anything close to the shade of them in my life. Without a doubt, I could easily get lost in her, in *them,* if I allowed myself. And that's a problem.

A big *fucking* problem.

Fuck.

Running a frustrated hand through my hair, I blow out a breath, staring out the privacy window in my office. There is only one reason why I am here, and I grit my teeth as I wait for her to appear on stage. Like an obsessive stalker, I wait, just so I can catch a glimpse of her.

My door is pushed open, but I don't move, knowing exactly who has entered without even looking. There are only two people in this world that would come into my office without knocking and I know for a fact it's not my papà.

"Something interesting down there?" Dante drawls, humor lacing his tone.

Sometimes I hate the way he knows me so well. "Fuck off."

He barks out a laugh, coming to stand beside me and joining me in my staring mission. It's then that the object of my desire bounces out on stage, looking every bit as stunning as I remember. I straighten, my body heating with desire as she begins to move her perfect body to the music. I stare down at her, watching every single second of her set like my life depends on it. My cock hardens in my pants at the sight. *Christ*, she is seductive, enticing without even trying to be. She is by far the hottest thing I have ever seen in my life, and I can see why she is so popular.

Every set of eyes turns to look at her, lust-filled and wanting what's *mine*. My whole body tightens, possessiveness slithering through my veins like a living, breathing thing. Irrational anger courses through me, my hand reaching back on its own volition, wrapping around the handle of the gun that sits in the waistband of my pants. I would say that I am about five seconds away from going down there and shooting every one of the goddamn motherfucking perverts in the head for thinking they can look at her. A low whistle sounds beside me, snapping me from my murderous thoughts.

"Jesus. She really is stunning. Exquisite actually. Hottest

dancer we've had in this place. And Christ she can move that body."

I grip the gun tighter. For the first time in my life, I want to shoot my best friend in his asshole face. "Don't look at her," I growl.

He chuckles. "Man, I think I'm the least of your worries. Every fucker down there has eyes on her."

"Fuck," I curse, my free hand balling and slamming down on the shatterproof glass. I need to get my shit together. I don't let women affect me. Ever. And definitely not some little dancer that I am pretty sure has a few skeletons hiding in her closet.

"Jesus, Nic. You better pull yourself together." Dante repeats my own thoughts. "And fast. It's just pussy. And let's be honest here, you have plenty offering themselves to you on a platter. Let it go. Leave the girl alone. You know it can never be more than a fuck anyway. We *don't* fuck the dancers and you have..." He trails off, his gaze shifting to mine. My jaw clenches as I stare him down. Not only did he just remind me of the clause we have in place, but he also reminded me of what is expected of me. Blowing out a breath, he steps away from me and up to the bar cart where he pours us both a finger of whiskey. He's right. I know he is. But it doesn't stop these... I shake my head as if I can rid myself of this interest I have in the girl.

Ocean.

So fucking beautiful with her big innocent blue orbs that look exactly like the crystal-clear waters of paradise. I grimace. What the fuck? Why the hell am I even thinking of shit like that. Fucking clear waters of paradise? If Dante heard my thoughts right now, he would probably think I've gone crazy. Sighing, I throw one last glare at Ocean, who is just finishing up her set, then stride across to my desk and take a seat. This thing with the girl needs to be done with. I am all about control. I have to be in this life. And for some unknown reason, she makes me feel like it's slipping. I don't like it.

I need to forget about her and remember who I am. An underboss. Heir to a multi-million-dollar empire with a duty to my father. To my family. To the Cosa Nostra. And my responsibilities, they come before anything. Especially women. With those thoughts in mind, I push images of Ocean aside and decide to get out of here. Downing my whiskey, I push to a stand, my serious gaze locking on Dante.

"Let's get out of here."

***

"Ah, come in son." Sarcasm drips from my papà's voice as he pushes the whore on her knees at his feet away and zips up his pants. I'm disgusted at the scene in front of me, but I would be lying if I said it's the first time this has happened. I glower at him before shifting my disgust to the woman now scrambling to her feet. I will never understand why he constantly cheats on my mamma. Valentina Marchetti is a good woman. Beautiful. Classy. Loyal. And for some goddamn unknown reason, she loves him. "Leave us." He barks at the woman, making her squeak and rush out of his office like her ass is on fire. We are downtown at the high-rise building the Marchetti family owns and the place where we conduct meetings for our more...legitimate businesses. Construction. Property management. Restaurants. Nightclubs.

"Jesus. You don't even try to be discreet." I shake my head in disgust, running a palm down my face.

"When you are as powerful as I am, you don't need to be," he responds arrogantly.

"I don't get it. Mamma loves you. She is a good woman. Why would you even consider eating a burger when you have

Dancing In Sin

steak at home?" I would never refer to my mamma as steak but it's the only analogy I can come up with off the top of my head.

He huffs sardonically. "My boy. Come back and talk to me about this when you take a wife. You will see then exactly why I do the things I do. I have certain...tastes. Ones I would not expect *my* wife to take care of. Whores on the other hand, they will do anything if you flash them a bit of wealth and power."

I stare at him with disdain. Lorenzo Marchetti. My father. Mafia boss. Head of our *famiglia*. I can argue with him, but it will do me no good. He believes his words are law, therefore he will see it as disrespectful if I challenge him.

"You wanted to see me?" I grunt, taking a seat in front of his desk.

"Yes," he says, clearing his throat as he shuffles some paperwork. "It's about your sister." My spine snaps straight, tension filling every part of my body. This can only mean one thing. He has found a husband for her. "Franco Romano contacted me," he starts, and it doesn't relax me any. Franco Romano is the head of the Romano family and one of the five families in New York. It makes sense for my sister to marry into another powerful family. If Franco wants a deal with my father, then it must be his son Riccardo who is on the table. I have heard rumors about him. How he treats women. I don't want my sister anywhere near him and neither should my papà. No way can I agree to this shit.

"No," I say, cutting him off before he can say anything else.

His eyebrows raise in warning. "No," he repeats, his face twisting like he is sucking a lemon. "Last I checked, I am boss, Nicolas, and you will treat me as such." I don't miss the way he uses my full name. It's a thinly veiled warning to put me firmly back in my place.

"He will destroy Allegra." I hiss, not caring that I am being disrespectful. "She deserves better than someone like Riccardo Romano."

"That may be. But this alliance could bring us more power than we have ever had. It will give us a monopoly over the construction industry and Franco is willing to trade fifteen percent of his territory if the union happens. It makes good business sense." His voice leaves no room for argument, but argue I do.

"You would be willing to trade your own daughter for money? For more power? Don't you have enough? She isn't a piece of meat on the selling block for the highest bidder."

His face turns red in anger, and he pins me with a look. "Nico, stop. You know how our world works. This will be a good match. You have no say. I was just showing you a courtesy by telling you. Now remember your place and show me the respect a Don deserves." He growls, his meaty fist hitting his desk.

Pushing out of my chair, I laugh but it's humorless. "You are making a mistake," I bark out, but he just stares at me. "I won't let my sister be traded to that man. She will not survive it. He is a fucking animal."

"It's not up to you. I am considering it, so let it go. It's my decision and I will do what's best for the *famiglia,*" he roars with finality.

Shooting a look of disdain in his direction, I spin on my heel and stride to the door. It's not done. No way. As long as I am breathing, I will put a stop to this – even if it's the last thing I do.

Over my dead body will my sister marry Riccardo Romano.

Chapter 4

Ocean

The sound of knocking at my door has me groaning. Scrubbing the sleep from my tired, heavy, eyes all I can think about is the day I finally get my own place and won't have to deal with random interruptions from my sleep. Though, I am grateful that they had a space for me here – being it's strictly for women and safe – it will be nice to have peace and quiet. I sigh and remind myself of how lucky I am to have found this little hostel, even if I am irritated right now. Despite my irritation, I roll over, my gaze landing on the brown door.

"Yeah?" I croak before clearing my throat.

"Ocean, honey?" I recognize the voice as Valerie, the lady that runs the hostel. "I'm sorry to wake you dear, but I need you to open up so that the maintenance guy can check your bathroom. There is a leak somewhere in the building and he isn't sure where it's coming from." She tells me, regret heavy in her voice. Though some of the other staff don't mind, Valerie hates intruding on our space. It's one of the things I like about her. As long as you aren't doing anything illegal, she leaves well enough alone.

"Give me five. I just need to get dressed." I shout back. She doesn't respond, but I hear her mumble something to someone.

Dragging myself out of the bed, I pull on some sweats, my Converse, and a hoodie before moving to the bathroom. I make quick work of splashing my face with cold water and brushing my teeth. Stepping back into the bedroom, I grab my cell and pull the door open.

Valerie smiles at me. "Ocean, why don't you go down to the communal room? I made breakfast. Mr. Dobak is here for maintenance."

"Thanks." I nod, my eyes shifting to the man beside her. He stares at me lasciviously, his beady gaze roaming over my covered body. His eyes meet mine, a horrible smirk curving his lips. I shiver, suddenly feeling uneasy about him going into my room.

"Go on now, dear. I will help Mr. Dobak." She jerks her head, her eyes imploring me. I understand what she is saying without her saying it. She won't leave him alone in my room.

Moving past them, I make my way down the stairs and to the communal room at the end of the hall. Some of the other girls are already in here, drinking coffee, and eating waffles and pancakes as they chat. I spot Selena in the corner on her own and make my way over to her. It's Selena who told me about The Executive Club, having worked as a dancer there for around four months. She offered to put a good word in for me and as they say, the rest is history. I don't know her story and I haven't asked her. But I get the feeling it's dark. Though she tries to hide it, I see the haunted look in her eyes. See the pain she tries to cover with her beauty, humor, and smiling face.

"Hey," I greet, pulling a chair out at the table where she sits.

Her head snaps up. She smiles wide when she spots me, and I can't help but grin back at her. Like all the girls at the club, Selena is show-stopping gorgeous. What makes her different from most of the other dancers – and in my opinion better – is she is actually nice, kind, and genuine, which I haven't found in many of the other girls. I don't know whether it's because they think I am their competition, but for some reason the majority of them all took an instant dislike to me.

"Oh, hey Ocean. You okay?" She chirps enthusiastically, looking fresh, unlike me.

"I would be if I wasn't dragged out of bed after only a couple of hours of sleep," I grumble.

She chuckles. "Right, I would be pissed if I had to work last night and then was dragged out of bed early the next morning. Thankfully, I didn't but I did have a date, so I still had a relatively late night." She pauses, her head cocking. "Though, I bet it I was in bed earlier than you."

I blow out a breath. "Yeah. It was past four by the time I got into bed."

"I was home by one, so had a couple more hours of sleep than you," she frowns. "You work too hard Ocean. You should cut down on your shifts. None of the other girls work seven nights a week." She chides, shaking her head.

"I need the money." I shrug.

She eyes me for a long beat. "We all need the money, but girl, you are going to exhaust yourself and crash if you are not careful."

My chest tightens at the concern in her voice, but for right now, I am not going to cut down my shifts. I have a dream and I want to achieve it sooner rather than later. "Thanks for looking out for me, but I'm fine. Promise."

Her eyes narrow in on me playfully before she sighs. "I'm going up for another pancake. Do you want anything? Coffee?" she asks, changing the subject and I'm grateful for it.

I shake my head, grinning. "I look that bad, huh?"

Her eyes widen. "What? No. You're fucking stunning, Ocean, even on a couple hours of sleep."

I chuckle. "I'll go up and grab something. Those waffles look good too." I say eyeing her plate of waffles and berries.

Selena laughs. "They are. If you want one, go now before they all get eaten."

I am out of my seat before she finishes her sentence, rushing over to the side table that is stacked with food and an assortment of cold and hot drinks. Grabbing a plate, I stack it with a couple of waffles, some chopped banana, strawberries, and whipped cream before pouring a mug of coffee and making my way back over to the table.

Selena takes her seat opposite me, and without a word digs into her pancakes. Her eyes close as she chews. "Damn, I'm going to miss these when I eventually move out of here," she groans. "In fact. I may just stay for Ms. Valerie's breakfast."

I laugh, taking a bite of my breakfast. I almost moan out loud as the sweetness of the fruit and waffle hits my tongue. I agree with Selena. I would also stay just to have this breakfast every morning. Fortunately for us, breakfast is included in the weekly rate we pay for our rooms. It makes the cost a little higher but it's worth it. No other meals are included but that's okay. I work most nights and Leo always makes sure the girls are fed. It works out perfectly, really. Most days, I don't have to waste money buying food.

"Good?" Selena asks.

I nod. "So good." I drop my fork, grabbing my mug. "So, tell me about this date?"

She blushes. She holds up a finger, silently asking me to wait for her answer while she finishes chewing. Swallowing, she takes a sip of her coffee before speaking. "Eric is great," she sighs dreamily. "He is in finance, stocks to be exact. He is tall, dark,

Dancing In Sin

and so gorgeous." She chews her bottom lip in contemplation, before whispering out. "I think he might be out of my league."

My eyes bug out of my head. Out of her league? Has she seen herself? "No. No way. You are stunning, Selena." And I mean every single word of it. With her olive skin, hazel eyes, and chocolate hair, she is beautiful. "No one is out of your league."

"Yeah but…" she trails off, blowing out a breath. "No. You're right. I'm just being silly." She picks up her fork, running it through her food but never picking it up. I can tell she has more to say, so I wait patiently for when she is ready to talk. It doesn't take long. "It's just, don't you ever feel…I don't know, like we are less because we take our clothes off for a living?" Her eyes dart to me, wide with a look of shock, as if she can't believe she just said those words.

I chuckle, shaking my head. I get where she is coming from. I mean, taking your clothes off can be demeaning, but it can also be empowering. It all comes down to perspective and I will not be made to feel less just because of my job. "No. I don't. Especially not at The Executive Club. I guess there are seedy places around that would make me feel gross but not there. We are protected and we make good money. There is nothing wrong with what we are doing." I assure her.

She nods, a thoughtful look on her face. "I haven't told Eric that I'm a dancer." She blurts out. I glance around to see if any of the other girls are listening to our conversation, but they are all too engrossed in their own to worry about what we are talking about. "Well, he knows that I am a dancer, but he doesn't know where I dance or that I take my clothes off," she rushes out before sucking in a breath.

Reaching over, I take her hand, giving it a comforting squeeze. "Be honest with him. If he doesn't like that you do what you have to do, to keep a roof over your head and food in your belly, then he isn't the man for you."

***

"Ocean?" My name being called has my hand pausing, just as I am about to coat my lashes with mascara. Lifting my head, I meet Leo's gaze in the mirror. I frown. He doesn't usually disturb any of the dancers, unless it's for something important, like paperwork or shift changes.

Anxiety swirls in my stomach as I stare at him through the mirror. He looks tired. Weary. What does he want? Is he going to take me to that office again? Leave me to sit in that room and be interrogated by that intimidating man. *Nico.* Equal parts gorgeous and terrifying. It's a lethal combination and one I should stay the hell away from. I don't want to go to his office again, but if that's what Leo is here for then I have no choice.

Forcing a smile, I speak. "What's up, Leo?"

He eyes me, stepping closer. I suck in a breath, my body tensing. From the look on his face, this isn't good news. Rubbing a hand through his hair, he blows out a breath. My pulse kicks up, waiting for whatever he is going to tell me. Then increases when a big grin curves his lips as he pulls something out of his pocket. "This is for you. One of our best clients left it with Sykes last night." He shoves the envelope into my free hand, startling me. A nervous laugh bursts from me, my shoulders sagging in what can only be described as relief.

"Jesus, Leo. You nearly gave me a heart attack. I thought you were going to take me to the office again. Or worst, fire me." With one hand clutching the envelope, I rub my chest with my free one as if it can alleviate some of my stress.

His eyes narrow, but I see the humor in them. "Now why

would I do that? You're my best girl right now." He drawls with a wink.

I chuckle, shaking my head. "Well, next time you have something like this for me, maybe don't act so damn serious. And wait until my shift is over." I add.

He barks out a laugh, saluting me. "Whatever you want darlin'." He winks, laughing as he spins and saunters out of the changing room like he didn't just cause me a coronary.

Laughing, I shake my head only to freeze when I feel eyes on me. Glancing around the room, I watch as some of the girls scowl and shoot daggers at me. I sigh. I shouldn't be surprised. When women feel threatened, they go to their default mode.

Bitch.

Ignoring them, I peel the seal open, my eyes widening in shock when I see a stack of dollar bills wedged inside. Pulling them out, my mouth drops open. I thumb through the one-hundred-dollar bills, my heart rate picking up when I finish counting and find ten thousand dollars inside.

What the fuck?

Clenching them in my fist, I briefly wonder which of the men from last night would leave me this sort of money and why. I don't know and I'm not about to analyze or question it right now. For some reason, he thought that my dancing was worth thousands of dollars to him. Shaking my head, I shove the money into my backpack before finishing off my make-up and pulling on my outfit. Standing, I grab my belongings, shove them in my locker, and make my way out to the stage.

Chapter 5

Nico

Though I told myself I wouldn't come to The Executive Club unless absolutely necessary, I once again find myself standing at the privacy window, watching Ocean as she moves her body on the stage. Frustration slithers through my veins, and I grit my teeth. I don't know why, but she seems to have some weird hold on me. A hold that is completely out of my control and making me do irrational shit. Like fucking stalking her like some obsessive creep.

My eyes follow the roll of her lithe body, tracking every little move she makes. She is so fucking sensual; hypnotic, that her dancing like this in public should be illegal. The way she moves her perfect body to the music is an art and adds to her beauty... well, let's just say it's a lethal combination. One look at her, she pulls you in, keeping you there and making you beg for more. I would never admit it, but I for one, am caught up in her, enthralled by her. I can't seem to tear my gaze from her. And it's not just me. Every pair of eyes in my club are on her right now. As if she has bewitched everyone in the whole place with some twisted magic until she is all that you see.

Fuck.

Forcing my eyes away from the spell she is casting down below, it takes every bit of self-control I have in my body to move away from the window and toward my desk. Dropping down in my chair, I shake my head in disgust at myself. I am acting like a fucking teenager who just discovered his first crush. It's infuriating and inconvenient that I seem to have developed this... interest in her. She is a distraction.

Groaning, I run a hand down my face. Christ. What the fuck is wrong with me? My life was fine before she came along. I was cool, calm, and rational. Right now, I feel anything but those things. I should just have Leo fire her ass, then maybe I could get back to my normal self and concentrate on business. I snort. Somehow, I know that's a lie. Whether Ocean works here or not, something tells me that my obsessive thoughts about her won't stop. Not now I have met her. Not now I know that she exists. I frown, wondering why out of all the women I have ever met, she seems to be the one bringing out this side of me. Hmm. Maybe she really is a sorceress with magical powers, casting spells over everyone she encounters. At this point, it seems like the only explanation. I don't get like this over pussy. *Ever.*

So again. Why her?

This girl, I don't even know or trust. I see the secrets in her ocean-blue eyes. What is she hiding? Shoving my hand through my hair, I tug at the dark strands in frustration as I try to talk myself down.

She is just a woman. A fucking dancer, no less. She takes her clothes off for money. That's beneath you, Nico. You are a fucking king and will marry a queen. Not some stripper that every rich asshole in New York is getting a good look at every night of the week.

I chant the words in my head, hoping I can make myself believe them and end this weird infatuation with her. But deep down, I know it's pointless. I can feel it in the way my blood heats with possession every time I even so much as think about her. I laugh, though arguably none of this bullshit is humorous.

With that one interaction, she fascinated me, *enraptured* me. And until I have had a taste, I don't think I will be able to just walk away or let this go. Logically, I know that I need to get as far away from her as I can. But that doesn't change the fact that, for the first time in my life, a woman has made me feel something other than pleasure and that has never happened. What that something is, I am not sure, but for research, I should maybe find out.

My door is shoved open, startling me from my thoughts. Dante steps in, his breathing harsh. My eyes narrow in annoyance, but he ignores it, grunting out, "We have a problem."

My spine snaps straight; my body fills with tension. My eyes shift to the window as I grip the edge of my desk. Did something happen to Ocean? Did some motherfucker put their hands on her? Who am I going to have to kill? These are the first thoughts that race through my mind, and I hate that I am so distracted by her.

"Not her." he rolls his amused-filled eyes. I relax back in my chair, jerking my head for him to continue. "The Russians. Somehow, they found out about our coke shipment. The one that came in tonight. All of our soldiers are dead." He blows out a weary breath. "Well apart from Luigi. He is the only one that got out of there alive. He called me. Confirmed it was the Bratva that hit us."

My fists and jaw clench. Red-hot rage thrums in my veins, burning up my body with the need for revenge. But the news of the Bratva killing my men is not the only thing causing the anger. It's the girl. While I was here, obsessing over and distracted by fucking Ocean, my warehouse and men were getting shot up by the fucking Russians. My jaw ticks. This

Dancing In Sin

confirms what I already know. I need to get my shit together and thoughts away from the girl. And fast.

Exhaling a breath, I try to calm myself down and get my head straight. Pinning Dante with a serious look, I speak. "Where is Luigi right now? And does my father know?"

"He has a minor wound on his stomach where a bullet grazed him. The doctor is patching him up. And yes, Lorenzo is aware of what happened." He tells me all this, his voice cool, calm, like we didn't just lose a dozen men and millions of dollars. His rationality is one of the reasons I will make him my underboss when the time comes. Dante, just like me, knows how to keep his shit together, no matter the situation. *Your shit's not together right now,* a voice in my head taunts, but I shove it aside so I can take care of more urgent matters. Like my *fucking* business.

I nod, pushing out of my seat. "Take me to my papà."

***

"How the fuck did this happen?" my papà's fist hits his desk in anger. We are at his home in the Hamptons. My childhood home and the estate where my mamma and sister both still live. It is secluded, the grounds patrolled by guards twenty-four-seven. The estate is so protected, it would be harder to break into than Fort Knox. Which is perfect considering the two women I love most in the world live here.

Dante had anticipated that I would want to see my papà immediately after breaking the news about the Russians. He had already contacted our pilot, Hansen, to fuel up the Marchetti helicopter. Within the hour we were up in the air and on our way.

"We have a rat." Giuseppe Greco, Papà's consigliere and

long-time friend mutters as he blows smoke out of his mouth from the cigar he is smoking.

I nod. "It makes sense. How else would they know about the shipment? The exact location it was going to? It's our smallest warehouse. One we only acquired recently. Giuseppe is right. We have a traitor *or* traitors within our organization."

Papà blows out a breath, falling back in his seat. With narrowed eyes, he looks at me. "Find them. I want names within twenty-four hours." His tone leaves no room for argument. Though he needn't worry. I will have what he wants in less than the time he asked for.

I nod. "Of course."

"We cannot allow this to happen again. It makes us look weak." He roars through clenched teeth.

I stand, Dante following suit. "Agreed and it won't," I say, though I can't guarantee it. "Now, it's late. Dante and I will stay the night," I tell him, because what is the point in flying back to the city at three a.m. when I can sleep for a couple of hours in my childhood bedroom. Dante can take the guest room and Hansen can bunk in one of the guardhouses. "Tomorrow we will get to work. Find the rat and make them pay."

His eyes gleam with satisfaction, no doubt at my mention of revenge. "Very well. Your mamma will be happy to see you. She was just telling me at dinner how you don't come to visit her anymore. She misses you," he grunts.

I chuckle, shaking my head at the absurdity of my mother missing me. No matter how old I get, or how much blood I have on my hands, in my mamma's eyes, I will always be her little boy.

***

"Oh *figlio mio*. Mi sei mancato." *I've missed you.* My mamma says, her sweet voice soft as tears fill her eyes.

Smiling, I pull her into a hug. "I've missed you too, Mamma."

She slaps my chest, staring up at me with a smile on her face. "Don't leave it so long next time," she admonishes.

"I won't. Promise." I press a kiss to her head, then move further into the kitchen where I find my sister and Dante already at the food-filled breakfast table. They sit opposite each other in silence, staring at one another. My gaze flicks between them and I frown when I find something on both their faces that I can't quite decipher. They haven't noticed me yet, so I pause, watching them for a long beat. I don't know what I am looking for but there is something... Hmm. Interesting. Shaking my head, I make a mental note to ask Dante about all this later.

Clearing my throat, I grin as two sets of eyes snap at me. Rounding the table, I drop a kiss to my sister's hair, before taking the seat beside her. "Hey, Sis," I grunt, the smell of coffee and bacon hitting my nostrils and making my mouth water. Christ, I didn't realize I was so hungry.

"Hey, Nic. Nice of you to visit us." My sister's voice is full of sarcasm.

My brows raise at her insolence, but she knows that she is one of the only people in the world that I would allow to get away with speaking to me like that. "Some of us have work to do, Allegra."

She huffs, shaking her head. "It would be nice to have my brother around once in a while." I look at her. Studying her face for any sign of what could be wrong. Something is definitely off with her. She has never given me an attitude like this. It's not in her nature. She is soft. Submissive. Like mamma. Then I see the sorrow in her eyes. The loneliness. *Sadness.* I frown at what could cause the look on her face. Does she know about the deal

Papà set up with the Romanos? No. No matter how much of a monster he is, Papà wouldn't have told her yet. Not until everything is set in stone.

I shake the thought of her potential arranged marriage away because honestly, that shit is never going to happen anyway. Grabbing the glass carafe of coffee, I pour myself a mug full just as Mamma takes her seat.

"Juliana prepared breakfast. Your papà will be joining us shortly and then we can start." She informs us before lifting her glass of orange juice to her mouth and taking a sip. Annoyance slithers through me. I don't know why. It's been this way since we were children and had family dinners. Even if it takes an hour, we will not start eating until *Papà* has arrived.

Turning to my sister, I frown when I find her eyes on Dante. My eyes narrow in on her face, then flicker to my best friend. Like they are in some staring contest, they just watch each other as if their lives depend on it. Like I watch... Ocean. I grit my teeth when the unbidden thought enters my mind. Wanting to break their stare off, I clear my throat and speak. "How's school?"

Allegra's head snaps up, her eyes wide with a mixture of fear and embarrassment. Her cheeks turn a dark shade of red like she just got caught with her hand in a cookie jar she was not supposed to have it in. And she is *definitely* not to have her hand anywhere on or even near Dante. "Good. I'm on track to be valedictorian." She squeaks out.

Ignoring her weird behavior with my best friend, I smile, impressed at her achievement. Allegra goes to a private, all-girls, school around two miles from here. She always has two guards protecting her at any given time, and at her old school she was embarrassed by having men following her every move. But having bodyguards at The Weststone Saints Academy for Girls is normal. The daughters of the elite, of some of the richest and

Dancing In Sin

most powerful men and women in the world, attend the academy. Ninety-nine percent of the student body has security with them. In fact, it is perceived as weird if you don't have guards. "Good. Let me know when your graduation is. I want to be there."

She beams at me, a real smile and the first one I have seen from her since I sat down at the table. Her mouth opens to respond only to snap shut when Papà walks in. "Let us eat." His loud voice booms around the room as he takes the seat at the head of the table. Juliana rushes over, loading the table with dishes of delicious food.

Papà digs in first, silently telling us to do the same. And just like that, the boss has spoken, all conversation stops, and we eat.

Chapter 6

Ocean

Pulling open the staff door to the club, I step inside only to come to a complete stop when I spot Nico and Leo standing in the hallway, deep in conversation. My heart rate kicks up, beating against my ribcage just at the sight of Nico. I swallow past the lump in my throat, hoping that they are so deep into their discussion, that I can slip past them and into the changing room unnoticed. But when the heat of both their gazes land on me I know I'm not that lucky.

    The air turns thick in the small space of the hallway, almost choking me with the sudden tension. I shift on my feet, my stomach dipping with nerves. I keep my gaze trained on Nico, waiting, but for what I am unsure. I feel like prey, caught up in his predatory pale blue eyes. They rake over my body, burning every inch of my skin they touch and leaving goosebumps in their wake. When his gaze finally locks on mine, I feel warmth rush to my cheeks. His head cocks, and a flicker of confusion flashes in his eyes before he hides it. He watches me for a long intense beat, an expression I can't quite decipher covering his handsome features. I stand like a statue, too scared to move in case he pounces. Satisfaction, followed by annoyance, flashes in his eyes, as if he likes what he sees but he isn't happy about it.

"Hey," I squeak out past the thickness in my throat, break the awkwardness.

Leo smiles but I can tell it's forced. "Ocean. How're you doing?" he greets.

"Good. I was just getting here for my shift." I blurt, then roll my eyes. I have no idea why I said that. Leo knows I work Saturdays. But for some unexplained reason, I have this sudden need to explain myself.

A smirk curves his lips, no doubt at my awkward behavior. "Go on ahead to the changing room, sweetheart." He jerks his head in the direction of the room as if I don't know where it is. Nodding, I exhale a shaky breath and as if of their own volition my gaze shifts to Nico. All the air leaves my lungs when I see the dark murderous look on his face. His jaw is clenched tightly, and his pale blue orbs have darkened to an almost black color. He looks...angry. Really angry. I want to ask him if I have done something wrong, but I don't think I could speak right now, not with that penetrating stare laser focused on me.

Swallowing down my fear, I force a smile before rushing past the two men, not stopping until I make it to the end of the hall and into the changing room. It's only once I am inside that I release the breath I was holding.

Fuck. What was that all about and why does he set me on edge?

Questions swirl in my head, all wanting answers that I don't have.

Was Nico's anger directed at me or was it for Leo?

If it were aimed at me, then does he know that...that I lied?

No. Surely, I would have been fired by now if that were the case. I shake my head, knowing I don't have time to delve into this right now. And do I even want to? Just from looking at Nico,

I can tell that he is a man of power. A man not to be messed with. After all, I should know. I've been surrounded by men of power and wealth my whole life. Men like Nico. My body shudders as if it is rejecting even the smallest thought of my past and I shove the thoughts aside, telling myself that no matter what, I need to stay away from Nico Marchetti. No good can come from getting caught up with someone like him.

Finished with my little pep talk, I move further into the room, to my designated chair and mirror. Dropping down, I grin when I spot Selena bounding toward me.

"Hey," she chirps, eyes meeting mine in the mirror. I smile back at her, genuinely happy to see my friend.

"Hey. I haven't seen you for a couple of days." I say, because she has been MIA from both work and our current home.

She blushes, her hazel eyes lighting up with excitement. "You know I told you about Eric? Well, let's just say things are heating up and I have been staying at his apartment the past couple of nights."

"Well, it must be good if you are canceling work for him." I tease, waggling my brows before my face sobers. "No, but seriously. I'm happy for you."

She giggles. "Thank you. I have really gotten to know him over the last couple of days. He is amazing Ocean. He treats me like a queen..." A big smile curves her lips, and she leans in, covering her mouth and winking conspiratorially. "Well unless we are in the bedroom."

With a smile twitching my lips, my face screws up in mock disgust. "Too much information, Selena."

She giggles before it cuts off. Selena watches me and I literally see the cogs working in her head. "You know, Eric has some friends. Want me to set you up? We could double date."

Don't ask me why, but my mind immediately goes to Nico. Even though not five minutes ago, I promised myself that I would stay away from him. I frown, annoyance slithering through me at the direction of my thoughts. It's fucking ridiculous. Thinking about Nico Marchetti in any capacity but the man who owns the place where I work. We are going to be nothing else but employer and employee. Not that I think for one second he would be interested in me in that way, but still. I need to remember my place. I inwardly roll my eyes. I am losing my mind over a man. I need to pull my shit together and remember why I am here in the first place. To make enough money so I can move the hell on. Maybe go to school and buy a small house with a picket fence. I don't care about being rich. I just want to survive comfortably.

Shifting my thoughts back to the now, I realize I haven't responded to Selena. Smiling, I tuck a lock of blonde hair behind my ear and speak. "I'm not really looking for anything right now."

"Well, if you change your mind..." she trails off, but the implication is clear. I need to put her straight. Though I like Selena, I don't need her setting me up with anyone. I don't need the distraction of any man right now and I *definitely* don't need to be getting caught up in any situation that I can't get myself out of. Relationships mean trust and honesty. I have no trust to give, and I can't be honest about who I am or my past, so therefore it's easier to be on my own. Maybe one day in the distant future that will change, but for now, I need to keep things simple.

"I won't," I say, with finality.

***

With my shift finished, I get cleaned up, pull on my sweats and coat, and prepare for my walk home. Pushing the staff door open, I shiver when the cold night air hits me in the face.

Pulling my coat tighter around my body, I step outside into the dark early hours of the morning.

After my last dance, Selena and a couple of the other girls asked if I wanted to grab pizza with them, but I declined their offer wanting nothing more than to just go back to my room and sleep. It's most likely done me no favors in making friends in this place but, to be honest, I don't care. I am exhausted and right now, sleeping is more important than anything.

Closing the door behind me, I start down the dark back alley, heading in the direction of my building. I only make it a couple of steps when my name is called by a deep, masculine voice. My steps falter and I come to a complete stop. Just like every other time I have been around him, my heart rate kicks up in my chest. Fear trickles through my veins, all the hair on my body standing on end. Everything in me screams to run but for some reason, I stay put like an idiot. What the hell is wrong with me? I should not be alone with this man, especially in a darkened, secluded alley, where he could do anything to me without anyone witnessing it. Adrenaline pumps in my body, making me lightheaded. I suck in much-needed air, preparing myself for when I come face to face with him. Telling myself to get this over with, I spin around just as Nico steps out of the shadows, like a dark presence.

"Ocean," he repeats, irritation thick in his voice.

"Nico?" His name is a question from my lips.

His stare drops to my lips before coming back to my eyes. Distaste flickers in his blue orbs and then he speaks. "What are you doing out here alone," he glances at his watch. "At three o'clock in the morning?"

I swallow, shifting the strap of my duffle up my shoulder. My gaze flickers back to Nico before I mumble out. "I'm going home."

He studies me for a long beat. His pointer finger comes up

and runs across his full bottom lip. My eyes zero in on the movement. I never thought something like that could be so sexy but Jesus... I wonder what it would feel like to run my tongue against the pink flesh. Taste him.

"And where is home?" the rasp of his voice snaps me from my thoughts, hitting me right in my sex. A pulse thrums deep inside me, moisture seeping into my panties. Pressing my legs together, I try to alleviate the sudden ache causing a maelstrom of emotion inside me. I have never felt anything like this before, and I certainly don't want to feel anything toward this man, but it's as if I have no control over it. Glancing at Nico, I can tell he is aware of my current turmoil when a smirk curves his sinful lips. Damn him. The man doesn't miss anything. "Answer me," he demands, making me jump.

Shifting on my feet, I chew my lip as I search his face. I don't want to tell him where I live, but I also get the distinct feeling that he won't let me leave this dirty alley if I don't give him something. "About three blocks away," I tell him. I am being vague but that's all he is getting.

Slipping his hands into his pants pockets, he watches me with that intensity that I have come to expect from him. Butterflies erupt in my stomach, tension filling the air with something I can't explain. I should walk away. Break this connection between us. The electricity. Does Nico feel it too? Or is this... feeling... all one-sided? Surely a man like him could have any woman he wants. So why would he want me? I mean, I know I am attractive but so are all the other dancers at The Executive Club. Some of them are even models. I'm not experienced with men, and I don't understand what's going on here. But I need to get a handle on it and fast. Need to remind myself to stay the hell away from him.

"You walk? Alone?" he grits out, making me jump and breaking me from my reverie.

I nod. "It's not far. And anyway, it's not like there won't be people around. This is the city that never sleeps." I laugh, but from the clench of his jaw, he doesn't see the humor in it.

"I will take you." His voice leaves no room for argument. But I don't care. There is no way am I getting in a car with him.

"No, thank you. I'm fine to walk. I do it most nights." I spin away from him, ending the conversation. Without looking back, I rush down the alley towards the street and hopefully where other people are, but before I make it to the end, a solid arm wraps around me, pulling me into a hard, muscular chest. I yelp, trying to push away from him but he just holds me tighter.

"You are not walking on your own. If you are not comfortable with me giving you a ride, I will have one of my men take you," he growls and... did he just smell my hair? I stiffen, my heart pounding in my chest. He smells so good. Masculine. I want to bury my nose in his chest and breathe in all things Nico. My eyes widen at my errant thoughts. I need to get away from here. Now.

"Let me go." I push at his chest, trying to wriggle out of his hold and the lust fog he has cast on me. "I've been working here for about three weeks now and have walked home every single night. I don't need one of your men to chauffer me. I can look after myself," I grate the words out through clenched teeth because fuck this guy. He doesn't get to control me or tell me what to do. He isn't my father. I barely know him.

Growling, he shoves me away from him. I stumble, but before I hit the ground, I manage to steady myself on the cold brick wall of the building. My head snaps up to find Nico glowering down at me. Nose in the air like he is better than me. I glare back at him, my mouth parting, ready to give him what for, but he beats me to it.

"Fine. It's your funeral. Don't come crying to me when you are getting gang raped or killed behind a dirty dumpster. And all because you are too stubborn to accept my offer." His voice is detached, cold with every word out of his mouth. I shiver, knowing everything he said is a possibility, but still, it won't make me accept his offer.

I will take my chances. I am aware of the dangers that lurk in this city. *In every city.* As long as I keep my wits about me, I should be fine. I have been so far. I don't need a man to protect or save me. No way. With men like him, nothing comes for free. Every offer of help has a string attached to it. A string I am not willing to give. He may not want anything from me now, but he will. They always do. Of that much, I am sure. It's not happening. I refuse to be in debt to anyone. Even if it is for something like a little car ride.

With those thoughts in mind, I shoot him a sweet, patronizing smile, turn on my heel, and run before he can stop me again.

Chapter 7

Nico

*S*tubborn fucking woman.

I glare after her as she all but runs down the alley toward the street. I shouldn't care that she is walking alone in the dark. Yet, as I watch her walk away from me, that pert, heart-shaped ass bouncing, something claws at my chest, commanding me to go after her. To make her submit to me. To punish her for her insubordination… for being so reckless. And I would punish her. Hard. Just the thought alone makes my cock twitch in my pants with a need so strong my legs almost buckle.

"Fuck," I bark out, running a frustrated hand through my hair, my eyes lasered in on the spot where Ocean just disappeared.

Before I can question it, or stop myself, I'm striding down the dirty, dark alley, following after her. I shouldn't be walking these streets alone, not after all the shit with the Bratva we have going on. But I have this incessant need to know where she lives, *who* she lives with. Does she have a boyfriend? Someone at home waiting for her to return so he can sink his cock inside her. Cuddle with her. Red-hot anger snakes up my spine, jaw clenching on its own accord. There better not be any fucking man. I don't want to have to kill an innocent. Though I will if they are in my way.

Shaking my head, I try to shove down the strong emotions Ocean seems to elicit from me. What the hell is wrong with me? Why do I seem to lose all rationality and control over this girl? I have never been possessive over a woman before. Ever. The fact that I seem to have become an unhinged stalker over Ocean, despite telling myself to stay away, only angers me further. It's only a matter of time before I do something stupid. I know it.

Following her down the mostly empty street, I make sure to keep at a long enough distance, so she doesn't see me. I track her every step with my eyes, glaring when she takes out her cell, giving it all her attention. Does she realize that she is putting herself at unnecessary risk? Does she understand the dangers that lurk in this city? The predators who are just waiting to take a bite out of someone like her?

You included, asshole, and you are the biggest predator of them all. That voice in my head whispers but I shake it away, staring at her like it is my job. Fury unfurls in my chest when after five long minutes she is still engrossed in whatever is on that damn phone, oblivious, with no idea of the monster that is tracking her.

We continue walking for another ten minutes, in the direction of a more... rundown part of the city. Rundown is being nice; this area is rough and has one of the highest crime rates in New York. Adrenaline pumps through my veins and I will her to continue walking to a nice neighborhood. I know my thoughts are pointless when she comes to a stop outside a brick building with a sign hanging out front. *Book and Bed Hostel for Women.* My brows shoot up in disbelief. She lives here? In a shithole building in one of the worst areas in the city?

Everything inside me prays that she is just here visiting someone, a friend, but when she punches in a code, pushing the door open in the next second, it's confirmed. Ocean lives here. In a hostel for women. Though I hate the place, I can't help but be a little relieved that it's not mixed accommodation. I can rest easy that she isn't at risk of men hitting on her when she goes home. I chuckle at my thoughts, though the situation is not humorous at all.

My eyes go back to the building, lips turning up in disdain. Is this why Ocean didn't want me to give her a ride? Is she embarrassed? My eyes narrow in on her just as she steps inside and closes the door. I hate to admit that I stare, long after the door closes, but I do. The girl is an anomaly, one I was intrigued by before, but now even more so. She told me her parents were dead, which would explain why she is working for me and living here. But surely, she has relatives that can help her out, find her somewhere better to live? Even if she doesn't have family, I know for a fact that she is one of our best earners and makes good money at The Executive Club. So why here? Surely, with the money she is earning, she could afford something a little better than a hostel?

My eyes roam over the building, looking for any sign of her in the windows as I try to make sense of everything I have learned. Something isn't adding up. I want to know everything.

Pulling my cell from my pants pocket, I scroll through my contacts until I find the name of my PI. Clicking the message icon, I type out a text before hitting send. My eyes go back to the building. A smirk curves my lips, my heart pumping wildly in my chest with the anticipation of what comes next. I glance at my cellphone screen, reading over the words.

> Me: Find out everything there is to know about Ocean Embers.

***

"Christ, Nic, you shouldn't be walking around this city alone. Not with the Bratva on our asses," Dante snaps, running his hands through his hair in frustration as he paces the floor in my office.

I know damn well that I shouldn't have gone after Ocean on my own. But I can protect myself and, best friend or not, he needs to remember who he is talking to. "I'm aware, Dante. Now watch your mouth." I bark, pinning him with a look that dares him to argue with me.

Shooting me a glower, he shakes his head before dropping down on one of the chairs in front of the desk. "What were you doing anyway?" he asks, curiosity lacing his tone.

Ignoring his gaze, I glance at the pile of papers on my desk, picking them up and shuffling them around just so I don't have to look at him. If I make eye contact with Dante, he will know that I'm lying when I speak my next words. Not that I care. But if I tell him what I was really doing – stalking Ocean – that is going to lead to questions I don't have answers to right now. Clearing my throat, I speak. "I was tracking a patron. I thought he might have been a spy for the Russians. Turns out I was wrong." It's vague but it's all I've got, and I don't owe Dante answers.

I feel his eyes on me. Scrutinizing me, but I don't look up. "Yeah. Well, next time make sure to take me or one of the other hundred guards that work for you. Things are tense right now. You shouldn't have been so reckless, Nic." he admonishes.

"Sure," I drawl drily, my gaze meeting his.

He chuckles, shaking his head. "Man, did you see the new girl tonight? Fuck, she had the whole club caught up in her spell, dancing on that stage. I'm beginning to think she has special powers of some kind. The whole fucking club was entranced by her." He says with a hint of awe in his voice.

My eyes narrow in on him, searching his face. Is he trying to goad me? Dante knows me better than anyone. He has seen the interest I have clearly shown in her. Is this his way of finding out how deep my fascination goes? He smirks, proving my thoughts. My jaw clenches as I try to keep my anger at bay. Exhaling a breath, I ignore the asshole and whatever game he is playing. "She brings in a lot of money," I drawl nonchalantly.

His face is blank for less than two point five seconds before he bursts out laughing. I grit my teeth as I watch him, reminding myself that he is my best friend and not to kill him. His amusement finally stops. He wipes his eyes, shaking his head. "I give it a month before you have her in your bed and your cock buried inside her."

Though I would take the same bet, I won't give him the satisfaction of knowing he is right. I should stay far away from Ocean, but the truth is, I already know I am going to fuck her. Nothing or no one will stop me. Not even myself. "Pay up now asshole. It's not happening. We have rules in place for a reason." The lie tastes thick on my tongue.

"You say that now, but I know you, Nic. She is exactly your type. I have seen the way you watch her. You want her and you never deny yourself anything." He pushes out of his chair, shooting me a smug look. "A month," he repeats, moving toward the door.

A slither of annoyance rushes through me, but I shove it down. "Where are you going?" I shout after him.

"Leo has tonight's earnings," he throws over his shoulder, before pulling open the door and leaving.

I slump back into my chair, running a thumb over my bottom lip, my thoughts going to the woman who seems to have consumed my mind. Even though I know the rules, I will fuck her out of my system. Who the hell is going to tell me no? I am the boss so I can do what the hell I like. Maybe then, after being inside her cunt, this interest I have will go away, though there is

Dancing In Sin

a small voice in my head telling me, warning me, that it's naïve to think like that. There is little about Ocean Embers that I don't want to explore. A hunger inside me that will only be satiated by taking a bite out of her. The forbidden fruit, the one that should be off limits to me of all people, but isn't that what makes it all the more exciting?

Because I am a man with no boundaries, no restrictions. No one stands in my way, and I always get what I want. That's not ego. It's truth. I was raised as a king and that is what I am.

Even as my mind screams at me that Ocean will be my downfall... It only makes me want her more.

And that's a problem.

A big fucking problem.

Because I know, no matter how much I tell myself to stay away, I will take what I want.

And right now, I want the girl with the striking blue eyes and blonde hair.

Chapter 8

Ocean

"Nico wants to see you in his office."

Those eight words have all the air leaving my lungs, and my stomach churning with anxiety. Leo appears in my mirror, a grim, sympathetic look on his face. My heart pounds in my chest. Fuck. This can't be good. Is it because I was fifteen minutes late for my shift tonight? It was a one-off. I have never been late once since I started here, so surely, he won't fire me over that.

I knew I shouldn't have gone out, but today is my eighteenth birthday, so I decided as a treat, I would take myself out and do normal things girls my age do. Like shop. Eat at a nice restaurant. Get my hair and nails done. Though I am trying to save money, I decided one day of splurging for my birthday wouldn't hurt. Maybe I was wrong. I was so caught up in the freedom of being able to do what I wanted; I was late to work. Now I might lose my job over it. Panic surges through me at the thought. I can't get fired. I would never earn even a fraction of the money I make in a night here, anywhere else.

Pushing out of the chair, I turn to face Leo with frantic, apology-filled eyes. "Leo, please. I'm sorry I was late. It won't

Dancing In Sin

happen again. Don't fire me over this. I need this job." I rush out my plea, hoping with everything inside me, he will fight in my corner on this. I don't care what I have to do, I am keeping this job. I will get on my knees and beg if I have to. Even in front of all the other girls. Even in front of... Nico.

Leos' brows furrow, confusion flickering in his eyes. "Fire you?" he repeats.

I glance around, my cheeks heating when I find all the other girls' attention on me. Ignoring them, I turn back to Leo. "Isn't that why *he* wants to see me?" I whisper, suddenly confused. Maybe I got this wrong. But what else could he possibly want?

Leo shrugs. "No. Well, I don't think that's what it is. Honestly, I'm not sure why Nico wants to see you." He jerks his head towards the hallway. "Come on. Nico doesn't like to be kept waiting."

Nodding, I start toward the door on unsteady legs, my mind racing with a million different questions. What does Nico want? And why do I get the feeling that I've caught his attention? Unintentionally, but still. Our paths keep crossing, like some twisted fate. Maybe this is my karma for running... I shake the thought away before it can form. I am a good person and if Karma should come to anyone, it should be the people I ran from.

"Relax, Ocean. I'm sure it's just some problem with your paperwork or something." Leo's voice, though light, startles me from my thoughts. He strokes a hand down my back. It's a move meant to soothe me, but I can't help but tense at his touch. Leo frowns down at me, a hurt look in his chocolate eyes and I almost feel guilty. But why should I? It's my body. My choice of who I allow to put their hands on me.

Shifting away, I'm relieved when Leo's hand drops away, and he doesn't mention it further. He is quiet as we move up the back stairs, then down the hallway to the ominous door that leads to Nico's office. My feet stop moving on their own volition, my breaths coming out fast. I feel dizzy. Like I might faint. I don't want to go in there.

Noticing I have stopped, Leo pauses, his sympathetic eyes searching my face. He sighs, wrapping a hand around my bicep, and giving it a gentle squeeze. This time I don't push him away. In fact, I think his hold is the only thing keeping me standing right now.

"He won't hurt you. I won't let him," he murmurs, determination in his voice even though I know he is only trying to placate me. I know if push came to shove, Leo would do Nico's bidding. He sighs. "Come on. Let's get this over with."

Nodding robotically, I suck in a calming breath before exhaling. "He doesn't have the power to hurt me," I whisper with a confidence I don't feel. I am sure that if Nico ever wanted to hurt me, he would do it before I could blink.

Leo chuckles under his breath, his eyes softening as he watches me. "I shouldn't be telling you this, but not showing weakness is key when dealing with someone like Nico. If you show him fear, he will use it against you. Be confident when you go in there. Hold your head high."

I nod, trying to take Leo's advice on how to handle Nico. Straightening my spine, I keep my face a blank mask of indifference. Though I may look cool on the outside, that doesn't mean my body isn't trembling with fear when Leo knocks on the door and pushes it open. I follow him inside, staying hidden behind his broad back as if he is my shield. As if he can protect me. He can't. I know it. He knows it.

The air turns frigid. Thick with tension. I suck air into my lungs, preparing myself to face Nico. And then I hear it. His deep masculine drawl sends a shiver down my spine. "Leave us." He demands.

My body stiffens and I wish he would be more precise. Does

he want me or Leo to leave? My question is answered when Leo grips my wrist, pulling me in front of him to face the handsome devil sitting at his desk like a king. I swallow at the sight of him. All man and so handsome, it should be illegal. With his pale blue eyes, sharp jaw, perfect nose, and dark hair, surely he is every woman's dream man come to life.

"Sorry. You're on your own, girl." Leo whispers for only me to hear, startling me from my perusal. Nico's eyes darken, narrowing in on Leo's face.

"Go." Nico growls, low and deadly, making me nearly jump out of my skin. Glancing at Leo, I watch in absolute horror as he literally runs out of the room without another look in my direction. The door closes behind him, latch clicking into place with a finality that feels ominous. A forewarning of what is about to happen. "Sit," he commands, the silky, smooth tone of his voice making me turn to face him. My eyes lock onto his, heart skipping a beat at the intensity staring back at me. My stomach tightens, with fear or desire I'm not sure. His head cocks, as he studies me with a hint of... something I can't quite decipher in his pale blue orbs.

Swallowing down my fear, and despite the tension in my body, I exhale before moving toward the chair in front of his desk. Rounding the expensive, wingback executive chair, I drop down into the buttery soft leather. Nico tracks my every move, his jaw ticking with annoyance, but I see the flash of desire in his gaze. I'm only thankful that I didn't get changed into my lacy dance lingerie already and am still wearing leggings with a baggy sweater. The minutes tick by and Nico doesn't say anything, which only increases my anxiety. He watches me as if I am some mythical creature he has never encountered before, making me squirm and fidget.

The silence is putting me on edge. Not able to stand it any

longer and wanting to get out of here, I blurt out. "You wanted to see me?"

A hint of a smirk crosses his face, but he just leans back in his leather chair, getting comfortable. With his eyes locked on mine, he runs his thumb across that full bottom lip of his. I briefly wonder what it would feel like to have that plump flesh pressed against mine before I quickly shake the thought away. I need to stop thinking about Nico in that way. It will not do me any good fantasizing about his perfect lips. Just looking at this man, I know he could destroy me if I allowed him to, and in more ways than one.

"Why are you living in a hostel?" the deep baritone of his voice breaks the silence.

My eyes widen at his question, my pulse kicking up to an unnatural speed. How the hell does he know where I live? And why have I been called up to his office to discuss my living arrangements? I may work for him, but where I live is none of his business. He is out of line thinking he can call me in here to ask me questions that don't concern him.

Pushing my fear down, I jump up out of my chair, shooting him a deadly glare. I am playing with fire, and shouldn't be acting this way toward him, but how dare he invade my private life like that. How. Fucking. Dare. He. Outside of The Executive Club, my life has nothing to do with him. And I am about to tell him just that.

"How dare you? Where I live is none of your concern. None. I may work for you but that does not give you the right to look into my private life." I spit, my heart jumping with every word out of my mouth. I should stop. I should not be antagonizing this man, but I can't seem to stop myself. Spinning around, I move to get the hell out of here but don't even make it a step before he growls.

"Sit. Down." Two words. Two words that have terror

snaking up my spine, making me freeze. My heart pounds in my chest and I don't know how I am still standing. I want to run away, never come back. The only reason I don't is because I need this job. Swallowing, I turn to look at him. I wish I hadn't. He looks murderous. Like he wants to wrap those big hands around my throat and squeeze the life out of me. I want to defy him and stay standing, but there is being brave, and there is being stupid. And I have a feeling that stupidity will get me killed, so I sit. Satisfaction gleams in his eyes, no doubt at my submission. Clearing his throat, he speaks. "I asked you a question, Ocean. I expect an answer."

My palms turn clammy, sweat drips down my spine. I just want to get out of here, but I know that he won't let me go until I have answered his question. It's like Déjà vu from my first time in this office. Eyes on Nico and with trembling lips, words tumble out of my mouth. "It's safe. And cheap." I add, dropping my gaze when embarrassment heats my cheeks. I'm not embarrassed about where I am living, honestly, I am grateful I have a place at the hostel. It's just this man that reeks of money and power... well, I don't want him to know anything about me or where I live.

When the silence gets too much, I lift my head to find him studying my face intently. He is no doubt looking for a sign that I am lying, but he won't find one. It's the truth. Finding somewhere safe to live in this city is a feat in itself. It may not be in the best part of the town, but it's perfect for what I need right now.

"Hmm," is all he murmurs when he seems satisfied that I am telling the truth. The sound from his sinful mouth has desire heating my blood and moisture seeping into my panties. My pussy clenches around nothing and I almost whimper at the need pulsing between my thighs. Slowly, almost imperceptibly, I squeeze my legs together, hoping to ease the ache he started without him noticing the effect he has on me. The smirk that curves his lips tells me my effort is no use. He leans in, well, as much as he can with a desk between us, a predatory spark in his eyes. My chest heaves in anticipation of his next words, my head feels light, as if I can't get enough oxygen into my lungs. I suck in a much-needed breath. I am pretty confident that if I wasn't sitting down already, I would have collapsed to the floor by now.

"What's wrong, Ocean?" he croons, and I suppress a shiver. His smile widens, eyes going to my neck where I am sure he can see the erratic pulse trying to break free from the delicate skin there.

"Nothing," I blurt. "Can I go now?" I don't think I can take much more of this head fuck. I just want to leave.

"No," that one word is final, absolute.

Pushing out of his chair, he rounds the desk, and my pulse quickens with every step closer he gets. Dropping his hands to the armrests, he cages me in, blocking any chance I had of escaping this. He is so big, a massive presence in front of me, I have to tilt my head back just to look at his face. His masculine scent envelopes me, sending my pulse haywire. My nose wrinkles when a familiar smell washes over me. I wrack my brain, trying to remember where I have smelt it before. My eyes widen when it hits me. His cologne. *Bleu de Chanel*. Exactly what my brother wears. I would know that aroma anywhere.

Oblivious to my inner turmoil, he leans in close, his hot breath hitting my neck and making me gasp. "Next time I offer you a ride, you will take it, *Ocean*. You will not walk around *my* city on your own at night. I followed you last night." My breath hitches at his words. "You were distracted by your cell. Unaware of the dangers surrounding you. Any monster could jump out of the shadows and take advantage of you. Do *anything* to you." I feel rather than see his smile. "Like me. *I am* that monster. I could have dragged you down a dark alley, had my wicked way with you, and there would have been nothing you could do about it." I feel my eyes widen in shock and... desire? Jesus Christ, I must be sick. Because the thought of him taking away my will, dominating me and doing to me as he pleases has moisture seeping into my panties. "You would enjoy it, though." He pulls back to look at me. By the smirk on his face, he likes what he sees on mine. He winks, the look so hot I nearly drop to my knees and beg him to do the things he is saying. "Don't worry, *Tesoro*. Our time will come." His voice drops, husky and so full of desire, I nearly come on the spot. "That's a promise."

My mouth drops open. I stare at him. This gorgeous man, who seems to have taken an interest in me. It would be so easy to fall into him. To be caught up in all things him. But I can't allow that. It's dangerous. For him. For me...

"Can I go?" I say over the thickness in my throat.

Pushing himself upright, he grins. "You can. For now."

He doesn't need to tell me twice. Before he can say any more, I am out of my seat and pulling open the door. Its only when I get back to the changing room that my wits come back to me, and I silently question what the hell just happened. No way did he call me in there to ask me about my living situation. Pushing the thoughts aside, I make a mental note to stay away from Nico Marchetti. Now and in the future. No good can come from it.

Taking a seat in front of the mirror, I blow out a breath and get to work applying my makeup. A small smile tugs at my lips and I thank everything holy that I didn't get fired. But it drops just as quickly when I remember Nico's words.

Maybe being fired would have been the best outcome.

Chapter 9
Nico

I grunt with every hit to the punching bag.

My irritation is at an all-time high and I feel like I am about to snap, so I needed to do something to work my frustrations out. Usually, I would fuck it out of me, ramming my cock inside a beautiful woman's cunt. But fucking seems to be out of the picture for me right now. Because there only seems to be one woman I want to sink my cock into, and she should be off limits to me. So, beating the shit out of this bag will have to suffice. For now.

For the first time in my life, my head is a mess, consumed by a woman of all things. I don't know why Ocean has me twisted up in knots, but it's frustrating to say the least. I barely know the girl, yet everything about her screams to me on a level I didn't know existed inside of me. It's primal, possessive... fucking annoying.

I don't do relationships. Never have. From a young age, I knew what was expected of me, so I didn't see the point. Didn't like a woman enough to take that next step. Fucking women; leaving straight after we have both gotten off is what I do best. What I am good at. So why has this girl, some fucking *dancer,* that I don't even know, achieved the impossible and managed to worm her way beneath my skin? She is an itch that I desperately want to scratch. Yet a part of me, a smaller part, warns me to stay the fuck away from her.

"Fuck," I curse, fury slithering through my veins at my erratic, contradicting thoughts. I punch the bag harder. The sound of my fist hitting the leather is like music to my ears. For years, I have had a roster of women for the sole purpose of taking care of my needs. They know the deal, and though some of them have wanted more, I always made sure to let them know where they stand. If they get too clingy, I don't see them. I use these women strictly for pleasure. But that's as far as it goes. I know some of them fuck around with other men, but it has never bothered me. I don't give a fuck what or who they do in their free time. I always make sure I wrap it up, keeping me safe, from not only an STD but pregnancy. I know what's expected of me in this life, and when the time comes, I will fulfill my duty. My marriage will consist of mutual respect between me and my wife but not love. Never love. I can't afford to have weaknesses. Though eventually, I will; when my future wife bears me children. They will be a weakness, but through forming allegiances with a marriage, I will be able to protect them and my wife.

My thoughts shift back to the woman I should be forgetting. An outsider like Ocean would never be accepted, let alone protected. By going near her, I would be putting a target on her head. It would be frowned upon for me to be with someone like her. Not that I am even thinking about something serious with Ocean – I just want to fuck her – but still. I am the future Don of this *famiglia*. I will be expected to marry a good Italian woman from another mafia family to form alliances. Just like it's expected of my sister.

Blowing out a breath, I frown at my jumbled thoughts. Logically, I know what I need to do, but that doesn't change the fact that I feel this protective possessiveness toward Ocean that I have never once felt toward anyone before. I hate that she is living in a fucking hostel. Hate that I am still allowing her to dance in my club. The only reason I have let it go on so long is because, if she wasn't working at The Executive Club, then she would be dancing at some other club in the city. I wouldn't get to see her. I couldn't just show up to where she works, or go to her hostel every night, like some creeper. Or could I... Hmm, now there's a thought. I know in this moment, that I would if I had to. Who would stop me? No one. I run this fucking city and could buy that damn building if I wanted to.

I shake my head and not for the first time do I think that maybe she has cast some sort of spell over me. It's the only logical answer. I can't possibly be having these sorts of feelings for a woman... can I?

"Fuck," I growl, my irritation growing with every erratic thought in my head. Punching this bag was supposed to ground me, yet it isn't doing shit for me – no matter how hard I hit it. Pulling away, my eye twitches with rage that, even with an hour's worth of hitting the punching bag, I am still in no better shape than I was before I started. Grabbing my towel off the bench, I bring it up to my face, wiping the sweat off in anger. My gaze shifts to the corner of my gym when I spot movement. Dante. With one leg crossed over the other, he watches me with a knowing smirk.

"Good workout?" he asks, but I hear the teasing in his voice.

"What do you want?" I grumble, as I continue to wipe the sweat from my face and neck.

His grin grows wider. He leans back in his seat, getting comfortable as he hitches a shoulder. "Nothing. I was just wondering if you are going to The Club tonight?"

Dropping my towel, I grab a bottle of water, twist the cap

off, and gulp it down. Draining the cool liquid, I throw the empty plastic in the trash can. Folding my arms across my chest, I eye him with suspicion. "Maybe. Why do you ask?" My gaze narrows on him, muscles tensing. I know what is going to come out of his mouth before he even says it.

"No reason." His voice is filled with humor. "I just have it on good authority that Jensen Harkins has booked out most of the club and has specifically requested *your* girl to perform for him in a private room."

My whole body stiffens with every word he speaks. My heart rate kicks up to an abnormal rhythm, red hot possession slithering through my veins. Jensen Harkins. A millionaire investment banker and longtime patron of The Executive Club. He has never taken interest in any of the dancers, much past them performing, and has never requested anyone specifically. So why Ocean? Has she bewitched him too? The more I hear, the more I am beginning to think it's a possibility. Yes, without a doubt, she is the most beautiful girl we have working at the club, but every other dancer in the place is stunning and has been working there longer. Why does he have a sudden interest in the blond-haired, blue-eyed witch?

Clenching my jaw, I take a breath, forcing myself to relax. Dante knew exactly what he was doing, coming in here and telling me this. But I refuse to give him the reaction he wants. Eyes locking on his, I grit my teeth at the smug smile curving his lips.

"Get Leo to up Jensen's spending minimum. If he wants special treatment, he can fucking pay for it." I drawl nonchalantly, like I'm not about to kill one of my clients.

Dante searches my face for a long beat. He must find what he was looking for because he bursts out laughing.

"Whatever you say, man. But a bit of advice? Don't go to the

Club tonight. People will notice if someone like Jensen Harkins disappears."

***

I don't know why I fucking came here.

I knew I should have taken Dante's advice stayed away.

But that possessive, primal part of me insisted that I come and torture myself like a fucking masochist. Make sure that entitled prick Jensen keeps his hands to himself.

Sipping my whiskey, I stare down at the stage where she dances. Jensen and his associates all stare at her, licking their lips like she is a fucking Wagyu steak they want to devour. My eyes lock on her body as she writhes gracefully. She is art. The way she performs is *art*. Like a priceless Monet or Van Gough. Just watching her you can tell she has had extensive training. She wasn't lying when she said she was a ballet dancer. The delicate way she moves, at one with the music like it was made just for her. My jaw clenches. She should be on stage with The New York Ballet, not taking her clothes off in my club. Though high-end, she is still better than this place.

Movement down below catches my eye. My gaze shifts to it, just in time to see one of the motherfuckers reach out to grab her. Anger pulses in my body. And I'm done. Spinning around, I place my glass on my desk before pulling the door open and striding out of my office. Without even thinking about what I am about to do, I step into my private elevator and make my way down to the basement.

Once inside, I enter the room that holds the power supply and with one flick of a switch, I plunge the building into darkness and silence. A smirk curves my lips as the music disappears. Panicked voices shout and scream but I pay it no mind. Fishing my cell from my pants pocket, I hit the flashlight and make my way back up to the main room. The club is dark except for the light of flashing cellphones. Raised, confused voices bounce around the otherwise quiet building, but it's Leo's deep timbre that stands out. I grin at the clear panic in his voice.

Ignoring them, I head straight for the stage where I see Ocean's silhouette standing stock still against the pole. When the light from my cellphone hits her eyes, I see the fear shining in them. A feeling of protectiveness surges through my veins, as I scoop her up into my arms in the next second. She squeaks in shock, her whole body tensing. Her palms slam down on my chest, pushing at me and trying to fight her way out of my grip.

"Stop it," I growl. She freezes in my arms, and I swear I hear the loud thrum of her heartbeat.

"Nico?" she whispers.

"Yes," I confirm, carrying her backstage and away from the assholes in the room.

She relaxes a little in my arms and that primal part of me roars to life. "What happened? The lights went out. I nearly fell off the stage."

I grunt. It was a risk. Me cutting the power. She could have hurt herself. But even knowing that, I would do it all again. I couldn't stand their eyes on her any longer. "Power went out," is all I say.

"Oh." She responds and even in the dark, I know she is chewing that pouty bottom lip.

Coming to a stop outside the changing room, I drop her to her feet, pushing her against the wall. The other dancers' murmurs come from inside the room, but I ignore them and focus on the witch in front of me.

Her breath hitches, and in the near silence I hear the erratic beating of her heart. Leaning in, I run my nose up her cheek. "Get dressed, *Tesoro*, before I lose all my resolve and fuck you against the wall." My voice is a whisper, a caress against her soft skin. I can't help but dart my tongue out, licking a trail up the delicate skin of her neck and to her ear. She tenses, a small whimper leaving her lips. I grin. "Hmmm, you taste like my new favorite thing." I'm not lying. She does. My mouth waters just imagining how good her pussy will taste on my tongue. My cock hardens and before I do actually fuck her in this hallway, I take a step back. Self-control. I have always possessed it. Ocean makes it slip and I need to start exerting it more where she is involved. "Go." I say, my voice filled with pure lust.

I don't have to ask twice. She wriggles out of my hold, scrambling down the hall and through the door.

I smirk.

I just lost a lot of money with that little stunt I pulled.

Worth it.

Chapter 10

Ocean

Moving into the changing room, I release a breath when I find it partially lit up by cellphones. The girls all chat excitedly amongst themselves as I step towards my locker and mull over all that has happened in the last ten minutes or so.

The power went out. Check.

Nico carried me off the stage. Check.

He *licked* my neck. Check.

His cock was hard when he pressed against me. Check.

Him telling me he was going to fuck me against the wall. Check. Check.

My stomach clenches almost violently just thinking about him inside me. Stretching me... destroying me with what can only be described as a weapon of mass destruction... Jesus.

I don't have anything to compare him to, but he is big, really *big,* and that dirty mouth of his.... I know with absolute certainty that I will never survive someone like Nico Marchetti. But even knowing this, it doesn't stop the moisture dripping between my thighs or the way my pussy clenches with a need so strong, I almost begged him to do as he said he would and shove his cock inside me. I've never really thought about sex. Never been bothered by it. But with Nico... I want him to do all the dirty things his whispered words promised, no matter how much of a bad idea it is. I'm a contradiction right now. On one hand, I want to stay away from him and on the other... I want him. More than I have ever wanted anything in my life.

"Interesting night, right?" Selena's voice breaks into my Nico fog, dragging me from my thoughts.

Shaking my head, I huff a laugh. "Yeah. You could say that."

She chuckles. "Shall we get out of here? I got my period and could really use a bag of candy or something equally as sweet and full of sugar." Her eyes light up. "Like pancakes."

I open my mouth to answer, only to snap my mouth shut when the lights flicker on. Smiling, I exhale in relief. I hate the dark. "Looks like it's back to work," I murmur, slamming my locker shut. I start toward the door, pausing when Nico appears in the doorway. The chatter stops, the whole room falling silent as he stands there like a menacing presence. His gaze locks on me, a frown marring his face when his eyes rake over my near-naked body.

"Get dressed," he demands, his tone leaving no room for argument.

Shifting on my feet, I wrap my arms around myself. My body burns with the weight of curious, albeit jealous, eyes on me. Everyone is witnessing this. I swallow, self-conscious and embarrassed that he is addressing me in front of the other dancers. I squirm under everyone's attention, particularly the intense stare of Nico. My cheeks heat and though I know every person in the quiet of this room will still hear me, I lower my voice to a whisper. "The power is back on. I still have an hour of my shift left."

His eyes spark, predatory gaze never leaving mine when he steps further into the room. My heart jumps into my throat when he moves closer, and I want to look at the other girls. See the expressions on their faces, but I don't dare look away.

"Your shift is over. I'm taking you home." His repeats, his tone non-negotiable. It angers me. Who does he think he is? Coming in here, embarrassing me in front of all the other dancers. He doesn't realize it, but he has just put a bigger target on my back. Apart from Selena, I am deemed an outcast amongst the others. The girls aren't necessarily nasty to me, they just don't acknowledge me. They are a clique – one I am not part of.

With Nico showing me interest, surely this will only make them hate me more and will cause me more issues. I don't want that. I just want to keep my head down and make money. Keep myself to myself. I don't want his attention, especially not right now when he is going to make things harder for me at work.

Pushing aside my fear of him, I straighten my spine, narrowing my eyes as I grit out. "No."

His eyes flash with challenge, a smirk curving his lips and I only fear I have awoken the beast. He shoves his hands in his pants pockets, watching me like I am an insolent child. "I wasn't asking. Get dressed, Ocean. I won't tell you again," he responds coolly. A whisper of shocked gasps sounds around the room and my cheeks heat in embarrassment. Nico glances around the room, daring anyone to go against him, before his detached eyes come back to me. My heart pounds in my chest and I know whatever he says next, I will not like. He speaks, his words cold, threatening. "I could always force you. But I am sure you don't want me to do that in front of prying eyes. You have five minutes, Ocean. Not a minute longer." He finishes, pinning me with a look that has my breath lodging in my throat. A smirk curves his lips and without another word he turns, leaving the room.

My mouth drops open in shock as I watch him leave. What

the hell? He is a fucking asshole. Sucking in a much-needed breath, I try to control the conflicting emotions coursing through my body before I even dare look at anyone else. When a couple of minutes have passed, I glance over my shoulder at Selena. She stares at me, in shock and bewilderment, but I don't miss the questions in her hazel eyes.

"What was that all about? Do you know who he is?" she whisper-hisses, concern lacing her voice.

Rolling my eyes, I turn back to my locker, pulling out my yoga pants and hoodie. "It's Nico. And no. I don't know what that was all about." I say in a hushed voice, trying to keep our conversation private. I mean, yes. I have an idea what his little display of authority was about. I'm not stupid. He clearly has some weird...infatuation or whatever it is with me. Why else would he keep calling me to his office for no reason, carrying me off stage and all the other shit he has pulled?

"Ocean, that was Nico Marchetti. It's rumored he is..." she trails off, swallowing. Her worried eyes dart around the room before she shakes her head at whatever she was going to tell me. "Never mind. I will talk to you at home."

I nod, pulling on my clothes. "Okay. We could still get pancakes if you want?"

She forces a smile, but I don't miss the worry on her pretty face. "No. It looks like you already have plans. I will talk to you tomorrow."

"Okay." I sigh, shooting her a soft smile.

Grabbing my bag, I make my way to the door without looking at any of the other girls. I already know what I will see on their faces.

***

Staring out of the window of the moving SUV, I nearly

choke on the thick tension suffocating the small space. Nico is silent next to me, but I can feel his heavy gaze, burning into the side of my cheek.

After I dressed, I found him leaning against the wall outside the room. The same wall he had me pinned up against not even ten minutes earlier. My cheeks heated at the sight of him standing there, all big and powerful as he focused on his cell phone. It took mere seconds for him to lift his head and spot me, as if he could sense my presence, and within a couple of minutes, he had me in his car, insistent on taking me home.

Now here I am, locked in a car with a man I don't know but I'm pretty sure is dangerous. Not able to stand the silence any longer, I glance over at him and blurt. "Why have you taken an interest in me? I mean, you could have any woman you want. So why me?" My eyes widen and as if I can take those words back, I slap a palm over my mouth. Oh god. Did I really just say that? To him of all people.

His lips curve up, those pale blue eyes glimmering with amusement and my heart crashes against my chest waiting for him to answer. "Hmm. Now isn't that the million-dollar question. Why have I taken such an interest in *you* when I could have anyone I want?" It's not a question even though he asks it as one. He looks thoughtful for a long moment before confusion furrows his brow. He looks as perplexed about the situation as I feel. Like he can't understand why his attention is on me.

My own brows furrow as I watch him watch me. His hand darting toward me catches my attention but before I can blink, he has my belt unbuckled, and I am pinned to the seat beneath him. My breath lodges in my throat and I stare up at him with wide eyes. He hovers over me, staring down at me with a hungry look in his eyes. His chest heaves, nostrils flare. My heart rate kicks up, but it's more in...desire than fear. I swallow. There is something wrong with me if I am getting aroused right now.

Nico searches my face and by the smug look on his, I know he can see every bit of the effect he is having on me. His hand moves under my hoodie, traveling up my bare rib cage and toward my breast. My stomach tightens, breathing turns ragged.

"What are you doing?" I whisper, my gaze shooting to the man driving the vehicle. I relax a little when I find he isn't paying any attention to us. His eyes are pinned to the road ahead, oblivious or accustomed to whatever is happening.

Shifting my eyes back to Nico, I shudder as his pools of blue dilate with pure hunger. His eyes never leave mine as he runs gentle, soothing, circles with his thumb across my skin. Everything inside me comes alive, sparking to life like a firework waiting to explode. If I was thinking rationally, I would push him away. Tell him to get off me. But something deep inside me, something I have never felt before has been awoken by him. It's a deep-seated ache that for some unknown reason, only this man can sate. I shouldn't want him to satisfy any urge I have. I should run far away before he completely consumes me. And he will. Of that, I am certain.

"*Tesoro*," he growls that word again. And though I have no idea what it means, it feels as if it's a pet name of sorts. My eyes widen when I feel him harden against my thigh. I squirm, and pant, wanting to both push him away and pull him closer. "I want to devour you. Every inch of your perfect body." he rolls his dick into me, making me moan. "Shove my cock so deep inside your sweet pussy, they will have to surgically remove me." I gasp at his dirty words. At the visceral reaction surging through my body when he speaks like that. He grins as if he knows exactly what I am thinking and without saying another word, his mouth crashes down on my lips. I whimper at the feel of him. At the bruising, primal way he attacks my mouth. This isn't kissing, it's claiming. An ownership.

Before I can think about it more, his free hand comes up to

grip the back of my head and holds me exactly where he wants me. His tongue stabs at my mouth, wanting entrance. I open up for him, allowing him to push his tongue inside and conquer me further. I moan in pleasure as he explores and tastes every inch of my mouth. Wetness seeps into my panties, my stomach tightening with need. My body rolls against him, desperate and full of desire. Moisture coats my panties and thighs, and I am suddenly concerned about whether I should be this wet from just a kiss.

Nico breaks the kiss and I whimper at the loss. He smirks, lifting his nose and sniffing the air. I am confused about what he is doing until he speaks. "So responsive to just a little kiss. I can smell your cunt from here." My cheeks heat in embarrassment, but he just grins smugly. I can only be thankful that he doesn't look disgusted by my reaction to him.

The car stops, snapping me out of my lust-filled haze. Nico glances out the window, anger clouding his features before he sighs. Sitting upright, he runs a hand down his tie. I scramble up in my seat, looking through the tinted glass to find that we are outside of my building. I grimace, wishing I lived further away. Looking at Nico, I nibble my lip, suddenly feeling shy, and exposed. The Nico fog has cleared, and I can see clearly. I shouldn't have let this happen. Clearing my throat, I force a smile. "Thank you for the ride."

He smirks. "Oh sweetheart. That was a just little teaser of what's to come. This was only the beginning." He leans in, dropping his voice so only I can hear. "Believe me when I say, that when I finally get my cock inside you, you won't be able to speak, let alone walk." My breath catches in my throat. He pulls back to look at me, jerking his head toward my building. "Now go, before I completely lose my control and fuck you raw in the back seat, with Christopher here as my witness."

I whimper. Not because I'm scared. I almost stay where I

kelly Kelsey

am, in the warmth of the car just to see if he will make good on his promise. Instead, and because I don't want my first time to be in an SUV with an audience, I climb out, rushing to the door of my hostel and locking myself inside before I do something I will regret.

Chapter 11
Nico

Adrenaline pulses through my veins as I make my way through the cold, damp, warehouse, with Dante by my side. Just like I told my papà, I found the rat bastard that has been leaking information about the business dealings of the *famiglia* to the Bratva.

It wasn't hard once I started asking questions. Turns out that one of our soldiers isn't happy with his place within our organization. The fucker was playing double agent and making extra money at my expense. Now he is about to find out just what happens when someone crosses a Marchetti.

Pushing through the metal doors into the refrigerated room where he is currently being held, I pause when the smell of piss, shit, blood, and sweat hits me. "Christ," I mutter, my nose scrunching up in disgust.

Dante chuckles. "Why is it these assholes always soil themselves before we torture them. The smell really ruins my mood when I'm cutting someone up." I grunt in agreement. I'm a sadistic bastard, but Dante is even worse than me when it comes to torture techniques. If I had a heart, I would almost feel sorry for his victims. Fortunately, I don't, so I revel in his punishments as much as he does.

My eyes shift to the traitorous bastard, strung up in the middle of the room. *Federico.* His arms are pulled tight, stretched up to the ceiling by cable and ropes. His muscles strain with the tension, veins popping as his limbs twist abnormally. My gaze moves from his bloodied, bruised face down to the wet patches that line both legs of his jeans. Disgust and the need to exact revenge, surge through me. Fucking traitor.

"What did he tell you?" My question is aimed at Dario, an enforcer of ours.

"Nothing much. He begged. Screamed. Promised he wasn't the rat. You know, all the usual shit that comes when someone has been found out." His hands are in his pockets, eyes cold, almost dead. Dario is one of the scarier men in our *famiglia*. He has no issue following our every command, whether it be taking a life or blowing up a rival's building. It's why he was promoted up the ranks quicker than most.

I step closer to the body hanging like a pig. Federico pales, his eyes widening as much as they can with the damage Dario has inflicted. "You think you can betray us? Turn rat?" I hiss, my voice low and deadly.

"It wasn't me. I swear it, Nico." Spittle flies from his mouth when he speaks, and I step back as he starts to cry. Then as if he finds a little extra fight in his battered and bruised body, he thrashes around, kicking out at me and screaming for help as he tries to get free. It's no use. He knows that. I know that. If he could escape his shackles he would have done so already.

I tsk, shaking my head. "This will be easier if you stop lying. We already know it's you. We traced some of your calls and texts with someone within the Bratva, confirming shipments, and locations." I push the sleeves of my black dress shirt up my arms. "You fucked up, Federico. And you know what happens to people who fuck up."

Tears pour down his blood-soaked face. He knows this is the end. Knows that this is the place he will take his last breath and die. "Please, Nico. Show me mercy. I have a family. My children need me," his voice is getting hysterical, and I almost laugh at how he thinks he can change my mind. That he thinks I will just let him walk away. I won't. I can't. One day I will be boss, and these men need to learn to respect me. If I show leniency in any way, then it will make them believe they can get away with this kind of treachery.

Sighing, I pull my Glock from my waistband. I could drag his torture out, but I want out of this shithole. Federico's eyes widen, tears slipping down his now resigned bloodied face. Without another word to the traitor, I lift my gun, aim and shoot him straight between the eyes. Quick and easy. Done. News of my killing him will spread and hopefully deter anyone else from getting ideas of talking to our enemies.

"Get the clean-up crew here," I say to no one in particular but knowing they will do as I say. Shoving my gun back in my waistband, I turn, making my way back towards the doors.

"Clean-up is on their way." Dante says coming up beside me. I nod my acknowledgment. He clamps a hand down on my shoulder, sighing. "Come on. I think you need a drink and some pussy."

I bark out a laugh. "Drink yes. Pussy no."

"Come on Nic, you need to get your dick wet. It's been what? A month?"

I look at him out of the corner of my eye. I mean yeah, I could do with getting laid but there is only one woman I want to stick my cock in right now, and it's the one woman I should stay well away from. Maybe Dante is right, and I should hit up one of my regulars. Take out my frustration on one of them. I scrub a palm down my face, suddenly exhausted. "I need to go to the club first. I have some business to take care of."

He chuckles and I grit my teeth, knowing what he is going to say. "Yeah. That business wouldn't have anything to do with a blonde-haired, blue-eyed girl with a body made for sin, would it?"

Possessiveness shoots through my body and I will myself not to wrap my hands around my best friend's throat. Instead, I pin him with a murderous look that wipes the smile straight from his face. Blowing out a calming breath, I shake my head. If I carry on like this, I'm going to lose my damn mind. Or stop her dancing altogether ... I can't bear the thought of people's eyes on her, which is why I cut the power the other night. How I am still letting her dance is beyond me, but it does show that I have a little self-control when it comes to Ocean, even though the caged beast inside me demands I put a stop to it. But what right do I have? She isn't mine. She never will be... For some reason that thought feels all wrong.

Sliding into the back of my SUV, I lean my head back, closing my eyes. My erratic thoughts about her are beginning to take their toll and I know it's only a matter of time before I do something stupid. Like lock her in a room. Hide her away from the world. Fuck. I need to get my shit together and quickly.

Dante climbs in beside me, breaking me from my reverie. My driver, Christopher, turns on the ignition, waiting for instructions on where to go next.

"Take us to The Executive Club," I instruct, no other words are needed. Putting his foot on the gas, Christopher takes me to the place that has become both my heaven and my hell.

***

I wish I had gone home and stayed away.

I should have listened to Dante, had a drink, and called up some of my regular pussy.

But no. Being the masochist I seem to be when it comes to Ocean Embers, I find myself standing at my damn window. Red-hot, pent-up anger, and another emotion I can't think about right now, courses through my veins, demanding I release it on every asshole down on the club floor.

My eyes roam over the *piccola ballerina,* and I watch in fury as she sways her hips, hypnotizing every mother fucker in this place. Even every member of staff on my payroll watches with rapt attention, mesmerized by her. As infuriating as it is, the attention she is receiving, it's Leo that caught my attention. My gaze narrows in on him, at the way he watches her. The way his eyes light up like a fucking bonfire and he licks his lips like she is his next meal. My hand tightens around the glass so hard, I'm surprised when it doesn't break. I am going to fucking kill him.

Friend or not, he doesn't get to look at her like that.

Fishing my cell from my pants pocket with my free hand, I unlock it, scrolling to Leo's number. Pressing down, I bring it to my ear. He frowns as he looks at the screen before answering.

"Yeah?" he greets over the music. His voice is so blasé that it spikes my irritation further.

"Bring the girl up to my office." My voice is deathly calm and at complete odds with how I am feeling. He looks up and though he can't see me, he knows that I'm watching. He also knows exactly which *girl* I am talking about without me having to say her name.

"Why, Nico?" he sighs, and I almost miss it over the loud club.

My hand grips the phone tighter. Fury like I have never felt before surges through me. Who the fuck does he think he is to question me?

"Because I fucking said so." I roar and I watch as he pulls

the cell from his ear before bringing it back. He blows out a breath, running a frustrated hand through his hair.

"Yeah. Okay. Let her finish up her set and I will bring her up." He concedes before ending the call.

Striding to the bar cart, I pour myself another scotch, knocking it back in one go. Pouring another drink, I stride to the leather couch that sits against the wall. Taking a seat, I get comfortable and wait for Ocean. Not even ten minutes later, a knock sounds at the door. My heart pounds in my chest. My blood heats and it feels like pure lust has been shot into my veins as my cock thickens in my pants. My reaction to this girl is not normal, yet I can't seem to bring myself to care tonight. Tomorrow I may think differently, but for tonight I am going to allow myself a little taste.

"Enter." I call out when a couple of minutes have passed. I don't want to look to eager.

The door is pushed open, and Leo appears. Ocean is tucked partially behind him, but I see her worried face. She chews that full bottom lip, and rage ignites inside me when I find myself jealous of her damn teeth. I want to be the one nibbling the plump flesh. Drawing it into my mouth. Driving her wild...

"Dante is downstairs checking on shit. Tell him not to interrupt me. Now leave us." I tell Leo, but my gaze has shifted back to Ocean. She shifts on her feet as she watches me, a look of complete fear covering her beautiful features. The door slams shut, letting me know that Leo has left. Adrenaline courses through me. I have Ocean alone. *Just how I like it*. The thought hits me so fast, I grit my teeth.

My gaze locks on Ocean, studying her to see what she will do next. I watch with amusement as she pushes down her fear, straightening her spine. The scared doe-eyed look is gone, now replaced with false strength. I know it's fake because I can see the pulse point in her neck, jumping erratically. She sighs indifferently, and I have to bite back a laugh at her little display. She is about as frightening as a Chihuahua right now, but I have to give her points for how she is handling this. Even if it is all a façade. She is trying to force confidence, but I see the nerves swimming in her blue eyes. The girl is a complete paradox. A mixture of innocence and sin. Self-assurance and apprehension. Maybe that's why she intrigues me so much.

"What do you want Nico? This is getting a bit tedious now, don't you think?"

"Dance for me," I demand before I can stop myself.

Her mouth drops open in shock, those pools of blue widening almost comically. "Wh-what?" she wheezes out, all signs of her confidence now gone, the fear shining through. If she can dance for a room full of men, then she can fucking dance for me.

Taking a sip of my whiskey, I let the smooth liquid wet my throat. My voice is husky when I speak. "Did I stutter? Dance. For. Me." I enunciate the last three words.

Ocean shakes her head, her arms wrapping around her body protectively as if that will save her from me. My gaze drops to where she has pushed her tits up and it's only then I notice what she is wearing. It's the same outfit she had on while she was downstairs dancing, but I see it clearly now. A crystal-encrusted bra and matching panties. Christ, is she trying to kill me? I can't say I would be opposed to going that way. Death by Ocean Embers.

"Why?" she blurts, snapping me from my thoughts. My eyes lock on her face. I harden at the fear flashing in her blue orbs, at the way her lips tremble. I want to shove my cock between them, fuck her mouth as the plump flesh vibrates around my length. My cock twitches, liking that thought, but I shake it away, remembering I haven't given her an answer.

"Because, I want to see what has all those men down there

so enraptured by you." It's a lie. I know exactly why they are so fascinated, but if it gets me what I want, I'm not above lying. "So, dance. If you want to leave my office any time tonight, then you will dance for me." I growl out.

Her face pales as she no doubt mulls over her options. She only has one option. That's to give me what I want. I will not let her leave until she has moved that body for me, so she better get to it. I see the moment resignation sets in. Watch the emotion in her eyes when she realizes that she will not be leaving until she does as I ask. Straightening her spine, she pins those blue eyes on me.

"There's no music." She points out the obvious, her voice exasperated. Feeling's mutual, Ocean. If only you knew the shit going through my head.

I grin at the defiance in her voice, wanting nothing more than to make her submit. That will come another day. For now, I want to see her body move up close. Dropping my tumbler of whiskey to the table, I grab my cell. Punching in the passcode, I open my playlist, quickly finding a song and hitting play.

The dulcet tones of Debussy's *Clair de Lune* sound around the otherwise quiet room. Ocean stares at me in surprise, no doubt at the fact that I picked a classical tune more suited to ballet rather than what she dances to here at my club. Inhaling a breath and with a small smile, she starts to move her body. I smirk, hooking my arms over the back of the couch as I watch her find her rhythm. With the ease only a professional dancer could have, her body moves sensually, seductively, at one with the music playing. It's an experience watching her, one I want to bathe in. My cock hardens, stabbing against the material of my briefs, and begging for release. I grip the fabric of the couch and it takes everything in me to stay where I am.

Moving into a pirouette position, she twirls several times before coming to an abrupt stop when the music ends. It's by far the sexiest thing I have ever seen in my life. Her chest heaves, breasts lifting with the movement. And then she looks at me. Shy, innocent eyes stare back at me, and fuck... she is everything I want.

"Crawl to me," I demand, my voice thick with unrestrained lust. I don't know why those words just came out of my mouth, but there is a sick part of me that wants to see her on her knees, just for me. Only for me. I want to push her boundaries; to see how far she will go to please me.

Her eyes widen, but at this point she knows I won't take no for an answer. But still, she thinks about it for a couple of seconds before slowly lowering to her knees. My heart pounds in my chest at the sight. Fuck, she is exquisite when she submits to me. I groan, my gaze tracking her every move when she starts crawling toward me. My cock turns to steel, and I almost lose it completely. I haven't even been inside the girl and yet this is the single most erotic moment I have ever experienced with a woman.

When she makes it to the coffee table, my self-control slips, and I have to touch her. Pushing off the couch, I pause when she comes to a stop, backing up against the table as if it will protect her from me. It won't. Nothing will save her from me. Closing the distance between us, I bend. My hands hit the oak wood, caging her in. Her breath hitches when I get in her face. I smirk, dropping my face to her neck. I breathe in her sweet scent, groaning in my throat at how good she smells. The pulse in her neck jumps erratically, making my cock harden to steel, and I want her so bad, I can't see straight.

"What is it about you that makes me want to break every rule I have ever had? Hmm? I want to ram my cock so deep into you, I will be imprinted in your cunt forever. I want to paint you with my cum and mark every inch of your beautiful skin." I murmur, bringing a finger up and running it across her arm.

She startles at my touch but doesn't push me away. "Yo-You can't say that to me." her words are stuttered, and I know I affect her just as much as she affects me.

Pulling back, I smirk. "I just did, *Tesoro*. Now what are we going to do about this...attraction?"

Her cheeks turn pink with desire or embarrassment, I'm not sure. She watches me with parted lips and wide eyes. I know she wants to break our staring and run far away from me, but she also wants to show me she can be brave. I inwardly grin when the latter wins. Defiance flashes in her narrowed blue orbs, her teeth bared as she snarls. "I don't know what you're talking about."

I smile. I'm going to enjoy every second of making her submit to me. "Oh, but you do. I can smell your desire in the air. You want me." I run a finger down her cheek. Her skin is soft, with only a little makeup. She doesn't need it though. The girl is stunning.

Leaning in closer, I breathe in every little puff of air she releases. Her tongue darts out and she licks her lips. My eyes zero in on the movement. Like a hungry lion about to eat its prey, I move in. Ready to take her mouth, to feel if it's as soft as I imagine it to be. I am so close, mere millimeters away, when the door is pushed open abruptly and I'm interrupted. Ocean jumps backward, startled by whoever dared to barge in here.

Straightening to my full height, I turn around to find Dante. I glower, ready to pull out my Glock and kill the asshole for disturbing me. His eyes dart from me to Ocean, where they linger for a long beat. Possession heats my blood and I have the sudden urge to hide her from his view. As if he knows exactly what I'm thinking, he smirks. I grit my teeth, pinning murderous eyes on him.

His face sobers and he clears his throat. "We have a situation." By the tone in his voice, I know it's serious. Know I will have to deal with whatever it is and leave this office. Leave Ocean. I glance down at her. Her eyes dart to Dante and back to me. I frown, wishing we could go back to a minute ago, caught up in our... well, whatever it was. But I have business to attend to. Irritation slithers through me and it takes me a split second to decide I am not done with her tonight. I want more. So much more.

Glancing down at her on the floor, I pin her with my *don't argue with me* look.

"Wait here for me. We have things to discuss. I won't be long."

Chapter 12

Ocean

What the hell just happened?

Shaking my head, my gaze remains locked on the door Nico just disappeared through. I'm in shock at what has transpired in the last fifteen minutes or so. My head lands in the palms of my hands. What did I do and why does it feel like I just opened Pandora's Box?

I danced for him.

Crawled for him.

Why did I submit to him so easily?

Heat fills my body, moisture seeping into my panties, as images of what I just did play on repeat in my head. At how he played a song that I haven't danced to in a long time. The way my body moved to the music, never missing a beat. The way I willingly dropped to my knees, eager to please him. The satisfaction that sparked in Nico's eyes at my easy submission. How I... I liked it. Want more of it. To see that look of desire in his blue orbs, knowing I'm the one to have put it there. It's addicting. A rush.

I shake my head at my errant thoughts, pushing up off the floor to stand. What is wrong with me and why does Nico make me lose all sense of reason? Pacing the floor, I start to feel out of sorts and embarrassed at my behavior. Though I can't deny I liked dancing for him, now that the fog has cleared, I'm mortified. Where do we go from here? I can't lose this job. I should have kept it professional and told him no. I groan. Something tells me he wouldn't accept the word no and I wouldn't have been allowed to leave this office until I gave him what he wanted. And right now, that seems to be *me*. Coming to a stop, I chew my lip anxiously as I stare at the door, debating my next move.

"Stay here."

Yeah, no.

Not happening.

Maybe I should listen to his demand – he does own the place – but when I signed up to work here it was Leo who interviewed me. Leo who hired me. Leo is my boss.

My eyes shift around the room, landing on the window. Tentatively, I move toward it, pausing when I step up to the tinted glass and see the view below. Does Nico watch me from here? My stomach dips as I picture a man like Nico, standing here, drink in hand, as he watches me dance. I know for a fact, that you can't see anything through the window when you are on the club floor, but I have a clear view of the whole place from his office. He must have some one-way privacy glass or something. It would make sense.

Selena sashaying out on stage, dressed in what I can only describe as a go-go get up, snaps me from my thoughts. I have never seen her in this outfit before so it must be new. My guess is she wants to make extra tips, so she is changing up her performance this evening. That's one of the good things about working at The Executive Club. We have full control over our choreography, and can perform what and how we want as long as it brings in the clients and money.

My eyes track Selena as her body moves sensually to whatever music is playing. I grin at the big, beautiful smile on her face. She may have questioned working here, but I can see in her eyes she is happy when she is dancing. Just like me. I sigh wistfully. It might not be the dancing I dreamed of doing growing up, but at least I get to dance. Had I stayed with my parents, it would have been taken away from me, along with many other things.

A couple of minutes later the song must come to an end, because my friend takes a bow, waves to the crowd and saunters off stage, looking like the cat that caught the canary. Grinning, I shake my head before getting back to my predicament. I mull over my options but really, I only have one.

Mind made up, I turn for the door and make my way back down to the changing rooms. Fuck Nico. He doesn't get to tell me what to do. Maybe I am a little compliant, but I feel the defiant side of me begging to break free. And right now, my rebellious side is winning.

Consequences be damned.

***

The sexy beat of Sam Smith's *Unholy*, sounds around the club. I spin around the pole a couple of times, in my element as I dance. Legs crossed at the bottom, I drop my ass to the stage before lying flat on the stage and arching my back. My eyes close, a grin curving my lips when I hear the catcalls. It's my last dance of the night, and it's also the one that makes me the most money. I can make thousands in those last couple of minutes. Thousands to add to the already healthy stash of green I have hidden in a secret location at the hostel.

Unlike most strip clubs, patrons aren't allowed to throw money at us - The Executive Club is way too classy for that.

Instead, hostesses walk around, collecting the money in black crystal bowls that each have our names on them. Once they have collected it, they will bring it backstage and hand it over to the dancers. It feels less seedy than shoving bills into a thong, so I prefer The Executive Club's way of doing things.

I haven't seen Nico since he left me in his office and that was well over an hour ago. Did he really think I would wait around for him to come back? I smile. Of course, he did. He is Nico Marchetti. All the girls go crazy over him here, so why would he think that I'm different? He is about to learn. Because instead of doing what he asked, I am out here doing what I love. Dancing. Dancing like no one is watching even though I know there are hundreds of sets of eyes on me.

When the music stops and the emcee begins to talk, my eyes snap open. Time's up. My dance is over. Rising to my feet, I ignore all the eyes I feel on me, collect my bra, and move to head backstage. Just as I go to take the first step, a hand wraps around my wrist, pulling until I tumble off the stage and into a warm, *hard,* lap. His cock digs into my ass, and I want to be sick. My whole body stiffens when arms lock around me, holding me in place. I wriggle, trying to get out of his hold only to freeze when a husky voice hits my ears.

"I've been waiting to get my hands on you, gorgeous." he slurs. His hands start to roam my body, cupping my breasts. Panic courses through me, and I try to wrestle out of his hold.

"Let me go." I snap, searching around for security to come and do their damn job. They can see me, see that this man is breaking all the rules right now, but for some reason everything seems to be happening in slow motion. It's as if they can't get to me.

The man laughs, clamping his hands down around my thighs to hold me still. "Nah, beautiful. I don't think I will. Not now I have you." He grinds his cock into me, and I go still. Bile fills my throat with every roll of his hips. "Feel that? You did that." He thrusts up into me, his dick sliding between my ass cheeks. I've had enough.

Balling my hand into a fist, I turn, raising my arm to hit him in his perverted face but I don't get the chance to make contact. I am yanked out of his hold and pulled protectively into a hard chest. I don't have to look up to see who it is. I can smell him. Feel him. Feel the power radiating from every pore in his body. Nico.

The music cuts off, and the club goes silent. Glancing around, I notice all eyes on us, watching with rapt attention. I swallow nervously, turning my head back to Mr. Pervert in front of me. He goes deathly white, his eyes widening in horror. "Mr. Marchetti," he squeaks out, all signs of the asshole that just manhandled me gone.

"Shawn. Why are you touching *my* girl? Are you looking to lose a hand?" Nico's voice is calm, but I hear the threat in his tone. Hear the possessiveness when he says, *my girl*. Does he refer to all the dancers that way? I shake the thought away. I don't have time for that right now. Glancing up at Nico, I recoil at the sadistic, twisted smile on his face. It's a smile I would imagine a predator wearing, just before they take down their prey.

Shawn, as Nico called him, shakes his head. "Sorry man. I wasn't thinking. One too many whiskeys." He laughs nervously, reaching up to wipe his sweaty forehead.

Nico shoves me behind him, stepping closer to the pervert. My heart rate kicks up. I just want to go back to the changing room and put some clothes on. I look around the club, trying to locate anyone who can help me out of this mess. My eyes eventually lock onto Leo's face. He frowns, but there is something else on his face. Fear? Pity?

A murmur of gasps bounces around the club, drawing my

attention back to Nico. He has a hand wrapped around the man's throat; his mouth dropped to his ear as he speaks. I can't hear what he is saying, but I know it must be bad because there is no hiding the look of absolute fear in the pervert's eyes. My assumption is confirmed when his beige chino pants darken with the wetness seeping down the fabric. He just soiled himself.

My head snaps up when, with his free hand, Nico, grabs the man's arm, yanking him up out of his seat. Nico's gaze drops to the stain, a look of disgust crossing his gorgeous face. "You make me fucking sick." He hisses, passing him over to one of the security guards. They drag him away, but I don't have a chance to see where they take him because Nico grabs my arm, pulling me into him. His gaze roams over my half-naked body and he scowls. "I told you to stay put. My office now," he growls, releasing me so he can remove his suit jacket.

Throwing it over my shoulders, he makes sure I am covered before gripping my elbow and escorting me across the club floor and in the direction of his office. I don't even attempt to pull out of his hold. There's no point. I disobeyed him. He is angry and now I am pretty sure that I'm going to pay for my insubordination.

"Ow. You're hurting me." I whimper when his fingers dig harder into my arm.

He looks over his shoulder as he loosens his grip on me. Not completely but enough so it doesn't hurt. His friend, the one who is always with him, steps up beside him. He doesn't acknowledge me as he speaks. "Ray has taken him to the basement." His voice is low, with no hint of emotion in it.

My heart rate spikes. Basement? Him? Is he talking about the pervert? Oh my God. What are they going to do to him? No, he shouldn't have touched me, it's club rules, but he doesn't deserve to be hurt over the small infraction. I knew Nico was powerful, he reeks of power and money, but who exactly is he? I come from an influential family, and though they live by their own rules, and run my hometown with an iron fist, my father or his associates wouldn't kill a man for such a small violation. I can't allow this to happen. I don't want blood on my hands.

"Nico," I start, swallowing over the lump in my throat as he drags me through the doors that lead to his private elevator. He glances back at me as does his friend. "I don't know how you normally deal with things, but he made a mistake. I am sure if you just cancel his membership and ban him from the club, that will suffice. I don't want you to hurt him." His eyes flash with something I can't quite decipher but I hope I somehow got through to him.

Pulling me into the elevator, he hits the button that will take us to the floor where his office resides. I suck in a breath, the tension in the small space palpable. Nico and his friend are so big they take up all the room, making me feel claustrophobic. Nico turns to face me, an evil smirk on his face. "I'm sure it would. But you have no say in his punishment. You should have listened to me, Ocean, and stayed put." He drawls. I shiver at the tone of his voice.

Shifting his gaze away, he talks to his friend. "Dante, have Leo speak with every patron here tonight, and tell them that I would appreciate their discretion. Get him to give them a drink on me."

"On it," the man I now know as Dante says, fishing his cell out of his pants pocket.

The elevator comes to a stop, the doors opening in the next second. Nico takes my hand, dragging me down the hall. My heels click on the tiles as I struggle to keep up with his long strides. Pushing open his door, he pulls me inside before closing the door with a resounding click.

"Sit." He demands, his tone leaving no room for argument.

Dancing In Sin

Scrambling to the chair, I drop down, obeying him. Taking his chair, he steeples his fingers, staring at me with a calculating look. I shift in my seat, uncomfortable under his intense scrutiny.

"I didn't mean to cause a scene." I blurt the apology even though I know what happened wasn't my fault.

His pale blue eyes spark, pleasure leaking into them. "Ocean. Ocean. Ocean." He hums my name repeatedly as if he is tasting it on his tongue. "You have left me with no other choice. You will quit dancing."

My mouth drops open, eyes widening in shock or incredulity I'm not sure.

Am I hearing things, or did he just demand I quit my job?

I stare at him. He stares at me. His face is impassive, but I know with certainty he means every word he just said.

What the fuck am I going to do now?

Chapter 13
Nico

She stares at me with parted lips and a look of complete shock on her face. I bite back a laugh, though the situation isn't funny. I didn't plan on ending my night by taking some fucking grabby asshole's hand. But I guess being who I am, I should always expect the unexpected, though arguably, I doubt I would be exacting the same punishment had it been any of the other dancers he pulled into his lap.

Being as she hasn't responded to my request, and concluding she didn't hear me, I repeat my demand. "You will quit dancing."

There is no other choice for Ocean now. Not now I have unleashed this possessive, primal need to keep her all for myself. I don't want her on that stage any longer, or any more beady eyes viewing what is mine. I told her to stay put when Dante called me away. She didn't listen. Usually Leo, being the manager, would deal with any drama within the club, but as it was the Feds that showed up, it was something I needed to handle. Had I not left the office, I would probably be buried balls deep inside her right now, and not in a fucking situation where she forced my hand. Made me demand this crazy shit.

My jaw clenches when I realize how deep my attraction for this girl goes. At the hold she has over me.

Her eyes widen, mouth drops open. She laughs nervously only to stop when she realizes my face shows no hint of amusement or that this is all some big joke. It's not. She won't be dancing here... or anywhere else for that matter.

Her eyes narrow in on me, muscles lock into place. She is going to fight me on it. "No." One word, but somehow, I knew that would be her answer.

"It wasn't a question, and this is not up for discussion, Ocean. You will not be dancing here any longer." My words are final, face blank. She doesn't want to fuck with me right now. My monster is lurking, trying to push its way to the surface and if she denies me this request, she will see just who she is dealing with.

She shoots to her feet, defiance flashing in her blue eyes. My cock hardens. I both love and hate the fire she has inside her. I don't want to completely put that flame out, but she will submit to me. "No. You can't do this. I didn't do anything wrong."

Standing, I brace my palms on my desk and lean in toward her. "I can and I will. This is non-negotiable. I have other businesses you can work at. Businesses where you..." my gaze drops down her body which is now covered by my suit jacket. I clear my throat. "Can keep your clothes on."

She growls, the noise so damn cute, I have to hold down the laugh that is bubbling up inside me. I shake my head. The fuck? Nico Marchetti doesn't laugh.

"Who the hell do you think you are, telling me where I can and can't work? I like dancing. I *want* to dance. I am staying here." She thinks her words are final, but this is my club. She is *my* girl. And she will do what the fuck I tell her to.

"No. You. Are. Not." I enunciate the words in case she is hard of hearing. Maybe the music down there is so loud, it has fucked with her eardrums or something. "Pack your shit. Leo will pay you what you are owed. You are done here. I have a spa a couple blocks from where you are living. Come see me tomorrow. Eleven a.m. You can work the front desk." I shove a business card towards her, with *Bellissima,* the high-end spa I own, and details.

Ocean glares before glancing at the card and back to me. She makes no move to take it. She will though, even if I have to force her to. And she can scowl all she likes; it won't get her anywhere. My mind is made up. She won't be taking her clothes off to earn a buck. Not on my watch.

Straightening her spine, she smirks. "You don't want me working here?" she taunts, "That's okay. There are plenty of other clubs in this city, that I am sure will be looking for dancers." She turns on her heels, heading for the door.

I'm around my desk, spinning her to face me, and pinning her against the wall in less than ten seconds. Her breath hitches as my hand wraps around her throat. Not tight but enough that it warns her I am not to be messed with. Those deep blue eyes dilate with fear and a hint of...lust? I smirk, leaning in so my mouth hits her ear. "No other club will hire you. I will make sure of that. I will have you blacklisted from every strip joint in the city. In the whole damn Tri-State area if I have to. Don't push me on this, *Tesoro.* You won't win. I am a very powerful man. You can work, but you will keep your clothes on. My word is law. Don't test it. Now be a good little girl and go get changed. One of my men will take you home." I finish, pulling back to look at her.

Her answering glower makes me want to press my lips to her and wipe the look from her face. I could make her feel so good. Have her screaming my name... My cock hardens just thinking of her tight cunt wrapped around my dick and I bite back a groan.

She swallows, the movement making her throat roll against my hand. I loosen my grip slightly. "Why are you doing this?" her voice breaks, defeat leaking into her eyes. I almost feel bad for her, that she has caught my attention. So many women before her have tried and failed. Though they think I am a prize, there are not many things worse than having the attention of Nico Marchetti. The look in Ocean's eyes confirms it. "I don't even know you," she continues. "I'm just some girl that works in your club. Have you given any of the other dancers the same ultimatum?"

I shake my head, the move so small, that if she wasn't so close, she would have missed it. "I don't have to give you a reason as to why. It's just what I want. And as for the other dancers? No. Just you. Take that as you will, Ocean. All I know is I don't want men looking at you. You are for my eyes only."

She sucks in a breath, her hands dropping to my chest as she tries to push me away. It's no use. I'm big. Lean and muscular. Ocean is so petite. Tiny compared to me. She feels so good, pressed up against me. Like she was made just for me. Perfectly molded to fit *me*. My cock turns to steel, pressing against her. She gasps, shoving at me. "Let me go." she whispers, her blue orbs turning watery.

A tear falls down her cheek. My eyes track the clear liquid, like a hungry lion. I want to lick it up and taste it on my tongue. Before I can stop myself, I lean in to do just that. My tongue darts out, licking a trail up her tear-soaked skin. Ocean flinches, her body tensing but she doesn't stop me. I lick up her pale, flawless cheek, lapping at the salty tear as if I am a thirsty man in the desert. She tastes so good. I want to eat her up. Taste every inch of this perfect woman, who has embedded herself under my skin somehow. It's a shame really. My poor little *Tesoro* really doesn't know what she has gotten herself into.

Pulling away, I search her face. Her eyes are wide, lips

parted, her breathing shallow. Fuck she is stunning. Exquisite. I have never seen anyone as beautiful as this girl in my life. Suddenly, I want to know everything. Every thought that has passed in her pretty little head. I want it all. And for some reason that makes me angry. With a growl, I release her and step back. She startles.

What is it about Ocean that makes me act this way?

Feral.

Unhinged.

Out of control.

It's both a fucking a revelation and an irritation.

Shoving the card in her hand, I turn back to my desk. "Go. I will see you at the spa tomorrow. Leo will arrange for one of my men to take you home." Without another word, she is dismissed. I hear rather than see the door open, then close.

Dropping down in my chair, I sigh. Fuck. I need to practice my restraint when it comes to Ocean. Otherwise, I am going to end up in a situation I have no control over.

Simply put, that cannot happen.

***

"I'm sorry Nico," Shawn screams as I start cutting through the last remaining finger on his right hand. The hand that touched Ocean. The hand that touched something that he had no business touching. Someone who is mine.

I huff a sardonic breath. "I'm sure you are Shawn, but the thing is, if I don't make an example of you, people will think they can get away with touching *my* shit. They can't. You touched something that doesn't belong to you." I tsk. "It's only fair that you pay the price," I growl out, as I slam the knife down, breaking the bone and slicing straight through. He cries out, tears pouring down his face, snot dripping from his nose, as the tip falls to the floor and blood gushes from the wound. I lean into his ear. "Forget what I said earlier. I want you to let the whole city know what happened here tonight. I want them all to know that there will be consequences for messing with what's mine."

My jaw clenches when a dark chuckle sounds behind me. *Motherfucker*. Straightening, I glance over my shoulder to see Dante with a big grin on his face. I glower. He knows exactly why I have done this. And it's not just because Shawn ignored our no-touching policy. It's because of *who* he touched. He holds his hands up in surrender. "I don't think anyone will touch *anything* that belongs to you when they see the state of this asshole."

I grunt, moving away from the fingerless fucker who is now writhing around on the floor, crying in pain. I don't know what the big issue is. He still has the fingers on his left hand. He just needs to remember to keep them to himself and he will be in no danger of losing them, too.

"Get him out of here and call in the clean-up crew." I bark, pinning Dante with a *don't fuck with me right now* look. He nods in acquiescence, pulling his cell from his pants pocket to do my bidding.

With one last look of disgust at Shawn, I leave the cold basement to head back to my office. Anticipation thrums in my veins, the closer I get. There is one more thing I need to do before I leave this place tonight.

It's completely irrational of me, but it doesn't change anything.

Ocean will not work at any other club.

I will make sure of it.

Chapter 14

Ocean

The asshole wasn't lying. I have been to twelve strip clubs today, begging for a job, but came out of each one even more deflated with every no. As soon as I gave my name I was turned away without so much as a reason why. I then realized that Nico had done as he said he would – he had me blacklisted from every damn club in the city. It's frustrating to say the least. I need a job, but I refuse to bow down to Nico's demands and work at his spa. I want to dance. Yeah, I didn't grow up dreaming of becoming a stripper, but circumstances didn't give me much choice, so it's where I am. It's honest work, I earn good money, and even though I have to take my clothes off, I also get to dance. Well, it's past tense now considering Nico's interference.

"Fuck," I growl, rubbing my temples as I stare at the white table. I'm tired, irritated and have a tension headache that just won't quit. After walking around for hours, I decided to stop at a local diner and take a much-needed break. I want coffee and need to think about my next move. I could always leave New York and go somewhere else. But why should I? I already ran once. And though I don't have much, I was making it okay on my own. I can't let some obnoxious asshole, whom I barely know, think he can take over my life just because somewhere along the line he decided I am his property. It's bullshit.

My shoulders slump, angry tears pricking my eyes. Why is this happening to me? I didn't ask for or want his attention. Yes, I admit I like it and last night when I was on his office floor with him invading my space? Well, it was the single most erotic experience of my life. He does things to me and affects my body in ways I don't want to even think about right now. There is something between us, something I can't explain, but the question is... Do I really want to get into anything with Nico? My head tells me no, but the butterflies taking flight in my stomach and the pulse beating between my thighs tells me that I do.

I blow out a frustrated breath. I am a walking contradiction right now, not knowing which way is up or which way is down. I could always talk to Leo about what is going on. Ask him to go against Nico and put me back on the roster, but with the sympathetic look he threw me last night I would bet my life on it – he won't disobey the boss' orders. No way.

I drum my fingernails on the table, my mind racing. I could always just show up at The Executive Club like nothing ever happened. But even as the thought forms, I know it would be pointless doing that. Something tells me I wouldn't even make it to the stage before I was stopped. There are too many security guards that have surely already been informed about the situation. My lips purse. My attempt to go back to The Executive Club may be pointless, but for right now it's all I have. I need to at least try. Fuck Nico. He doesn't get to tell me what to do. I have lived my whole life with men controlling me. It's why I ran. I am not about to fall back into that pattern. I need to fight back.

Determination surges through me. I smile. Tonight, I will go to The Executive Club as normal, to test things. See how far I get before I am stopped. I grin wider. There also might be a small chance that Nico hasn't informed anyone yet. It's highly unlikely, but I am willing to try anything at this point.

Dropping some bills on the table, I climb out of the booth and leave the restaurant. With renewed hope and a spring in my step, I make my way towards the hostel. It's only a couple of blocks away. I will have time to rest for an hour or so, shower, change and get to the club for my shift.

Coming to a crosswalk, I take a left down the street where my building is located. I only make it about ten steps before I come to a complete stop. My mouth drops open, eyes widen in disbelief, at what I find waiting for me.

Nico.

Leaning against a shiny, black SUV like it's a normal occurrence.

What the fuck is he doing here?

Shaking off my shock, I move closer to him. Slowly. Cautiously. He licks his lips, eyeing me like I'm a scared animal and could bolt at any moment. When I am within arm's reach, I blurt. "What are you doing here?"

"You didn't show." He states, pushing off the car. Those pale eyes spark with curiosity and a hint of anger. Like he is proud that I didn't turn up to the spa, but also pissed.

"Ten points for observation." I deadpan, shoving past him. I know he isn't a man I should be antagonizing but screw him. He is single-handedly fucking up my life. And the worst thing? I think he is getting some sort of sick enjoyment from it.

"Stop," he says so low and threatening, I freeze. Though every part of my body screams at me not to obey him, I do. "Turn around." He demands and without looking, I know his jaw is clenched tight.

Swallowing, I spin to face him. He stares at me with narrowed eyes as he runs his thumb across his full bottom lip.

My stomach clenches when I remember the way that mouth was on me last night. Licking up my tears, like it was his job. Like they belonged to him. Why did I like it so much? I should have hated it. Not secretly hoping that he wouldn't ever stop. He takes a step towards me, eliminating the distance between us. My breath hitches in my throat. His gaze holds its usual intensity and is completely focused on me.

Reaching out, his forefinger runs down my cheek. I stop breathing altogether. I have noticed it's a normal reaction, whenever I am in his proximity. "So, fucking beautiful." He murmurs softly before his face and voice hardens. "Now, *Tesoro*. I don't know whether it is defiance or stupidity, or both, but neither will wash with me. I told you to meet me at the *Bellissima*. You didn't. And why didn't you? Hmm?" It's a question but one he doesn't want me to answer. "Because you have been wandering around the city, hitting up other strip clubs and begging them for a job." He grips my chin, pulling my gaze to his. "You can try every damn place in New York baby. No one will dare go against my word and hire you. I already told you, I run this city. So, stop doing stupid shit, before I do something crazy and irrational. I am being accommodating to your needs and trying to let you keep a little independence here. But if you keep defying me, I will take it away completely. Understand?" It's a threat, but I nod my agreement, even though I want to push him away. His eyes spark with satisfaction before his head drops to my neck. He inhales, a deep groan rumbling in his chest. Despite my aversion to him right now, I shiver. My pussy clenches as moisture seeps into my panties. "You're aroused," he states confidently, as he nibbles my ear lobe. It's not a question, it's a statement. A true one at that. Like a shark sensing blood, he picks up on every little detail.

Pulling back, he smirks down at me. "Soon, *Tesoro*. Soon. Now. Back to your new job. You start tomorrow. Nine a.m. Leo passed on your number so I will text you the details. I would take you there right now, but I have business to attend to, so a message will have to suffice." He says all this like it's a given. I will be there as if it's of my own free will and not because he is steamrolling my life right now. Leaning in, he presses his lips to my forehead. My heart rate spikes, and I swear I nearly pass out. "Be a good girl, *Tesoro*. I will see you tomorrow, okay." He cocks a brow, daring me to argue with him. Again, I nod, because I seem to have lost my voice. He smirks, and without another word, strides to the SUV. Pulling the door open, he climbs into the back seat. Only then do I see Dante sitting inside, with the same man who drove me home the other night in the driver's seat.

Nico shoots me a look, before yanking the door closed. It's only when they drive away that I release the breath I was holding.

Jesus. Something tells me if I don't turn up at the spa, he will only show up here again. I don't want that. Any of it. Without actually leaving the city, I don't see how I can avoid his attention. He has taken an interest in me whether I like it or not. Surely, he will soon get bored when he realizes that I am not that interesting. I know with everything in me, I am going to do all I can to shake this attraction I have to him. He is rude. Obnoxious. Overbearing. Dangerous... Exactly the type of man I need to stay away from.

But I also need a job... and it doesn't look like he is going to let me dance anytime soon, even if I want to fight him on that. No matter how much I want to disobey him, I also don't want to run. Not yet anyway.

Shaking my head, I sigh, resigned to the fact that despite not wanting to work in a spa, I know I will be there tomorrow.

Chapter 15

Nico

Her defiance is an aphrodisiac. I like it almost as much as I know I will enjoy making her submit to me.

I'm so fucking hard, my cock throbbing with so much need, I feel like I could explode.

Ocean, la mia piccola ballerina - *my little dancer* - has no idea the beast she has awoken inside of me. The need to claim her and make her mine has taken root, deep inside my body. She will be mine. I will make sure of it.

Nonetheless, no matter how much I want her, I will have to keep it discreet. I can't have my papà finding out about my obsession. No way. He has his own plans for me. Plans that don't include the blue-eyed, blonde-haired beauty.

"I think I just won my bet." Dante drawls from beside me, snapping me from my thoughts. The humor in his voice has me gritting my teeth as annoyance unfurls in my chest.

Glancing at him, I glare when I see the big mocking smile on his face. "Fuck off."

He bursts out laughing, shaking his head. "Man, you are so screwed."

My jaw clenches, and not for the first time do I ask myself why this woman seems to have made me so unhinged. I look at Christopher, my driver, then back to Dante. Asshole has a big mouth. I trust Christopher – well, as much as a man like me can trust anyone – and he has driven Ocean home, so is aware of her existence, but still. Dante needs to shut the fuck up already. The less people that know about Ocean, the better.

"Where to, sir?" Christopher asks.

"The Marchetti Building," I grunt, settling into my seat and dropping my head back against the leather headrest.

"What do you think he wants to see you about?" Dante mutters.

I roll my head to look at him. "If I had to guess, it's about the Russians."

Dante sighs, running a palm down his face. "Yeah. The problem is we don't know how much information Federico leaked before you killed him."

"It's a fucking shit show," I grumble, thinking about all the trouble the Bratva could bring if we went to war with them. It's the worst time to start something with Ocean but even knowing all that, it still won't stop me. She is mine. I can keep her safe. I *will* keep her safe.

Thirty-five minutes later, Christopher pulls up to the curb outside Marchetti headquarters. Climbing out, I step onto the sidewalk, buttoning up my suit jacket. Dante comes to stand beside me. Craning my neck, I look up to the top of the high-rise with a sigh. My skin itches with irritation as I stare up at the extravagant building. The last thing I want is to be here, dealing with my papà, but I can't defy his orders. As my *Don* and father. Duty calls and The Cosa Nostra comes before anything. Unease slithers through me when I think about my last visit. He informed me of the marriage arrangement he was in talks with the Romanos about. For my sister. How he could even consider selling her to that monster I don't know, but he better not have gone ahead and agreed to it without discussing it further with me. I tense. Could his urgent meeting be about Allegra and not the Bratva? I fucking hope not. I don't know what I am capable of right now. I don't feel myself and I know this will just tip me over the edge.

"Whatever is said in here today, I want to make one thing clear. Do not mention Ocean. Even in a joking capacity. My papà cannot know about her." My voice is stern and absolute, face serious. No matter how much Dante likes to joke around about Ocean; he needs to remember who we are dealing with when it comes to my father.

Dante clamps a hand down on my shoulder. "I am loyal to the *famiglia,* Nico. But before that, I am loyal to you. Always." he replies, with sincerity.

Blowing out a breath I nod. "I don't know how some woman I barely know can fuck me up so much." It's an admission and the only one he is going to get right now. Dante knows me better than anyone. He sees how I am with her, so there is no point hiding the truth of my feelings from him.

"It happens to the best of us." He says cryptically. I glance at him, the way his face falls, the broken look in his eyes. Hmm. Interesting. I don't have time right now, but I make a mental note to ask him about it later.

"Let's get this over with." I sigh, starting towards the entrance.

Striding through the glass revolving doors, I ignore the people in the lobby, and we make our way towards the elevators. Hitting the button to the top floor, it opens immediately, and we step inside. Complete silence fills the small space as it ascends, and I am glad for it. Knowing my papà, he has cameras or microphones hidden somewhere in here.

The elevator comes to a stop, the ding snapping me from my

thoughts as the doors open. Stepping out, we stride down the hall that leads towards my father's office. His young secretary - who I know for a fact he is screwing - rises out of her chair, flashing us a white smile. "Nico. Dante." She purrs seductively and I scrunch my face up in distaste. "He is waiting for you."

With a nod of acknowledgment, we move past her, only to pause when I see more soldiers than he would usually have guarding the space.

"Something is not right," Dante murmurs, echoing my own thoughts.

"Whatever it is, we will deal with it." And with that, we carry on to the office, ready for whatever is waiting for us behind my papà's door.

***

"Fuck," I growl, shooting back my whiskey, then slamming the empty glass on the desk. Dante watches me, picking up the bottle of Macallan and pouring me another drink.

We are back at the club after the meeting with my papà and his consigliere. I thought news about my sister would be the worst thing that could happen. Or even the Bratva. I was wrong. What my father wanted to discuss was so much worse.

"Fuck is right," Dante adds, watching me with concerned eyes.

He has every reason to be worried. I have been unpredictable lately but even more so when I walked out of that building. Rage consumed me, and when a random guy walked into me as I was walking to my car, I ended up punching him, then nearly pulling my fucking gun on the poor asshole. It's not like me. I exert control in all parts of my life. But recently, I've felt it slipping. And it's all because of a woman. I grind my teeth so hard I swear they nearly break. The conversation with my papà should be the final nail in my Ocean coffin, but still, it won't make me walk away from her.

"I mean, I knew it would eventually happen but not this quick," I grumble, as fury at the whole situation heats my veins. Fuck. I either need to kill someone or fuck all this pent-up anger out of me. Preferably the former. I swear my cock has stopped working for anyone other than la mia piccola ballerina. That thought only seems to infuriate me further and I take a mouthful of whiskey, hoping the burn of the liquor will calm me some.

Dante sighs. "What are you going to do?" he takes a sip of his drink.

I shake my head. "Nothing. This is my destiny. My legacy. He is Don. I can't fight him on it."

"But what about–"

I cut him off, knowing exactly what he was going to say. "This has nothing to do with her. I will carry on as I am. She is mine, but I have a duty to fulfill, and I will do just that. She only needs to know what I tell her and nothing more."

He nods. "You're right. Hell, doesn't she think that you are a rich businessman? She has no idea that you're the underboss and future heir to the biggest organized crime family on the East Coast." His voice sounds as shocked as it should be. Everyone in this city knows who I really am. Well, everyone but Ocean. I would laugh if the situation wasn't so fucked up.

"And it will stay that way." I say firmly.

Because no matter my obligations to the *famiglia,* it won't change anything that is already set in motion. If I have to keep *her* hidden as my little secret, then that is what I will do.

Ocean is mine.

Nothing and nobody will change that.

Not my destiny.

And not even my papà.

Chapter 16
Ocean

"So, you just click on the date they want, find a time slot that suits them and then add the client, treatment, and therapist?" I confirm with Macy, the manager at *Bellissima*, the high-end spa Nico owns. After an hour of training on the computer in the reception area, I think that I finally understand how everything works.

After my brief interview this morning where I told both Nico and Macy that I have absolutely no experience working a front desk, I was told the job was mine. Nico left shortly after but promised to see me later. I was confused by that. We aren't dating and yet he is acting like we are. Apart from those couple of *small* encounters between us, we have barely kissed. Though I will admit, what happened in the back seat of his SUV and the moment in his office are by far the most sexual experiences I have ever had. The *only* sexual experiences really.

"You picked that up fast, honey. Well done." Macy praises with kind eyes. She is an older woman, I would say in her forties, and very glamorous. She screams wealth. Sophistication. The type of woman I could see Nico with... My jaw clenches as something a lot like jealousy slithers through me with that thought. I tamp it down quickly. I am not that person. The kind of girl that gets territorial and jealous... so why do I suddenly feel like the green-eyed monster over Nico? "You okay?" Macy's concerned voice breaks through my irrational thoughts.

Plastering on a smile, I speak. "Yes. Thank you for showing me everything. I never thought I would be working in a place like this." I wave my arms around the sparse, extravagant space. With its plush white couches, oak tables, soft, soothing music, expensive coffee, water, and juicing equipment, it is everything you would expect from a high-end spa.

"You are very welcome." She pauses, her eyes twinkling as she laughs. "Not that I had a choice. When Nico demands something, you do it." She teases with no malice in her voice which puts me at ease.

I huff a laugh. "Yeah. I'm starting to realize that."

She watches me, curiosity written all over her face. "How do you know Nico?" she asks.

With a sigh, I debated whether to tell her about my previous job. I am not ashamed of working at a strip club, but I have learned over the years that the less you tell people, the less information they have to use against you if they ever turn on you. But Macy is my boss. I should have a good rapport with her and be able to trust her. And anyway, it's not like I am telling her deep stuff. Things about my past...

Clearing my throat, I look her in the eye. "I worked at The Executive Club as a dancer. He decided he no longer wanted me dancing there and offered me a job here instead." I keep it short, giving her the basics. I want to form a good relationship with Macy, but she doesn't need to know everything.

She chuckles, shaking her head. "Wow. I don't even know what to say to that. You don't really look like the..." she trails off, blushing. "The stripper type. But then that's probably me being judgmental when I should be more open-minded." She shakes her head, laughing softly. "I've worked for Nico for eight years. He employed me as the manager of *Bellissima* when he opened the place. Poached me from another spa." She stares off before her gaze comes back to me. "Though I don't know Nico that well, I do *know* him if you know what I mean. I can tell you now, he has never done anything like this before." I don't miss the curiosity in her voice.

"It's not like that," I whisper, shaking my head and suddenly feeling exposed. I shift on my feet. I both hate and like what she is saying. But again, that little voice in my head asks, *why me?*

"Oh, it never is honey," she responds with a knowing grin.

Without saying another word, we get back to my training. I'm glad for the distraction and that Macy doesn't pry further.

***

At nine p.m. - closing time - I tidy up the front desk and shut down the computer. After, I head to the staff break room to grab my purse. Despite my apprehensions about working at a spa, I actually enjoyed myself. Not that I would ever admit it – well, not to Nico anyway.

Honestly, I thought I would be bored, but *Bellissima* is a revolving door of glamourous women wanting beauty treatments, their hair colored and styled or a mixture of both. It reminded me of happier times in my past life. A time when my mother and I would visit our local salon for the exact same reasons as the women who visit *Bellissima* do. Though I was hit with nostalgia, which then made me feel slightly homesick, I reminded myself of the reasons as to why I left. A shudder wracks through my body just thinking about what would have become of me had I stayed.

"All done?" Macy says, glancing at me as she enters the room.

I nod. "Yeah. Thank you for everything today. It's been great."

"No problem, honey. You get yourself home. I will see you tomorrow." She chirps, disappearing back the way she came.

Turning, I reach into my assigned locker, pulling out my purse. Spinning around, a scream leaves my mouth when I spot a figure by the door. In only a couple of strides, Nico is across the room, slapping a palm over my mouth and pulling me into his arms.

"Ssh *Tesoro*, it's just me," he croons, as if that makes it any better. He is scarier than any man I have met. Yet, surprisingly, I feel quite safe in his arms. He stares down at me. So formidable and big against my petite five-foot-five self. Nico pushes me up against the lockers, the cool metal hitting my back and a huge contrast to my now heated body. "How did you like today?" he drawls, his forehead dropping to mine. Head-to-head. Nose to nose. My heart rate kicks up. What is he doing? He breathes me in, sniffing me, like I am a pet. "Fuck. You smell good enough to eat." He growls and I feel his cock hardens against my stomach.

"Nico," I whisper on a sharp inhale.

A deep groan vibrates his chest. "My name on your lips, *Tesoro*. Christ, it does things to me." he runs his nose up my cheek, nuzzling me. "I want to do things to you that would scare you. I want to sink my cock in your pussy and fuck you until you think that you can't take anymore. But I wouldn't stop, I would fuck you through it, using your delectable body as I please." I shiver, my heart rate kicking up to an irregular speed and my legs nearly buckling. No one has ever spoken to me like this. "I want to watch as you wrap your full, perfect lips around my cock. Watch as that pouty flesh stretches around my thickness. I want to fuck your mouth until your jaw aches, then shove myself so far down your throat my cum will have no choice but to settle in your stomach." He rolls a finger over my throat as if to prove his point, then groans again, the sound hitting me straight between the legs. "Christ, I would stretch you so good with my thick cock. Taking you to limits you have never known. It would hurt, but in the best kind of way. You would love it. Beg for it even. And I would give it to you. Every. Single. Inch." He enunciates the last words and liquid heat floods my panties. Jesus, this man and his dirty mouth. Leaning back to look at me, a smirk curves his lips. He knows the effect he has on me. Can probably smell it. "Come on. I want to take you to dinner." My head jerks back at the complete change of subject. I shake it as if ridding myself of the words he just planted in my mind.

"Wh-what?" I stutter.

He smirks. "I am taking you for dinner."

I stare up at him, my chest heaving like I just ran a marathon. It's dangerous for my health being so close to this man, yet I can't seem to stop it. Have no choice over it. Nico's eyes drop to the way my breasts move with every inhale and exhale. He grins with pure satisfaction. Reaching down, he grabs my hand, threading our fingers together. Electricity courses through me, and I know he feels it too when his brows furrow in confusion. He clenches his jaw, gripping my hand almost painfully before loosening his hold. Sighing, he glances down at me before dragging me out of the staff room, through the spa and outside to his waiting SUV.

Chapter 17

Nico

I don't know what I am doing with this girl, but I do know she affects me in a way I have never felt before or can explain. It's fucking infuriating. Especially when she is consuming my mind so much, that I struggle to focus on anything else. On business. I simply cannot allow that. The *famiglia* is my life. My legacy. My birthright. No woman should come between that. Yet Ocean has, no matter how much I try to deny whatever it is I am feeling toward her.

I always knew I would marry someday, but in my world, it will not be a marriage of love but one of convenience. To bring more power to our family. Form stronger alliances. My wife will be someone that understands this world, and not interfere with business. They would be by my side and eventually have my children. We would have mutual respect but there would be no love. I don't think I am even capable of that emotion, to be honest. Lust, yes. And right now, I can definitely say that I am verging into obsession territory with the little dancer, but as for love, that will never happen for me.

Nonetheless, whatever it is I am feeling, I am done fighting it. I am confident, that once I finally fuck her, these feelings will subside. They have to, this thing with Ocean can only be temporary. *But what if the feelings don't go away?* The voice in my head whispers. My jaw clenches. Fuck. It's a possibility for sure. It's clear that I am irrational when it comes to Ocean, and if that's the case then I will have no other choice but to keep her as my... I shake my head again. No. Nope. Not going there.

A throat clears, snapping me from my thoughts. My eyes narrow in on where Ocean sits across the table from me, shifting in her seat and looking more uncomfortable than I have ever seen her. We are at one of the Italian restaurants I own, a couple blocks away from the spa, in a private back room. I chose this particular establishment because I know it's not one my papà or his men frequent. Though I would love nothing more than to show Ocean off to the world, I need to keep things discreet. I can't risk my papà finding out about her. Not now.

My gaze drops to her fidgeting hands before flicking to the throbbing pulse point in her neck. I make her nervous. Good. Because she makes me feel a whole lot of things that unnerve me. I huff a laugh, scrubbing a palm down my face. Jesus fucking Christ I need to be careful with this girl. Not for her sake, but for my sanity. My contradicting thoughts are making me crazy. Our server appears, drawing my attention away from Ocean. He places our dinner on the table with a nervous smile before disappearing and leaving us alone once again.

"Eat," I demand, picking up my utensils and digging into the delicious ravioli. With a glare in my direction but without argument Ocean picks up her fork, digging into her Bolognese. She wraps the noodles around the tines before taking a mouthful of the carb and meat deliciousness gracefully. My eyes shift to her mouth, cock hardening in my pants when I remember how her lips felt pressed against my own. Soft. Innocent. *Mine.* That word jumps into my head unbidden, making me grit my teeth.

Shaking the thought away, I clear my throat. "So, did you enjoy your first day at *Bellissima*?"

Swallowing her food, she reaches out, grabs her soda, and takes a sip as if she needs the time to give me an answer. I watch her delicate throat roll as she drinks the dark liquid. I want to lick my way up her neck and taste every inch of her perfect skin. Glass hitting the table has my gaze lifting back to Ocean's. She smiles, and the look is so breathtaking, I am grateful that I'm sitting right now as I think my legs may have buckled under her beauty. I inwardly roll my eyes. What the hell is wrong with me? I don't think shit like this. Ever.

"It was good. I enjoyed it more than I thought I would. And Macy, she is so nice. She really looked after me." She frowns before continuing. "I will miss dancing, though. Not necessarily the taking my clothes off part, but I have been a dancer my whole life." Her voice is solemn, and wistful, and I want to say anything, *do* anything to remove it from her voice, but I can't have her stripping no matter how much I want to see her happy. Not that I think taking her clothes off made her happy, she just confirmed as much. Maybe I can give her what she wants without that part?

I nod, speaking before I can stop myself. "We can find you a studio or whatever. You don't have to quit dancing completely. But your body stays covered. It isn't for anyone else to look at but me."

Her eyes widen before narrowing in on me. She watches me with fire in those blue orbs, and I know without a doubt that a feisty Ocean is about to appear. I am proved right when she speaks. "You can't tell me what to do, Nico. Don't think me working at *Bellissima* is me submitting to your demands. I don't have any other choice right now. No other club will hire me because of you," she spits, her voice pitching with her anger.

Though I like the stubborn, independent, fiery side of her –

she will need it for what I have planned for her – sometimes she just needs to learn to be grateful and accept what is. Dropping my fork to my plate with a resounding clang, I pin her with a stare that I hope conveys just how serious I am with my next words. "And it will stay that way. Your days of taking your clothes off are over. If you want to dance, I will find you a studio. Hell, I will buy you a damn *studio*. But you will certainly not be working at any club. You work at *Bellissima* now and it will stay that way. So how about a thank you to me for being gracious enough to give you a job."

Lifting her nose haughtily in the air, a disbelieving laugh bursts out of her. I grit my teeth, anger coursing through my veins. When she speaks, it takes everything in me to not put her over my knee and spank her defiant ass. "Thank you? You really are crazy. I had a job, Nico. One I liked." She smirks. "And anyway, I can always leave the city. Go somewhere else to take my clothes off." She finishes. Picking up her fork, she continues eating, her face smug as if she won this round. She didn't.

I snort to cover my laugh. *La mia piccola ballerina* has claws and a nerve, I will give her that. "*Tesoro*, if you do that, I will find you. Anywhere you go. There is no place on earth, or in this fucking universe, you could hide from me. No. Where." I enunciate before picking up my fork. "Now be a good girl and accept what is. It will make things a lot easier for you going forward."

She glowers as if she wants to fight me on it but, thankfully for her, she forks up some of her food, and continues eating. She doesn't say anything else and neither do I. We both eat in silence, the air thick with the tension rolling off Ocean as she occasionally shoots daggers from those piercing blue eyes. I bite back a grin. Such a spirited little thing. And though I will enjoy making her submit to me, I don't want to completely break her. After all, it is her attitude that draws me to her.

When we have both finished our food, and the server has

taken our plates away, I stand, rounding the small table and pulling Ocean to her feet.

"I will take you home." My voice leaves no room for argument. After our little back and forth this evening, I am done. We both need to cool off while Ocean comes to terms with what her life is going to be. I won't back down. Its time she learns that.

***

"*Mio Figlio*," Mamma greets me as I step inside the grand foyer of our family home. Her palms cup my face, she presses a kiss to my cheek and smothers me with love. "I have missed you." she says earnestly.

I chuckle, dropping a kiss to her hair. "I was here just last week."

She sighs, swatting my arm. "How many times do I have to tell you, Nico. You might be twenty-eight years old, but I will always miss you when you are not around. You will understand how I feel when you have your own children."

Well, that's not happening anytime soon. Instead of telling her that, I grin, smelling the air and the aroma of…. "I smell garlic and basil."

She beams up at me. "Well, since I knew you were coming to visit, I made your favorite." Her eyes move past me and she smiles softly. "Hello, Dante."

"Mrs. Marchetti." He greets, stepping around me and pulling her into a hug.

"Val is fine. You know that," her voice is scolding, but I hear the amusement.

"I know. But no matter how many times you tell me, you still won't convince me to call you anything else. I happen to like breathing. I don't want your husband to put a bullet in my head," he chuckles.

It's not that Dante doesn't want to call my mamma by her first name, but it's a respect thing, one my papà expects to be adhered to. He may disrespect Valentina Marchetti every day of the week, but God forbid someone addresses her in a way he doesn't like.

"Where's–" I cut off just as the person I was about to ask after descends the stairs, all regal and dressed like the mafia princess she is. "Never mind. Allegra." I greet my sister.

She rolls her eyes before they shift briefly to Dante. "Big brother." She hits the tiled floor, her heels clicking against them as she closes the distance between us and wraps her arms around me for a hug. "I need to talk to you," she whispers for only me to hear, the cockiness in her voice gone, now replaced with worry.

I squeeze her. "Okay." She pulls back, with a small nod.

Plastering on a smile, she glances at my best friend. "Danny,"

"Leg," he responds, his lips twitching.

I shake my head at the way they still call each other by the nicknames they gave each other when we were kids.

"Come, come. Dinner is nearly ready." Mamma claps her hands, breaking whatever energy is buzzing around the foyer. My narrowed eyes flick between my best friend and sister, and not for the first time do I make a mental note to talk to him about my suspicions. I am never usually wrong, but this time I want to be.

Because if what I think is happening, is in fact *happening*. Well, let's just say, Dante won't have to worry about my papà putting a bullet in his head for calling my mamma by her given name.

It will be because of this shit with my sister.

Chapter 18

Ocean

My first week at *Bellissima* passes quickly.

Though it took a couple days, I have finally managed to get the hang of everything and am settling into my new routine. It's nice to finish work at an appropriate time and wake early in the morning so that I can work out. Working nights messed with my sleeping pattern, and I would sleep in until lunchtime, most days.

I haven't seen Nico since the night he took me to dinner. The night he spoke dirty words to me, turning me on until my panties were soaked and my pussy ached with need. I would never admit it, but I feel a little empty inside not seeing him. It's almost as if my whole body has slowed down, waiting for the moment Nico returns so it can revert to its normal self. I won't delve into that emotion right now because, quite frankly, my emotions toward that man are all over the place and pure madness.

On a better note, one that doesn't involve Nico, I have managed to find a ballet studio. It feels good to get back into dancing in that environment. Had things been different at home, and my dreams of being a prima ballerina weren't going to be taken away from me when I turned eighteen, I would have worked hard enough to secure a position at a prestigious ballet school. Somewhere like The School of American Ballet, here in New York. From the moment my mom took me to my first ballet class, I knew it was what I was meant to do. I wanted – still want – nothing more than to be a professional ballerina, and it saddens me that I may not achieve those dreams. Life, well, my father if I am being specific, had other plans for me. Plans I wanted no part of. I shudder in revulsion just thinking about it, and quickly divert my thoughts back to ballet. To happier times.

Times when I was in my element at the ballet school I attended from when I was just a little girl, up until around six months ago. The place I took on big roles such as *Clara* in *The Nutcracker*. *Juliet* in *Romeo and Juliet*. *Odette* in *Swan Lake*. Though I am grateful for the opportunities I was given, if I am being honest, I wanted more than my teenage dance studio. I wanted to travel. To be the best ballet dancer the world had ever seen.

I can still try for my dreams again at some point, but most dancers work at their form and skills extensively every day, which is something I no longer have the privilege of doing, so it puts me at a disadvantage. I would have to work extremely hard to return to the level I once was. That doesn't bother me, and I know I would get there if I were to return to a professional school. But my need to keep hidden is bigger than my need to dance at that level right now. I know my family is still looking for me and will probably never stop. The first places they would look, given what they know about me, are places like dance studios and colleges with extensive ballet programs. So, it is better to stay away. Hide in the shadows. Dance in the dark... Maybe someday it will happen for me, but for right now, while I am running, hiding, I need to keep my head down and be as inconspicuous as I can. Hence why I chose a small run-down studio in Brooklyn, with its graffitied external walls and neglected look. If it weren't for the small sign on the door, no one would even guess it was a studio. Which means it is perfect for me.

The ding of the door opening alerts me to someone entering and drags me from my thoughts. My head snaps up, my stomach tightening when my gaze meets Nico's. I lick my lips as I watch him. His lean body. How he fills out that expensive, custom suit. He is so hot it should be illegal. His lips curve into a smirk as if he knows exactly what I'm thinking.

"*Tesoro*," he greets, humor in his deep raspy voice.

My spine snaps straight with that one word, and the rush I have been waiting to feel since the last time I saw him, explodes in my body, lighting up every nerve and making my blood burn hotter.

"Nico," I breathe, suddenly feeling a little lightheaded. I clear my throat, hoping I sound more confident than I feel. "Are you here to see Macy?" I blurt, because it's the only thing that makes sense. I thought, after not seeing or hearing from him in nearly a week, whatever was blooming between us was over.

His eyes locked on mine as he runs a thumb across that full bottom lip of his. That movement alone has liquid heat seeping into my panties. It's so fucking hot. I lick my dry lips, wishing more than anything Nico's were pressed against my own, owning me. Claiming me. Sucking the life from me...

The shake of his head snaps me from my reverie. Shoving his hands in his pants pockets, he stares at me with cold, calculating eyes. I swallow, shifting on my feet as I wait for him to respond to my question and when he does, my heart jumps into my throat.

"Nah. Get your things. I want to show you something." It's not a question but a demand.

My eyes widen, and I shake my head. "I-I don't finish work for another hour."

He pins me with an amused look, taking a step toward me. "Good thing you know the boss then, right? Macy is getting you covered. Don't make me ask again, *Tesoro*."

I stare at him in disbelief. Just then Macy sashays into the reception area drawing my attention to her. Spotting Nico, she comes to a stop, her eyes flashing with… is that lust? I grit my teeth, my fists balling when something a lot like jealousy consumes me. Does he have this effect on every woman that encounters him? I hold in a laugh, shaking my head. Yes. Yes of course he does.

"Mr. Marchetti, hi," she murmurs, her voice all breathy, filled with desire. I watch her. The way she flutters her eyelashes and bites her lip. She screams sex. Yet, I am just… well, I am just me. I may be attractive, but I don't know how to be effortlessly sexy.

"Macy," he greets her, his gaze shifting to her. "I trust you did as I asked, and have someone to cover the front desk?"

She clears her throat, along with the want written all over her face and nods with a proud smile. "I did."

"Good." His eyes move back to me. "Why are you still standing there? Go get your things and change out of your uniform." He glances down at the mandated all-black pants and smock top with gold writing. "Now, Ocean." He demands, making me jump at the slight bark in his voice. Glancing between them, I decide that now is not the time to argue with him. Nodding my head in acquiesce, I rush towards the staff room to collect my duffle and change.

Grabbing my bag out of the locker, I exhale with annoyance. Who does he think he is? But more importantly, why do I submit to his demands so easily? Sighing, I unzip my bag, pulling out the black yoga pants, sweatshirt, and Chucks I have stuffed in there along with my leotard, ballet slippers, and tights. I had plans to dance after my shift and now the arrogant asshole has ruined that. I could always argue with him, but I know there's no point. It will only waste my energy, and something tells me I need to conserve it whenever I can around Nico Marchetti.

Huffing, I quickly change and then make my way back out to the entrance. Macy stands behind the desk, her eyes conspicuously on Nico as he leans against a wall, looking down at something on his cell. Hearing my footsteps both of their gazes snap to me. I swallow, ignoring Macy's burning gaze in the side of my head and stride towards the man who is quickly taking over my life and, like a runaway train, I have no control over it.

His pale blue orbs spark with satisfaction when he spots me. Shoving his cell in his suit jacket pocket, he pushes off the wall, closing the distance between us. As if he needs to touch me, his palm lands on my lower back. Heat courses through me, creating goosebumps and warming every inch of my skin at the small contact.

"See you tomorrow," I mumble at Macy, my cheeks heating in embarrassment.

"Bye, Ocean. Have a good evening. You too, Mr. Marchetti." Though Macy's voice is chirpy, I don't miss the hint of jealousy. Great. Is she going to start treating me differently now?

"Macy," Nico drawls his goodbye, pushing me out the door and toward his SUV. It's like Déjà vu. And I can't decide whether I like it or not.

Opening the back door, he jerks his head, a silent way of telling me to get inside. Climbing in, I sigh as my ass hits the buttery leather seats. Nico chuckles, before grabbing the seatbelt and buckling me in. My chest tightens. It's a thoughtful thing to do, making sure I am safe. Once satisfied I am strapped in safely, he steps back, closing the door and leaving me with the man in the driver's seat. It's the same man from when I have been in the car with Nico before. He doesn't look at me, just stares ahead as if I'm not even here.

"Hi," I say shyly.

He glances over his shoulder, a small smile on his lips. "Good evening, Miss."

I grin at the polite way he greets me, but I don't get time to say more because the door opens, and Nico slides in beside me. His eyes lock on mine, so penetrating, so blue. So hypnotizing... Reaching over, he brushes a lock of hair behind my ear, snapping me from my trance. His gaze never leaves mine when he murmurs. "So beautiful."

I suck in a breath. The sincerity in his voice hits me right in the chest. Desire tightens my stomach. I cross my legs as if it will ease the ache building between them. I want to touch him. Reach forward, run my fingers over his lips. His face. His hair. Everywhere. I tentatively lift my hand, ready to do just that when a throat clears breaking me from my lust-filled fog. I shake my head, my face warming in embarrassment. What the hell is wrong with me?

"Where to sir?" the driver asks.

"My apartment," Nico responds coolly.

I stiffen when those two words hit my ears. His apartment? I don't really think that's a good idea. I open my mouth to say just that, but with one look in my direction I snap my mouth closed and the SUV pulls into traffic.

Guess I am going to Nico's apartment.

***

Said apartment is the penthouse in a very extravagant, modern building. A building that I just learned Nico owns. Overlooking Central Park, it is in a prime position and must have cost a fortune. I grew up in a prominent family, and we were considered one of the richest families in our town, but this? Well, let's just say it's next-level wealth. With its high-end appliances, floor-to-ceiling windows, and views people could only dream of, it is everything you'd expect for someone like Nico Marchetti.

"Wow," I whisper, as I look out towards the park. The evening sun is setting, and the autumnal colors popping. The scene draws you in so much that you never want to look away. It's the beginning of November and soon the orange, reds and yellows will disappear making way for winter.

Nico steps up beside me, handing me what looks to be a glass of rosé wine. I shouldn't be drinking, being underage and all, but he doesn't know that. "The view alone is worth what I paid for it."

I glance up at him, nodding with a small smile. "It really is." I agree. He sips his drink, whiskey if I were to guess, as he watches me closely. Searching every inch of my face and looking for what, I'm not sure. "Is this what you wanted to show me?" I whisper.

"Yes. A woman as exquisite as you, should experience the beautiful things in life. This is one of them." I shiver at his words. At the passion in his voice. "Come. Let's sit." He takes my free hand, pulling me gently towards the L-shaped black fabric couch. I'm careful not to spill any of my wine as I drop down.

My stomach pitches in a mixture of excitement, desire, and fear, when Nico sits beside me, leaving only a breath of space between us. There is no doubt in my mind that I am his prey, just waiting for him to hunt me. Exposed and vulnerable, ready for his attack. And he will pounce. I see it in his cold, calculating, predatory gaze.

He places his drink on the coffee table before his intense

gaze comes back to me. I swallow. I have a feeling that tonight is about more than just wanting to show me the view. I know I should probably be putting a stop to this. Know I shouldn't get caught up in someone like Nico. Especially when I am so inexperienced, and he is so... well, him. Do I want a man to like him to be my first? But then a little voice in my head whispers words that, up until this moment, I didn't know I needed.

If I am going to lose my virginity, who better than to a man like Nico Marchetti?

Chapter 19

Nico

She fidgets nervously on my couch, keeping a steel grip on the glass of wine I gave her.

My lips curve in amusement. I hook my arms over the back of the couch, getting comfortable. I stare at her, searching her face and wanting to know everything that is currently going through her mind. Ocean is a complete paradox. She can be defiant, sure, and confident at times, but then there are moments, like right now, where she is submissive, pliant, and hesitant. Hmm. Interesting. Maybe this is what draws me to her. The unpredictability. I don't know what side of her I am going to get from one hour to the next.

When you live in a world where every woman you encounter is predictable, and easy, it makes for a refreshing change. With Ocean, I have to work for it, whereas every other woman I have fucked – since I was fourteen - is willing to drop to their knees as soon as I walk into a room.

"Relax," I murmur, reaching across and running a hand through her blonde hair. "Tell me something about yourself, *Ocean Embers.*"

She stiffens, and her big blue eyes meet mine. So unique in

their color, like nothing I have ever seen before. I know I could easily get lost in them – that's if I let myself. I shake my head. *Jesus* Nico, get a fucking hold of yourself. You know that can't happen.

"There isn't much else to know. You know about my parents. You know I love ballet..." she trails off, chewing that full bottom lip. "Actually, I did find a studio." Her blue orbs sparkle, and I hear the excitement in her voice. I don't tell her that I already know that little bit of information. Or that I am having her followed by one of my men, a bodyguard of sorts, all because I want to know every little thing about her.

Not that he found out much. Just that she goes to work at *Bellissima*, dances a couple nights a week at a studio in Brooklyn and then goes back to the shitty hostel that she calls home. On one occasion she did eat brunch at a little diner with a girl. After sending me a picture, I recognized her as one of the girls that dances at The Executive Club, which Leo also confirmed. He told me her name is Selena, that she lives in the same building as Ocean, and they are friends. Apart from those small details, she seems to keep to herself, which honestly, I like. It will make things easier for me.

Ocean eyes me for a long beat. Almost as if she is thinking over her next words and whether she should say them. Being the inquisitive girl that I know she is, she can't help herself. "What about you?" she tucks a lock of hair behind her ear. "I don't know anything about you, other than you are a businessman."

I grin, biting back a laugh. *Businessman* is one way of putting it. Not that I am going to admit to anything else. Technically speaking, I am a businessman of sorts. I have my legitimate businesses, but I also have my... not so legal businesses. I have heard the rumors about me and maybe she has too. I know the girls sometimes talk at the club, though the majority of them are scared to voice the things they hear.

If Ocean has heard anything, knows anything, she doesn't express it. "Yes, I am. I own several businesses, restaurants, clubs, and spas. There are also the family businesses. Real estate, construction, waste management, casinos, hotels and again, restaurants, and clubs." That's as much as I am going to say. She doesn't need to know anything else.

Her eyes widen in shock. "Wow. So, you and your family are like rich, rich?"

I chuckle. "You could say that."

Clearing my throat, I reach forward taking her wine from her hand and placing it on the glass coffee table before interlacing our fingers. Her gaze drops to the contact, chest heaving as her pulse kicks up a notch. Leaning in, I brush my lips across hers. "I want to fuck you, *Tesoro,*" her breath catches, but she doesn't push me away, so I take that as a sign to keep going. "I want to eat your little cunt until you cream all over my face. And when you have come so much that you have no more left to give and you can't see straight, I will stick my cock in you. Stretch your pussy and claim you in a way only a man like me can." She moans, making me smirk. "You are mine, Ocean. Mine to do with as I please. But believe me when I say, you will enjoy every single second of what I do to you. The pleasure I will bring your body, you will crave it. Crave me." Her body trembles, eyes turning dark with desire.

Satisfaction thrums in my veins and without another dirty word, I smash my lips to hers. She squeaks, her mouth opening with her shock, giving me the opportunity to push my tongue inside. A groan rumbles in my throat. Just as delicious as I remember. Fuck, I could devour her. And not for the first time do I think, I could completely lose myself in her. That alone tells me I should run far away. But I don't think anything could stop this right now. Not even the building collapsing.

Gripping her hips, I flip her until she is underneath me,

never once breaking the kiss. Ocean whimpers in shock or desire, I'm not sure. Pulling back slightly, I run my tongue across her lips, her cheek, and then down to her neck, biting her erratic pulse point. She squirms beneath me, her quick, hot breaths hitting the side of my face.

Snaking my hand down, I reach under the waistband of her yoga pants, running a finger down her cotton panty-covered slit. My cock hardens at what I find, turning me almost feral with need. "Soaked," I growl. And it isn't a lie. She's drenched and just from a simple kiss.

"Nico," she cries, and the breathy way she says my name has me turning unhinged.

"I'm going to give you what you want, *Tesoro*. What you need."

Pushing up, I scoot down her body, taking her leggings and panties with me. She wriggles when her bottom half is naked, trying to cover her cunt with her hands. Anger slithers through me, that she is trying to hide what is mine, and I bat them away, staring down at her bare pussy in awe. Magnificent. Beautiful.

"Spread your legs." I bark, only to soften my features and voice when she flinches. "Wider. I want to see what belongs to me. I want to see your juicy, greedy cunt leaking and glistening for me before I eat you."

Sucking in a breath, she slowly, tentatively, does as I ask, widening her legs and exposing herself to me. My mouth waters. The most perfect fucking cunt I have ever seen. Wet. Pink. Tight. Swollen. Ripe.

Mine.

Dropping down, I grip her knees, pulling her closer to me. She moans, the noise hitting me straight in the dick. Leaning in, I run my nose up her wet slit, inhaling her, saturating myself in her. My tongue darts out on its own volition, tasting her. I groan. Fuck me. She tastes even better than I imagined. "Christ,

Tesoro, your pussy is heaven," I murmur, before pushing my tongue inside her tight hole.

She cries out at the intrusion, and she is so tight, I briefly wonder whether she is a virgin. I nearly snort at my thoughts, then grit my teeth in anger because I suddenly wish she were. I want to be the only person to experience what it is like to be inside her. Pulling out, I lick up her slit, tasting every inch of her freshly waxed cunt, before I latch onto her clit and push a finger inside. She is wet, fucking leaking everywhere. But even with one digit it's a tight fit. I frown, releasing her nub and pulling back to look at her.

"Are you a virgin?" I ask and pray with everything in me she says yes. If not, the sudden urge to go and murder any single man who has touched her crosses my mind.

She glares, defiance flashing in her eyes. "No."

Hmm, it's a firm no, but I don't miss the slight hesitation in her words or the way her face turns red. If she is a virgin, she doesn't want me to know that she is. Does she think it would stop this? It wouldn't. In fact, it would make me even more deranged, knowing that I am the first man to have her in this way. The first man to be inside her, claiming her innocence as mine. Instead of voicing my suspicions, I dive back in, eating her pussy like she is my last meal.

Adding another finger, I pump in and out, trying to stretch her as best I can, as I latch onto her clit. Her arousal gushes out of her, her juices running down my face and it's the best shower I have ever had. Lifting her hips, she begins to grind into me. My gaze shifts up, wanting to see the expression on her face. Her head is thrown back, eyes closed, caught up in her desire. It irritates me. I want her to watch me eat her, know it's me giving her this pleasure.

Releasing her clit again, I growl. "Eyes on me. I want you looking at me when you cum in my mouth." Her eyes snap open and I grin, sucking her little bundle of nerves back into my mouth. I pump my fingers faster, groaning at the way her tight inner walls suck me inside like they never want me to leave. With her blue eyes locked on mine, I feel her legs tense around my head and her body start to tremble. She is close.

With one last thrust of my fingers, I bite down on her clit, not hard, but enough to push her over the edge. She screams out my name, her pussy clamping down and convulsing around my fingers as she comes undone. It's the most exquisite thing I have ever witnessed in my life. If I died right now, with the vision of Ocean falling apart as my last image, I would die a happy man.

"Beautiful," I drawl, lifting my head and wiping my wet face. Her eyes snap open, the look in them making my cock leak. Pure lust stares back at me as she lays content and sated on my couch. I smirk, knowing full well that I am going to enjoy every minute of what comes next. Running a finger over my face, I scoop up her wetness, sucking it into my mouth. She stares at me with a look of pure horror. I chuckle. "Hmm, delicious." I say when I have finished tasting her.

Standing, my lips curve into a grin when her eyes drop to my erection, stabbing against my pants. She swallows, worry flashing in her eyes. If I were a better man, I would take this slow. Put her at ease. But I'm not. And nothing will stop me from taking her right now. Not even Ocean herself.

Reaching down, I pull her to her feet, then stride down the hall, tugging her along behind me. "I'm not going to fuck you on the couch like a cheap whore, *Tesoro*. When I claim you, it will be in my bedroom."

Chapter 20

Ocean

My heart races in my chest as he strides down the hall to his bedroom. I have no idea what I am doing, but the orgasm Nico just gave me has lulled me into a state of pure bliss that I never want to come out of. I am not this girl. The girl who is ruled by her hormones and willing to jump into bed with a man she barely knows – hence my still virgin status.

I should have told him the truth, and now that I think about it, I am not sure why I lied about being a virgin. It's definitely nothing to be ashamed of... Maybe I was so caught up in what Nico was doing to me, that I just wanted to believe I am more experienced than I actually am. Or maybe I didn't want him to look at me like I was just some silly, innocent girl, giving it up to the first guy who showed her some attention. I shake my head, knowing full well I wasn't in my right mind and that I wasn't thinking at all. But as he leads me down the hall, my body thrumming with nerves, I just wish I had been honest. Even more so after feeling his hard cock against my leg. He is big. *Really* big. One of his fingers barely fit inside me and when he added another it was painful until the pleasure took over. There is no way his dick is going to slide inside me without hurting.

A pulse thrums between my legs, my pussy clenching – in fear or desire, I'm not sure - just thinking about how he is going to stretch me wide open with his massive cock, and probably destroy my pussy forever in the process. Nico isn't a gentle man. There is no way he is going to take things slow and ease me into it. Especially not now he thinks I am experienced.

You should have just told him. A little voice in my head admonishes me. *You have made a rod for your own back now and it's time to face the consequences of your lies.* But I shove the thought aside, not wanting to hear it now.

I am startled out of my cock panicked haze, when the sound of wood smacking a wall hits my ears. Glancing up, I see it's a door. A door to his bedroom. In his rush to get his cock inside me, he must have kicked it open. I swallow, my body tensing with nerves. I'm going to die. I. Am. Going. To. Die. Death by dick. Oh my God. I should put a stop to this. Right now.

My eyes swing to Nico. As if he can hear every thought in my head, he grabs me by the hips, lifts me in the air, and strides to the bed, throwing me down like I am his little toy to do with as he pleases. Nico's gaze rakes over my body, and it's only then that I remember I am naked from the waist down. I feel exposed, on display, suddenly shy, scared... I cock my head. I am all those things, but the hungry look in Nico's eyes also makes me feel powerful.

Squeezing my eyes closed, I suck in a calming breath. I can do this. I started this and now I have to finish it. My eyes snap open, gaze raking down his still fully clothed body. In his black suit pants and white dress shirt, he exudes power. Raw masculinity. Pure sex. There is something to be said about this moment. Him dominant, a predator, with me at his mercy. I shiver wanting Nico exactly how he is. He smirks as if he just read my mind. Again.

"Take off your sweatshirt." He growls and from the look in his eyes, there is no backing out now. I don't want to. I just fear the unknown. Of how it will feel when he pushes his cock inside me. It's going to hurt, I know it will, but I think I trust Nico not to completely hurt me. Maybe once he realizes that I lied, he will be gentle. Wishful thinking on my part, and perhaps a little naïve, but it's all I've got to try and calm my racing nerves.

Knowing my fate is sealed and that I only have myself to blame, I resign myself to whatever happens next. Grabbing the hem of my sweatshirt, I make quick work of pulling it over my head. My heart pounds in my chest when my eyes meet Nico's. His tongue darts out, running across his bottom lip and he groans. Can he still taste me? My cheeks heat as I remember his mouth on my pussy.

"Bra too. I want to see your tits when I fuck you," he murmurs. The possessiveness in his voice has my stomach tightening and arousal seeping from me. Even in my worry, I don't think I have ever been so turned on in my life. At this moment, I decide that even if the pain is unbearable when he rips through my innocence, I want it. I want to feel all of it. All of him. Both of us stripped down to our baser instincts, raw and needy. For each other.

I frown, briefly wondering where these thoughts are coming from and how I did a complete one-eighty in a couple of seconds. While all the girls at my private school were sex and boy-mad, it never bothered me. It was drilled into me from my early teens that I would be with one person for the rest of my life. I didn't want the person I was promised to, so sex was the last thing on my mind. Never once did I imagine that I would have the freedom to explore my sexuality, in any way, let alone with someone like Nico Marchetti.

"I'm not going to fuck you with a condom," Nico states, snapping me from my thoughts. "I want to feel all of you. Every little part of your tight cunt when I push inside you. I want your arousal soaking my cock. I want to feel it all." He pauses, cocking his head. "Are you on birth control?"

Chewing my bottom lip, I nod. "Yeah."

He smirks and it is by far the sexiest thing I have ever seen. He is so handsome, the ache between my legs throbs with need. "I'm clean." He adds. "I've never fucked a woman bare before." He unbuttons his shirt, throwing it down on the floor. "I want to be with you. I don't want anything between us. Ever. Are you clean?"

Again, I nod, not one hundred percent sure I understand. If he means have I showered, then I did before work. Or could he mean... my eyes widen. An STD? I bite back a gasp. No. I *definitely* do not have one of those. So yeah, I am clean in both senses. Satisfaction flashes in his eyes. "Good. Because I am going to fuck you raw. Feel every inch of your perfect cunt. Fill you up with my cum until it leaks out of you. And then, when I am finished, I am going to do it all over again until you can't take anymore. By the time I am done with you, you will be sweating my essence out of your pores." He pushes his pants, then boxer briefs, down his legs in one swift move. His huge cock bounces free, smacking against his abs. My jaw drops open. I blink. Then blink again, just to make sure what I am seeing is real. Holy fuck it is. The hardness I felt against my leg had nothing on seeing him up close and personal. He is bigger than I imagined. So much bigger. Huge. The type of cock that should be on display for people to admire, not one to go inside any part of you. There is no way that thing is going anywhere near my pussy. He will tear me apart. Destroy me from the inside out. *Kill* me. I swallow. This was a mistake. I want an average guy with an average length. Not *Mr. Dangerous Dinosaur dick.*

With one hand he palms himself. I watch with rapt attention as he works his cock, only half listening when he speaks. "Tomorrow, you won't be able to walk without feeling me in every part of your body. And my cum will be dripping out of you for days. Just how I want it." He muses, stroking himself harder. And he isn't lying. The size of him, I think I will feel him until the day I die.

Scooting back on the bed, I start to rethink my obvious stupidity. God, I have no business messing around with a man like this. He is going to annihilate me. Literally. "May-maybe we should slow it down a little." I stutter.

Nico's head cocks to the side, his blue orbs lighting up with challenge. I know then, I am not getting out of here with my innocence intact. He is fucking me whether I want it or not. And I do want it. I'm just...scared. "I have waited for what feels like a lifetime to get inside that pussy. Nothing and no one will stop me from claiming you right now, *Tesoro*. Not even you." He climbs on the bed, grabs my ankles and pulls me towards him. "Because you are mine, aren't you? Your smart mouth, your perfect cunt..." he trails off with a groan as he peppers kisses up the inside of my thigh.

Throwing my head on the pillow, I resign myself to the fact that this is happening, and I have more chance of winning the lottery than walking out of this apartment with my virginity intact. I startle when his mouth latches onto my clit, my back arching in pure bliss when he pushes a finger inside me. He pumps into me, slowly building the pleasure before pulling out. "You are so fucking wet, I am going to slide right into you." he presses kisses to my stomach, between my breasts before sucking one nipple and then the other into his mouth. I moan. It feels so good and makes me forget all my fears.

Releasing me, he nips at my neck, chin, and lips and my gaze meets his. Blue on blue. For the briefest second, the thought of what our children would look like crosses my mind before I shake it away. One orgasm and I'm marrying the guy. I bite back a laugh at the absurdity. Pressing his lips to mine, he lines his cock up with my entrance. I tense, making him look down at me. A frown mars his face before he drops a kiss to my nose. "Relax, *Tesoro*. I'm big, but I've prepared you well enough to take me."

My guess is it doesn't matter how well he has prepared me. It's going to hurt no matter what. "Can you go slow?" I whisper over the lump in my throat.

He smiles, brushing his lips against mine. "I will, to begin with. You are so tight, and I'm a big guy. But when I have stretched you enough, all bets are off. I am not a gentle lover, and the sooner you get used to that, the better. You are going to learn very quickly exactly how I like to fuck."

He pushes into me, slow and gentle. All the air leaves my lungs. The pain is real, the burn intense, as stretches me wide open to accommodate him. Fuck. He really is going to break me. "Oh my God." I cry out in pain when his hips drive forward in one quick move, breaking straight through my innocence.

He smirks, his triumphant gaze landing on me. I know why. He just realized I lied. "Fuck." He breathes. "You were a virgin. Why did you lie? Did you think I wouldn't know?" he looks down to where we are joined, slowly pumping in and out as he stretches my pussy. I take it as a good sign that he hasn't stopped.

"I don't know." I gasp when he slides his whole cock inside me. The tight fit of his length stings when he pulls out a little only to plunge back in. I wriggle to try and ease the pain. I am so full of him. Surrounded by all things him.

A smug, satisfied grin takes over his whole face, his blue eyes holding me captive. "I am going to teach and mold you into what I want. You will learn everything I like and become everything I need. You don't know what you have gotten yourself into, *Tesoro*. The moment I broke through your innocence your fate was sealed. For better or worse, you are mine now." he whispers, licking a trail up my neck, before pulling back. Nico searches my face for a long beat before his left hand comes up to wrap around my throat. "You just created a monster, Ocean. I have always had a penchant for making people bleed. But they have nothing on what your virgin blood feels like soaking my cock." He groans cryptically before pulling his dick nearly all the way out only to slam back into me so hard, I move up the bed.

"Nico," I whimper, pain mixed with a hint of pleasure hitting every part of my body.

"I'm sorry, baby. I told you I would be gentle, but now I know that I am the first man to be inside you, it changes things." He growls, pumping into me, so hard, so deep I can't do anything but succumb to the way he fucks me. Animalistic. Feral. And with the most possessive gleam in his eyes, it has my stomach dipping. Whether in concern or excitement, I'm not sure. "Fuck. You are so fucking tight; your cunt is gripping me like a vise." He snarls, his thrusts speeding up. He slams into me harder, faster as if he is trying to break me in two. I cry out, the pain now subsided and pleasure lighting up my veins.

With his free hand, he reaches down, circling my clit. I whimper, my back arching up into him. Wanting more. *Needing* more. Trying to chase the high only he can give me. "Oh, oh, oh. Nico." I gasp at the sensations flowing through me.

He smirks, his head dropping to the crook of my neck. Hot breath hits my ear when he speaks. "Come for me, *Tesoro*. Come, so I can fill you up with my seed. Lay my white flag and mark you as mine."

My stomach tightens, legs shaking as I succumb to his brutal thrusts and dirty words. Before I know what's happening, an orgasm tears through me, so intense that I nearly black out from the powerful force of it. "Nico," I scream out his name, my eyes rolling shut as I slump back onto the mattress, sated. I can only hope his penthouse is soundproof, I dread to think what the other occupants might think if they heard me.

He licks a trail up my neck. "Good girl. You are so fucking good for me, soaking my cock. Now open your eyes and watch me as I fill your pussy." My eyes snap open. The look in his own has me nearly coming again. He picks up speed, his thrusts getting harder, jerkier. His gaze never leaves mine and I am completely consumed by all things Nico. I briefly wonder if I can stay in this moment forever, where only he and I exist. But it's a pipe dream. This, whatever this is, can never last.

An animalistic groan rumbles from him, pulling me from my thoughts. He goes stock still and I wonder if something is wrong. Then I see it. Pure undiluted desire and maddening possession stare back at me as his cock pulses and warmth fills my insides. He came. Inside of me. My stomach tightens, and my pussy clenches. I know he feels it when his eyes spark with satisfaction and a smile curves his lips.

"Good girl. You took me so well." He praises, breaking the silence. Leaning down, he presses a kiss to my forehead before pulling out. A surge of wetness runs down my sex and to my ass.

Glancing down, my eyes widen in complete horror when I spot the blood on my thighs. My gaze shifts to Nico's cock, my distress increasing when I find it smeared with my blood. "Oh my God. I'm so sorry." I blurt out, my cheeks heating with embarrassment.

He glances down at his dick. The possessiveness I witnessed in his eyes before burns even brighter. "I never want to hear those words from your mouth again – well, unless you're apologizing for neglecting my cock. But that won't happen because you are mine to do with as I please. Whenever. Wherever." He states confidently, as if it's absolute. "Now, back to the matter at hand. Its normal. My dick is bigger and thicker than average. It's your first time. Lay back. Relax. I will grab a washcloth and clean you up."

"I can do that myself," I say, starting to climb off the bed but he pushes me back down.

"No. You are mine to take care of now, *Tesoro*. I made this mess. I will clean it. Stay there." His tone leaves no room for argument, and I know there is no point fighting him on it.

Falling back into the pillows, I sigh. Maybe I don't know what I have gotten myself into, but for now I am going to enjoy it. It's been a long time since someone has taken care of me like this. Never in my wildest dreams did I think it would be Nico Marchetti, but it feels good, nonetheless. For the first time in a long time, I feel cherished, and wanted. I frown, nibbling my bottom lip when a worrying thought hits me. Not only do I like the way he cares for me, but I think I could get used to it. He said that I am his.

And the worrying thing is, I want to be.

Chapter 21

Nico

It's been three days since I had my cock inside the sweetest pussy I have ever felt in my life.

Three torturous days of having to wait to be inside heaven again, because I am caught up in Bratva shit. Since they torched one of our warehouses, they have stepped up their war against us, causing not only destruction and chaos but fucking inconvenience.

Unfortunately, due to the mess they are making, they have taken up all my time. Which means I haven't been able to see Ocean, sink my dick inside her, fill her with my cum, and own every inch of her delectable body. I'm distracted by all things her, which is dangerous considering I should be focusing on business. But every time I lick my lips, it's as if I can still taste her cunt on them. It tempts me, taunts me, begs me to go to her and do it all over again. And again. And again...

She was a virgin. *A fucking virgin.* I took her innocence, ripped through that little bit of resistance, painted my cock with her blood and now she is all mine. I remember how it felt as I pushed inside her. The way she looked at me with trust in her eyes. I'm not worthy of that trust, but I will take it. I will take

Dancing In Sin

everything she has to give, then take even more when she thinks she has given enough. I will conquer her, mind, body, heart and soul. I laid my white flag inside her pussy, claiming her as my own. Now I want everyone to know who she belongs to. I want to be her be-all and end-all. Her everything. I growl as a raw, possessive, primal feeling surges through my veins, heating my blood. Fuck. I'm obsessed. So unhinged and feral over this woman, it should scare me. But for some reason, it only makes me smile. She will submit. She will be everything I want her to be. I am never letting her go, no matter what is expected of me and soon she will learn that.

"What are you smiling about?" Dante's voice filters into my thoughts and my gaze snaps to his. He grins knowingly. I should have known the asshole would catch my unusual, happy disposition.

Clearing my throat, I give him a cool, one-word answer. "Nothing."

He smirks, shaking his head. "You fucked her didn't you." It's not a question but a statement that proves just how well he knows me.

"Jesus," I say, blowing out an exasperated breath.

His grin widens. He points at me. "You did." He laughs. "So, how was it? Was she everything you imagined and more?" There's a teasing lilt in his tone which irritates me. I don't know why. Usually, I have no qualms talking to Dante about hookups and vice versa. But for some reason, I want to keep Ocean to myself. I don't want him or anyone to know anything.

I laugh under my breath. Christ. She really is my *Tesoro*. My treasure. One I want to keep hidden from the world. I shake my head, huffing out a laugh, though the absurdity of the situation I have found myself in is not humorous at all. I have only been inside her once and I am acting like a pussy whipped idiot.

"I'm not discussing this with you." I pin him with a look that says not to challenge me. He holds his hands up in a surrender gesture, knowing not to push me on this, and backing down. "Now. Back to the Bratva and our damn warehouse. Do you believe it was Federico who gave them the information? Or do you think we killed an innocent man, and we have another rat? Or do you think Federico was working with someone else?"

He sighs, running a hand through his hair. "I hope it was Federico otherwise we have a bigger problem than we originally thought. It means that the Bratva have infiltrated the *famiglia* and we don't know how deep it goes or who we can trust."

I nod, agreeing with him. "Fuck. Papà is going to lose his shit if he thinks he has lost control of our soldiers."

"He will. I mean no disrespect Nic, but he is..." he trails off, sighing. "He is becoming unpredictable. The men don't like that. If they feel unsettled, it's easy for them to be paid off and used against us. There needs to be change. The soldiers, they respect you. Things will be different when you are Don." He finishes, looking a little uneasy. He has no reason to be, I agree with everything he is saying.

"You're right. But for now, Papà is boss and until he steps down, there is nothing we can do about it." I scrub my hand down my face, feeling tired. "He is in the Hamptons. Call Hansen to get the chopper ready. I want to be there within the hour."

***

After a long night of crisis talks with my father, his consigliere, Giuseppe, and Dante, I make it home to my penthouse at just past 6 a.m. I am fucking exhausted, but I cannot go another minute without seeing Ocean, so sleep will have to wait.

Hopping in my shower, I make quick work of scrubbing the

heavy night from my skin. My muscles relax and I let out a weary sigh. I know I should wait to see my obsession and get some rest. But I am also well aware of the fact that I won't be able to settle until I have laid my eyes on her. It has been too long as it is. Another minute will feel like torture, let alone a full day, so sleep can wait.

Dante, who has his own apartment two floors below me, has gone down to get some rest before we get back to work later. He thinks that I am doing the same. He couldn't be more wrong. Though he knows that I've fucked Ocean, he doesn't know how deep my obsession with her runs. Fuck, I mean, I knew I was feeling some kind of way toward her, but I wasn't aware of how intense my fixation with her ran. My need to see her consumes me, so much so, I can't stay away for another couple of hours. "Fucking pathetic," I grumble under my breath, irritation heating my blood. I wish I was done with her after that life-changing fuck, but it only seems to have fueled my fascination further.

Switching off the faucet, I step out, grabbing a towel. My cell, ringing from my bedroom, catches my attention. Wrapping the soft towel around my waist, I pad toward my nightstand, a smile curving my lips when I see the name flashing on the screen. With a quick swipe, I answer. "Mamma," I greet.

"*Mio Figlio*, you couldn't have waited another couple of hours to see your mother?" She scolds but her tone is soft, playful.

"Ah, yes." I run a hand through my wet hair. "Sorry, Mamma. I had business to attend to in the city. I had to get back."

"I know. I know. Business comes first." She sighs softly but I hear slight resentment in her voice. My chest tightens. Though Mamma was born into a mafia family, I know full well she hates this way of life. She was primed from the moment she was born and had no choice but to become the mafia queen she was groomed to be. It was instilled in her from a young age, that the *famiglia* will always come first. That doesn't mean she has to like it. "I have a couple of busy weeks but when things quiet down, I will come and spend the weekend with you and Allegra," I tell her, hoping it will make her happy.

"That would be nice, Nico," she says softly, the sadness in her voice now replaced by excitement. Though my mamma is constantly surrounded by guards and the staff, I know she is lonely. It doesn't help that my papà spends most of his time in the city, fucking other women and taking care of business.

I scowl, though she can't see it. "Well, it's settled then. I need to go, Mamma. I will talk to you soon."

"I love you *mio figlio*." She murmurs in way of a goodbye before ending the call.

Tossing my cell on the bed, I towel myself dry. Padding to my closet, I grab some boxer briefs, pants, a black dress shirt and my black Italian loafers before making quick work of dressing.

Once dressed, I pick up my cell, shooting off a message to Christopher, telling him to be ready in fifteen minutes. It may still be early, but I know for a fact that Ocean starts her shift at 8 a.m. and there is no time like the present.

I won't waste another second. I am seeing my girl.

***

Pushing through the door to *Bellissima*, a smile curves my lips when I spot Ocean at the counter. She nibbles her lip in concentration, staring at the computer screen as she holds the landline up to her ear.

"I have you down for a waxing appointment with Saskia on Thursday at 5:45 p.m." Her soft, velvet voice drifts through the room, hitting me straight in the cock. Fuck. Why does this woman have such an effect on me? It's bizarre really, though I am past caring or questioning it.

As if sensing me, her head lifts, gaze locking on me. Those blue orbs widen in shock before narrowing. A scowl crosses her beautiful face, as she shoots me a contemptuous look. Guess my absence the last couple of days didn't go unnoticed. I smirk at her reaction; at the way she challenges me. No one would dare look at me the way Ocean is right now. And I have no doubt in my mind that if Ocean really knew who I was, she also wouldn't be looking at me the way she is right now.

Ending the call, she places the phone on the holder before she looks at the computer screen and taps her fingers on the keyboard. My cock hardens and I smile wider, knowing exactly what she is doing. She is trying to ignore me, pretend that I'm not here. Unfortunately for her, I am.

Sauntering across the marble tiles, I close the distance between us. She still doesn't look at me. I sigh. Gripping her arm, I pull her around the counter, so she is standing in front of me. Her breath hitches, but still she keeps her eyes on the floor. Wrapping a finger around her chin, I lift until her eyes meet mine. Blue on blue. *Mine.*

"Did you miss me, *Tesoro*?" I tease, bending slightly so I can brush my lips against hers.

"No." she scoffs, her voice defiant.

My eyes narrow in on her. She may say no, but her face tells a different story. Vulnerability, hurt, anger. She probably thought me fucking her the other night was a one-and-done type of thing. It usually would be. But not with her.

My tongue darts out, running a slow path up her cheek. I grin, when the pulse point in her neck turns erratic and her chest starts heaving. "You're lying. I think you did miss me, baby, and that is why you have an attitude now. It's okay to admit it because I missed you too. I missed your perfect lips. I missed the way your cunt feels wrapped around my cock. I. Missed. You." I enunciate in a seductive whisper.

She moans, melting into me and I know I have her. "Where have you been?" she breathes.

I press a kiss on her hair. "I had business to take care of."

Stiffening, she huffs a laugh, pulling back from me. She twists her fingers together, a nervous, vulnerable gesture if I were to guess. "I thought..." she trails off, her cheeks turning red in embarrassment. Gathering herself, she takes a breath and continues. "I thought. Well, I thought that after we... You know."

I know what she is trying to say without saying it and she just confirmed my earlier thoughts with her jumbled words. Bundling her into me, I drop my lips to her ear, putting her at ease. "You thought that it was a one-time thing. That I got what I wanted and ghosted you?" I voice what she couldn't say.

She nods, looking up at me with her big sapphire eyes. "Yeah."

I laugh, but it's humorless. I almost wish that were the case. Unfortunately for her, it isn't. I am sure that by the time this is done, she would have wished it were the case also. I frown, my chest aching at the thought that eventually, one day, even if it is in the future, this will all be over. No matter how much I want to keep her, she deserves more than what I can give.

Pressing a kiss to her nose, I say. "You don't get rid of me that easily, *Tesoro*. Now come on. I will get your shift covered. It's been too long since I had my cock buried inside you."

Reaching for her hand, I pull her toward the staff area so that she can grab her bag. I also need to inform Macy that Ocean will be gone for the day. It's an asshole move and will probably leave my manager short-staffed. But Macy won't question me and will pick up the slack no matter what.

Because I'm the boss and I can do what the fuck I like.

Chapter 22

Ocean

My back arches as Nico hits a spot so deep inside me, I see stars.

The sound of skin slapping, and the smell of sex permeate the room. A noise, bordering on animalistic, leaves my mouth as he thrusts into me so hard, I hit the headboard.

After picking me up from *Bellissima*, his driver, whose name I learned is Christopher, brought us back to Nico's penthouse. Within seconds of entering his apartment, he had me stripped naked, on the bed and his head between my legs. I am still sore from when he took my virginity, but the soothing, gentle laps of his tongue that brought me to orgasm helped some and was just what I needed to soothe my tender pussy. The bliss of my climax lasted all of a couple of seconds before he thrust his thick cock into me, stretching me to my limits, and reminding me of why I am so tender in the first place. That was five hours ago. If I thought I was in pain after my first time, I am sure it will have nothing on how I am going to feel tomorrow. Nico is an animal. Feral and unhinged in his movements as he takes me over and over. Lighting up every part of my body like a live wire and bringing me pleasure I never knew existed.

"Nico," I cry out, black spots dotting my vision. Clawing at his back, my eyes roll shut, as my eighth - or is this the ninth - orgasm of the day barrels through me.

"That's it, *Tesoro*, milk my cock. Let me fill you up." He pounds into me harder, his dick stretching me wide open. Equal amounts of pleasure and pain shoot through my pussy as he uses me like his own personal fuck doll. I am still so new to sex, and Nico is abnormally big in the cock department. Long. Thick. Veiny. And perfect despite the way he is destroying my pussy right now.

"You are going to take every single drop of me *la mia piccola ballerina*. I want your cunt filled with my seed." He rasps, his Italian accent coming through. Jesus, it's hot. And for the first time in my life, I feel sexy. The fact that I can bring a man like Nico to his knees, make him fall apart, is empowering. "Fuck-kkk," he groans, his eyes rolling shut. He stills, his cock pulsing. And then I feel it. Warmth coats my insides as he fills me.

His eyes snap open, locking on mine. He smirks. "You are so fucking tight *Tesoro*. The way you grip me, the way you feel. You were made for me and my cock." He murmurs, dropping a kiss on my head.

My heart rate kicks up at the look in his eyes. Though it hasn't been long, whatever is going on between us, my feelings for him are growing at an unnerving speed the more time I spend with him. They are taking root deep inside, changing me irrevocably. I know with everything in me, this man could damage me in the worst way possible. He has the potential to break my heart into a million pieces, but even knowing that it's not enough for me to walk away. I want to dive into him headfirst, give him everything, *be* his everything. Dancing used to be the only thing that made me feel alive, and now I can add Nico to that list. It's equal parts thrilling and scary. A smile tugs at my lips. I once saw a quote that said *the best things in life always come from doing what scares you the most*. And Nico does scare me, so maybe whoever came up with that saying knew what they were talking about. Perhaps they had someone like Nico. And maybe, just maybe, Nico will be the best thing that ever happened to me...

My lips twitch with the need to smile at that thought, but I fold my lips between my teeth trying to hide my happiness. Glancing up, I find Nico's intense gaze on me searching my face. His brows are furrowed, and he watches me as if I am the world's most difficult puzzle to solve. Shaking his head, he presses a kiss to my lips, before rolling to the side, and taking me with him. His cock still inside me, he tucks me into his chest, holding onto me as if I might disappear. "Nico?"

"Hmm?"

"You-you're still inside me."

"Yeah. I am. And it's where I will stay until I fuck you again. Now sleep." I hear the humor in his voice, but he says it with such confidence, that I don't argue with him. Instead, I snuggle further into his chest as if it's where I belong.

It only takes mere seconds before my eyes grow heavy and my breathing evens out. Cuddled into Nico with his cock still inside me, I fall asleep.

***

"Fuck, *Tesoro*," a masculine voice grunts as I am roused from my sleep.

My eyes open to darkness and I feel full. Pressure builds between my legs, and I can't help the whimper that leaves my lips. Confusion hits me, my foggy brain trying to catch up with what is happening and where I am. I quickly sift through my memories. Nico. Picking me up from work. All the sex. Falling asleep. I startle, liquid heat coursing through my body when the stabbing sensation between my legs increases.

Blinking, I glance up, finding Nico's pleasure-filled face hovering over me. And then everything rushes to the surface, and what is actually happening hits me like a freight train. Nico is having sex with me. Thrusting in and out of me while I am sleeping. Should I be worried about that? Is it a normal thing for couples to do...? My thoughts are forgotten when he hits a particularly sensitive spot inside me, making me moan in pleasure. But even though desire is quickly coursing through my veins, the slight sting of pain is still there.

"Nico, I'm sore," I whine, hoping I convey just how tender I still am and that he what... just stops?

"I know baby, but I couldn't resist. You looked so sexy sleeping peacefully, with my cum running out of your pussy, I just had to fuck you. I have never been so hard in my life." He reaches down, running circles on my clit and making me forget my inner turmoil. He leans in close, his tongue darting out as he licks a trail up my face before his mouth drops to my ear. "I had to plug it in somehow. We don't want any going to waste, do we." He growls possessively and though it was asked in a way of a question it is rhetorical. "Now come for me, so I can pump your perfect cunt full of my seed again." I whimper, and as if he has a trained me to be his obedient little toy, I cry out when an orgasm hits, my pussy pulsing as I cum on his cock, just like he demanded. "Good girl." He praises, thrusting in and out of me faster. His moves turn jerkier, and I know he is close. With his eyes locked on mine, he buries himself so deep, I swear I feel his cock moving in my stomach. He groans, his forehead dropping to mine as he spills waves and waves of cum inside of me. "Christ. Out of all the women I have fucked, your cunt is by far the best thing I have ever put my dick in."

I scowl, despite him not being able to see me. The last thing

I want to hear about while he is inside me is the other women he has been with. It's disrespectful. How would he feel, had I not been a virgin, and I spoke about other men while he fucks me? I shove at his chest making him lift his head. A grin curves his lips when his gaze locks with mine and he searches my face. Asshole knew exactly what he was doing by saying those crude words. Knew I would react.

"Get off me." I hiss.

Nico laughs, angering me further. "Come now, *Tesoro*. Don't be jealous. It's a compliment."

I look at him incredulous. "A compliment? And how would you feel if spoke about another man's co-cock while we are having sex?" Despite wanting to sound confident, I stutter trying to say the word out loud, my cheeks heating in embarrassment.

His face turns hard, that blank mask locking in place. He narrows his cold, calculative eyes and fear shoots through me. Maybe I shouldn't have said that. But then, it's double standards if he is allowed but I have to keep my mouth shut. It would be a disservice to women all around the world, if I accept Nico's hypocrisy.

"Baby, I don't think I will have that problem. One, you struggle to even say the word *cock* without turning bright red, and two," he cuts off, pinning me with a threatening look. I shudder, my heart pumping erratically. "If another man ever touches you or you ever touch another man? I will make you watch as I kill him slowly. And then, just to prove my point, I will fuck you in front of his dead body, bathing you in my cum, so that even in death he knows you are mine."

I freeze, my blood turning to ice with every word out of his mouth. I stare at him, trying to find any hint that this is just an idle threat, but I come up empty. My heart pounds against my ribcage, my body so stiff I am like a statue. I knew he was dangerous but if he has no problem murdering a man for touching me then he is worse than I ever thought. I swallow, suddenly remembering the client who touched me at the club and Nico's reaction to that. Worry churns in my gut. "What..." I trail off, chewing my lip as I decide whether I want to ask him my next question.

"What, Ocean?" Annoyance and impatience flickers in his eyes.

I don't expect an answer, but I blurt my next words anyway "What happened to the man that touched me at The Executive Club?"

He smirks, but it's not a nice look, it's downright terrifying. He taps my nose. "I am not going to taint your pretty little head with nightmares of what happened to that asshole, *Tesoro*. But, what I will tell you is that he won't be touching you again."

I shiver, cold seeping into my bones and I suddenly have the urge to run far away from him. "I should go."

He shakes his head. "No. Let's shower and then I want to take you to dinner."

"But work..." I am grasping at straws; I know I am. He got Macy to get my whole shift covered today when he showed up this morning. But I feel like I am out of my depth with this man and that I'm playing with fire. Now that the lust-filled haze has worn off, I'm not sure I want to get burnt.

"Is covered." He pulls out of me, frowning when he glances at my pussy. Reaching down, he runs a finger through the liquid dripping down my thigh, pushing it back inside me. I gasp, desire coursing through me with that one touch. Nico shoots me a sexy smile. "If you continue to waste my perfectly good cum, I will have no choice but to have a bespoke plug made for your pussy just so it can't escape. I don't particularly like the thought of anything else but my cock inside your cunt, but I have businesses to run, and I can't keep my dick in you twenty-four-seven

even if I want to." He pauses, something a lot like jealousy flashing in his pale blue orbs. "Scrap that, it's torture just imaging a foreign object in *my* pussy. Nothing but my cock is allowed inside you. Understand?"

My mouth drops open, and I know with everything in me that he is being serious. I chuckle, trying to diffuse the sudden tension shrouding us, but it's uneasy. "Careful Nico, you are starting to sound a little crazy."

He grins, dropping his head and rubbing his nose against mine. "Oh. *Tesoro*. You haven't seen anything yet."

The scary thing.

I believe him.

Chapter 23

Nico

"I don't have anything to wear. We will have to stop by my place." Ocean says, eyeing me as she towels herself dry.

Smirking, I stride to my walk-in closet, pulling out the *Valentino*, champagne colored, backless, silk, slip dress and the matching nude pumps, I had my personal shopper pick it out for me. It's perfect and will compliment her skin tone beautifully. When I saw it hanging in my closet, it confirmed why I pay Davina huge amounts of money to shop for me.

"Wear this and put these on. No panties. I seem to be a masochist when it comes to you and want to torture myself with knowing your cunt is bare underneath your dress. I want to see your juicy pussy leaking all over the silk, needy, ready, and waiting for me to shove my cock into you again." I drawl moving back into my bedroom and handing them to her.

She gasps, her mouth dropping open, cheeks turning pink at my dirty words before recovering. Ocean shakes her head, glancing at the dress and no doubt trying to ignore me. She stares at the outfit in awe, her eyes sparkling with an emotion I can't quite decipher. Is she overwhelmed? I can't say that I blame her. The dress more than likely cost more than a month's worth of what she is paying to stay at that hostel.

Reaching up, I run a finger across my lip when a thought hits me. Hmm, I need to change her living arrangements. Now that she is mine, I need her somewhere that I can always have access to her. A place where I know she will be safe from my enemies. I would move her into my penthouse, but my father is known to stop by unexpectedly and I don't want him knowing anything about Ocean. Not until I can figure shit out anyway.

"Where did these come from?" she asks, breaking me from my thought. I don't miss the shock in her tone.

"I brought them for you," I say simply, stepping into her, wanting nothing more than to rip the towel from her body and bury my cock where it belongs.

"But they must have cost a fortune. They're designer." She states.

My head cocks at her comment. I don't know why, but I assumed from her situation, where she lives and the basic clothes she usually wears, that designer clothing would be the last thing she would have any knowledge about. I shake my head. That's on me. Judging her. For all I know, she is a massive fashionista with a love of designer brands, and a hope that one day she would own a couple of pieces of high-end clothing. Though Ocean has never struck me as materialistic, the awe covering her face as she looks at the dress has a sense of pride surging through me. If designer clothes are what she wants, then I can give those things to her. I can give her most things, whatever her heart desires. *Just not all of you,* that little voice in my head reminds me and I grit my teeth, shoving the thought aside before it can fully form and ruin our day together.

Forcing a smile, I glance down at her. "They are. Now put them on before I fuck you again and we never get out of here." I growl, wrapping my arms around her waist and pulling her into me, ready to say fuck it all and bury my cock in her sweet pussy.

A shiver wracks through her body making me smirk. I have never been with a woman so responsive to me. "I'm too sore. I don't think I could go again for a while, even if I wanted to," she murmurs, shifting her eyes to my chest.

Cupping her chin, I lift until her eyes lock on mine. "Never be ashamed *Tesoro*. Not in front of me. If you need some time to recover, then I will give it to you. I'm a big guy and you are still new to all this. You have been amazing at taking me. So good." I praise. "Your tight little pussy, stretching to accommodate me every time I fuck you... You were made for me baby." I press my lips to her forehead. "When we get back, I will draw you a bath, help ease any discomfort. And then you have twenty-four hours to recover. After that, all bets are off, and your ass is mine."

She chuckles, shaking her head. "So, kind and caring. Then you have to go and ruin it with your crude words."

I laugh. "Always. I'm not a good man, *Tesoro*. The sooner you realize that the better things will be for you."

***

Christopher pulls up outside *Ristorante Marchetti*, one of the upscale restaurants my family owns. The Marchetti's own over twenty clubs and restaurants in the city – not including my own - first started by my great-great grandpapà, over one hundred years ago in the Roaring Twenties. The first generation started acquiring restaurants and clubs and the following ones kept adding to the collection.

Obviously, over the years, we have updated the interior to keep up with the times, but even in doing that, you can still see the history that bleeds through the walls every time you enter one of our restaurants, or clubs.

It's risky bringing Ocean here. Not because I think we will run into my papà, -I made sure to find out where he was this evening, and I know he is in The Hamptons - but because he has associates that could report back to him. I know the staff won't say anything, but even so, I have booked a private room, will use the private elevator that takes me straight to said room, and will only use one server to limit our interactions with anyone who could potentially talk to my papà.

"Wow," Ocean murmurs, looking out the window and up at the high-rise in front of us. Even by New York standards, this particular building stands out. In a prominent position in the city, and with the best food and cocktails around, it is a playground for the rich and famous.

Pushing open my door, I step onto the bustling street. People are everywhere. On their way home from work, or ready for a night of sin and debauchery – either is a possibility.

Rounding my SUV, I pull open Ocean's door, taking her hand as she steps out. Wrapping a possessive arm around Ocean's waist, I lean just inside the door to speak to Christopher. "I will let you know when we are finished."

He smiles his acknowledgement. "Have a good evening, sir."

I nod, before slamming the door closed and pulling my woman toward the exclusive hidden elevator at the side of the building. Few people know about this, and it's only used when someone wants complete discretion. A married movie star, who wants to take his mistress out. A businessman, on the verge of a big deal, and wanting a private room to conduct said business. The *famiglia* when we deal with our allies and want to bring them somewhere a bit more grandiose than the meeting room of one of our clubs.

Fishing the fob out of my pocket, I hold it up to the panel and in the next second the hidden metal doors slide open, revealing the elevator. "Come on." I drag Ocean inside, pushing the button for the top floor and looking down when I sense her hesitancy. "What's wrong?"

She swallows, making my eyes drop to her delicate neck. I want to bite it. Leave my mark all over her soft, flawless skin so every knows she is owned. "Why aren't we using the main entrance?" Vulnerability flashes in her blue orbs and I know what she is saying without saying it.

Pushing her against the wall, I cage her in with my arms. "*Tesoro*, I am not hiding you, nor am I embarrassed about being seen with you, if that is what you are thinking; so get those thoughts out of your head. I just want privacy. I am a very..." I trail off wondering how to word what I say next. "I am a very rich and powerful man. If I walk through the restaurant, people will want to speak with me. I don't want to have to engage with anyone but you. I want to spend this time with you and only *you*, with no one interrupting us. I want you all to myself." I growl, nipping at her jaw.

Her eyes flutter closed, before they snap back open. A breathtaking smile curves her lips and I know she likes my answer. It's confirmed when she pushes up on her tiptoes, pressing a kiss to the corner of my mouth. My cock jerks in my slacks at her initiating something – even if it is only a quick peck of her lips. She has never instigated anything that has happened between us thus far. She is still shy and unsure when it comes to matters of sex, and I have noticed that she is mostly content for me to take the lead. It suits me. I like dominating her, showing her what I like. "Okay." She whispers.

"Okay," I repeat, eyes narrowing just as the elevator comes to a stop. The doors open, leading out to marble floors, expensive fixtures, and a small table set up for two. Beppe, our server for this evening, stands, waiting for us with a smile on his face. Being he is one of our longest-serving staff members, and he values discretion, he was my first choice for this evening.

Dancing In Sin

I search Ocean's face, waiting for her reaction to what she sees. Her wide eyes light up like the fourth of July, her pouty lips parted as she takes everything in. She likes what she is seeing. Satisfaction rumbles in my chest. Suddenly I get the urge to take her places and do things for her repeatedly, just to see her smile like she is right now.

"You did this for me?" I hear the incredulity in her voice, it's as if she can't believe that someone would go to such lengths for her.

"Yes," I say, taking her hand and stepping out. "And for your reaction alone it was worth it." I move us towards the table where Beppe is pulling out a chair.

Glancing at me, he straightens, greeting me. "Mr. Marchetti."

"Beppe," I reply, helping Ocean into her seat. By the time I am done, Beppe has pulled out my own chair and I drop down into it.

"Can I start you both off with some drinks?" he asks.

"Yes. Cristal. Two glasses." I don't see his reaction because I am staring at my girl, but I hear his retreating footsteps and know he is going to get what I asked for.

Ocean smirks. "You are really spoiling me tonight, Nico. I don't know how I'm going to go back to my boring life after this."

Irritation slithers through me that she is even thinking about when we end - because we won't. Not now. Not ever. - and I pin her with a dark look. "You won't. I already told you that you are mine, Ocean. And I look after what's mine."

She eyes me for a long beat, no doubt trying to find any hint of a lie in my words. She won't. I mean them. No matter what happens, or what plans my papà has in store for me, I mean every single word.

Clearing her throat, she smiles softly, and changes the subject. "What's good to eat."

Grinning, I wave her off. "I have the chef preparing several dishes for us. They are all exceptionally good and I promise you will love them." Her gaze drops, cheeks turning a lovely pink hue. Reaching over, I take a lock of her blonde hair, wrapping it around my finger. I lean in, my mouth dropping to her ear. Her breath hitches and I feel rather than see the rapid rise and fall of her chest. "Tonight is going to be an experience for both of us. There is nothing more erotic than watching a beautiful woman enjoy good food. And when we are done and Beppe brings out dessert, I am going to lay you out on the table, shove up your dress and eat my dessert – if you haven't guessed already, that will be your cunt - as you eat your tiramisu. You will watch me as I watch you."

"But I'm sore," she whispers.

I grin against her ear, knowing that would be her reply. "It will not hurt, baby. I am going to make you feel all better. I promise."

Pulling back, I look at her beautiful face enjoying the way her cheeks flush, chest heaves, and eyes dilate with pure lust. Pressing a kiss to her lips, I lean back in my seat just as Beppe arrives with the champagne.

Tonight, I am going to take us both to new heights.

Heights neither of us will ever come down from.

Chapter 24

Ocean

I can't help the big smile on my face or the way my mouth waters as our server, Beppe, strolls back into the room carrying a large round tray of food. Stepping up to the table, he starts placing dish after dish of delicious-looking carb goodness down on the table.

"Enjoy your dinner." He smiles when he places the last plate down before quickly disappearing and giving us our privacy. I watch as he leaves only for my eyes to snap to Nico when his hand grips my chin, pulling my gaze to his.

"Eyes on me. You will not look at another man. Only me." he growls.

I laugh, feeling a little drunk on the champagne, and a whole lot intoxicated just from being in Nico's company. He makes me feel things that I've never felt before. He makes me feel… alive. Like I could take on the world. It's a dangerous feeling. One I could quite easily become addicted to. Not that I will ever admit that to him. I don't want to further inflate his already very inflated ego.

"Eat," he commands, releasing his grip on me and jerking his head to the dishes.

I bite back a retort. There is no point in arguing with him. He is bossy, arrogant, demanding... but I like it. More than I should. Picking up my fork, I look over the food, before taking a little off each plate and loading it onto mine.

"It all looks delicious," I murmur with a smile.

"It is. Enzo is one of the best chefs in the city, hands down. He is old school and specializes in authentic Italian dishes. My father brought him to New York over two decades ago to run this restaurant." He says; his voice is passionate as he speaks highly of the man that created this yummy-looking food.

Nodding, because there is really nothing I can respond with, I fork up what looks to be a risotto ball wanting to know if it is as good as Nico just said. Slowly moving it towards my mouth, Nico's gaze doesn't leave mine. My cheeks heat when hunger – not for the food – sparks in his blue orbs. Biting down on the mixture of rice, mozzarella, sundried tomato, breadcrumbs, and spices, my eyes close in ecstasy when the flavors burst on my tongue. I swallow it down, my eyes snapping open, landing on Nico. His head is cocked, and I almost hear the silent question he wants to ask, so I give him an answer.

"Oh my God. Wow. That is amazing." I tell him honestly, pointing at the other half of the risotto ball left on my plate.

His lips twitch in amusement. He clears his throat. "Watching you eat is the single most erotic thing I have ever seen in my life. I can only be thankful I chose to dine in private, because had another man watched you with that risotto ball in your mouth, I would have had to kill them."

I choke on a laugh only to stop when I realize he is being serious. I shake my head. "Nico–"

I am cut off when he pins me with a dark, devilish look. Reaching across the table he takes my hand, bringing it to his lips and kissing me. My stomach clenches, moisture seeping between my panty-less thighs. Nico was right. At this rate there will be a big wet patch on my beautiful dress. "I mean it, Ocean. You are mine and any man who dares to look at you, I will remove his eyeballs. You are mine to desire. Mine to look at. Mine to fuck. *Mine*." The noise that rumbles from his chest is primal.

I stare at him, my lips parted in lust or shock, I'm not sure. "You're crazy. You can't go around killing people or removing their eyes. You will end up in a penitentiary."

He chuckles, dropping my hand and leaning back in his chair. "Oh, my sweet, innocent *Tesoro*. You have a lot to learn about me and what I can and can't do." His words are dark and cryptic. I search his face for what they could mean, but coming up empty, I decide not to ask more. Because quite frankly, I don't want to delve into anything right now that could interrupt me eating what I can only describe as the best meal I have had in a long time. Ignoring him, I fork up some noodles, popping them in my mouth, groaning as the flavors burst in my mouth and enjoying every single morsel of it. We eat in silence for a time before Nico speaks.

"You will be moving into a new apartment," he states coolly.

My noodle-covered fork freezes midair, hovering mere centimeters from my mouth. I cough, blink, and stare at him in disbelief, but his face doesn't change. He says all this as if it's a given, a done deal. What the hell?

Dropping the utensil onto my plate, I wipe my mouth with a napkin, giving myself a couple of seconds to find some calm before speaking. "Excuse me?" I ask evenly, though anxiety slithers over my skin.

His eyes spark with challenge, and in that moment I know I am going to have a fight on my hands. "You. Will. Be. Moving. Into. One. Of. The. Apartments. I. Own," he says slowly, as if his words are law. "I own a lot of real estate around the city and have condos in several different buildings. They are safe. You will be *safe.*" He enunciates the last word. The hairs on the back of my neck stand on end. I know I should be asking him what exactly he means by *you will be safe,* but first, I need to take care of the other situation.

I shake my head, imploring him with my eyes to listen. "No. I can't afford that. I like the hostel. I will stay there."

Before I even know what's happening, I am out of my seat and in his lap. A gasp leaves my lips as he gets right up in my face. "No. It is non-negotiable. It is close to the spa and a secure building. I want you somewhere I can keep you protected. And you don't have to afford it. You will live there for free. I don't want your money, *Tesoro.* I just want to know where you are and that you are looked after."

Anger explodes inside me. "Like some cheap whore? I don't want your money, Nico," I spit.

That blank mask locks into place, anger shining from his blue eyes. His jaw clenches. "You are not a fucking whore. You are mine. Mine to take care of. I can only do that properly if you are living somewhere secure. That hostel you call a home is *not* safe and quite frankly should have been condemned years ago." His voice is low, almost threatening.

I stiffen, swallowing, and though I don't want to argue, I suddenly feel protective over my little hostel. Yes, the building is not in great condition, and neither is it in a good area, but it's been my little sanctuary, somewhere I could lay my head down at night without worrying about being violated or robbed. But Nico doesn't see it that way. All he sees is a dilapidated building that I share with a bunch of other women. I chew my bottom lip. I mean, it would be nice to have my own space...

I sigh, shaking my head and knowing that I should say no to his offer. Should listen to the voice in my head screaming *red flag, red flag, red flag.* Unfortunately, red has always been my favorite color and the thought of having my own apartment is very tempting. I glance up at him, my voice a whisper when I speak. "I will think about it."

His eyes narrow, his face turns hard, ruthless. It equal parts turns me on and scares me. "There is nothing to think about. It is happening. I can have my men move your stuff tomorrow and get you all settled in before the weekend."

I open my mouth to argue more, but Beppe enters cutting me off. "Have you finished?"

"No. Leave the food but bring out dessert. Tiramisu," Nico grunts, his eyes never leaving mine.

His earlier words hit me with the mention of dessert. Heat builds between my legs, my stomach tightening with need. *"And when we are done and Beppe brings out dessert, I am going to lay you out on the table, shove up your dress and eat my dessert – if you haven't guessed already, that will be your cunt - as you eat your tiramisu. You will watch me as I watch you."*

By the smirk now curving his lips, Nico knows exactly what I am thinking about. Leaning in, his tongue darts out and he licks a trail up my neck. My eyes dart to Beppe, who hurriedly clears our plates without even a glance in our direction and makes a quick exit.

"I bet you are thinking about my mouth on your cunt as you spoon tiramisu into your own." He rasps, sending a shiver down my spine.

"Nico," I gasp, my pussy throbbing in anticipation. I want that. Now.

He grins, lifting and sitting me on the table in front of him. Running his hands up my legs he groans. "I can smell your greedy pussy from here. So needy for me. Begging me to give it what only I can."

I moan, pure lust coursing through me with every second that passes. Beppe rushes back into the room, dish in hand and snapping me from my desire-filled haze. Shifting, I try to scramble off the table but it's no use. Nico holds me in place, his strong hands pinning me down and not letting me move. Beppe, who never once makes eye contact, places down the small plates. Though he keeps his gaze trained on the job at hand, I can tell by the way his cheeks turn pink, he knows something is going on. Heat floods my body, but this time in embarrassment, hating that someone is witness to this.

"Leave us." Nico barks, making me jump and Beppe rush away.

"Nico," I hiss but he ignores me.

"Now, lay back and let me take care of you." Placing his big palm on my stomach, he pushes until I am laid back on the table. I glance around, noticing all dishes and glasses have been strategically placed near the edge of the table, I assume so I don't knock them over.

I don't have time to think about it further because Nico lifts the hem of my dress, pushing it up my body until it pools around my waist. His gaze zones in on my pussy, pure desire sparking in his blue orbs. He licks his lips, the hunger on his face making my stomach clench.

"Nico," I pant out.

"Hmm?"

"Wh-what are you doing?" I stutter between breaths.

"You know what I'm doing. Now take your spoon and be the good girl I know you are. Eat your dessert while I eat mine. I want your eyes on me, watching me while I eat my cunt."

"Oh God," I moan, back arching as moisture seeps from me.

He smirks, handing me a spoon. "No, *Tesoro*. Not God. The correct words are *oh my Nico*. I am the only God you will worship. The only name allowed to spill from your lips when you are like this. Now eat," he growls, his tongue darting out and running a line up my slit. My back bows, pleasure consuming me. I drop the utensil, not bothered about eating the tiramisu. Nico stops his ministrations. "If you don't eat. I don't eat." He cocks a challenging brow.

Rolling my eyes, I push up on my elbows, picking up the spoon and plate. "Happy?" I mock.

"Very." He smirks. Dropping his head, he runs his nose up my slit, inhaling me before he pulls my clit into his mouth. He sucks, nibbles, teases. It's heaven. The sensations coursing through me, lighting my body on fire. My eyes flutter closed, pure desire heating my veins. I don't know how I am supposed to eat, while he is doing this to me, but I try. Opening my eyes, I try to concentrate on taking a spoonful of dessert. I don't know how I manage, but I scoop some of the sponge and coffee-layered concoction. My gaze locks on Nico as he licks me, I bring the spoon to my mouth, gently pushing it inside. Nico watches me as I watch him, and I have never experienced something so erotic in my life. My back arches, eyes threatening to close as pleasure consumes me. "Mmmm," I moan, when the flavors hit me at the same time Nico pushes his tongue into me. Though the tiramisu is good, what Nico is doing to me is even better. My back bows, but I don't look away.

Satisfaction sparks in his eyes, no doubt at me following his orders and watching him. He starts to tongue fuck me harder, and the pleasure is so intense I drop the plate and spoon to the table. There is no way I can keep hold of them right now. Though Nico notices that I have stopped eating, he doesn't stop his ministrations. Pulling out of me, he moves back to my clit, sucking it into his mouth and pushing a finger into me. I wince, still sore from our all-day fuck fest.

"Nico," I whimper, reaching down and gripping his dark hair.

"That's it baby, ride my face." He snarls, before sucking me back into his mouth. His finger pumps inside me, gentler than I thought he was capable of, while he works his magic on my clit.

It doesn't take long before the familiar feeling of my orgasm building hits me, and I grind against him harder.

"Nico," I cry out when my climax barrels through me. I come all over his face, body turning limp with the power of my release. I fall back against the hard surface of the table, my chest heaving as I try to catch my breath. "Jesus," I mumble, trying to suck air into my lungs.

Nico swipes his tongue over my pussy, lapping at me as if I am the best thing he has ever eaten, before lifting his head with a smirk. My cheeks heat when I see his face glistening with my orgasm. Running a palm over his mouth, his lips twitch.

"You will move tomorrow and not a day later." His words leave no room for argument and neither does the pointed look on his face.

I sigh, knowing I need to pick my battles with him, and this isn't one of them.

Guess I am moving to a new apartment.

***

"I can't believe you are leaving me. First the club and now here." Selena whines, pouting from her position on my bed in the hostel. I haven't told her, it's Nico's apartment I am moving to. She doesn't even know that I have been... well, whatever it is we are doing. I know she is wary of him, and I don't blame her - he is a scary guy when you don't know him.

But for the first time in a long time, I feel genuinely happy, and I don't want her to put a dampener on anything right now. Though the hostel was safe, and it served its purpose, the whole point of working at The Executive Club was to earn enough money so I could move out. Now I can. And I don't even have to pay rent. It's a win-win.

"I know. I know. But we will still see each other. And

anyway, I have a sneaky feeling that you will be moving in with Eric soon." I wink teasingly. No matter what happens, I will still see Selena. She was my first and probably only friend in the city.

She sighs, flopping back on the mattress and staring at the ceiling. She chews her lip, a look of contemplation on her face. "Well..." she trails off.

My eyes narrow in on her. "He already asked you to move in, didn't he?"

She laughs, pushing up on her elbows and meeting my gaze. "He did." She says dreamily. "Eric is kinda perfect, but it scares me. I am so used to assholes that it's weird to have a normal guy, ya know?"

I snort. No, I don't know, because apart from Nico, I've never been in a relationship with a man in my life. Not even in high school. I was sent to an all-girls school, to make sure there was no chance of me...getting caught up with boys. Virginity is considered the most treasured, precious thing in my world - well, what used to be my world - and should be protected at all costs to ensure that you can be sold off to the highest bidder. It's archaic as fuck but it's how things were. No matter how much I wanted to change things, I would never have been able to achieve it. Not on my own against some of the richest and most powerful men in Seattle. So I ran instead. Shoving the depressing thoughts aside, I focus on my friend.

"Selena, Eric sounds great. Don't ruin a good thing because you are scared. If he treats you right and is good to you, then don't let fear spoil it. You deserve happiness." I swallow, knowing I feel the same when it comes to Nico, but also aware that I'm not going to let it stop me even with all the doubts.

She sighs. "You're right. I'm going to call him now and tell him the good news." She jumps off the bed, squealing with excitement and wraps me in her arms. "Don't be a stranger. I want to come visit your new place so message me the address and let me know when it's a good time to come over."

I hug her tighter. "I will. We can have girls' night."

She laughs. "Sounds good to me." she releases me. "Take care, Ocean. I will see you soon, okay."

"Okay." I jerk my head to the door to ease some of the sadness that's radiating in the room. "Now go tell your man that you are moving in."

She shakes her head, groaning as she points at me with a small smile on her lips. "If this goes wrong, I'm blaming you."

"You can blame away. But I get the feeling that it's all going to work out exactly how it should be." I frown, not sure whether it's Selena I am talking about now or me.

Waving, she moves toward the door, stepping outside and leaving me alone. Glancing down, I sag when I see the two small bags that currently hold all my worldly possessions. It's pathetic really.

But as long as I have my freedom, it's all I need.

Chapter 25
Nico

I sit in my office at The Executive Club, my eyes focused on the computer in front of me. I watch as Ocean walks around the apartment I moved her into. She doesn't know about the cameras that I had installed in every room and never will. I want to be able to watch her whenever I get the urge.

Would she find it creepy? Probably.

Do I care? No.

It's obsessive and maybe a little overkill, but it's for her safety also.

Christopher picked Ocean up - along with her measly belongings - from the shitty place she called home and dropped her off about two hours ago. I have two of my men situated in the lobby and one of my most trusted guards, Gio, will be living in the apartment next to hers. I have assigned him as her personal security. Not that Ocean is aware of what I have done, and again it will remain that way.

I watch as she moves to the bedroom, pulling her tank top over her head and revealing her perfect tits. I groan, my cock twitching in my pants as my eyes rake over her beautiful body. My hands move to my belt, and I begin to unbuckle it. Desire heats my blood, the need to jerk myself off as I watch her take in her new cage a living breathing thing. I am about to do just that when my office door is pulled open, and my papà strides in.

My eyes narrow, my hand leaving my belt as I make quick work of closing my laptop. Lowering himself into a chair, his cold gaze shifts to my computer before coming back to me. "Son," he greets with a smirk, but I see the tightness of his jaw.

"Papà, to what do I owe the pleasure?" I smile, but it's forced. He is a perceptive bastard and no doubt he thinks that I'm hiding something from him with my reaction to him entering my space. I am. But it's probably not what he thinks it is.

"Well, for one, I thought I would come and... wind down, and what better place to do that, than in my son's whore house." He grins, making me resist an eye roll. Yes, the *famiglia* owns brothels, but no, The Executive Club is not one of them. This Club is high-end. He knows this. He is just trying to bait me.

"And?" I say rolling my wrist for him to continue.

He pulls a cigar out of his pocket, bringing it to his mouth. Reaching across my desk, he grabs the box of matches and lights up. Taking a pull on the Cuban, he inhales before blowing out a thick cloud of smoke. His gaze settles on me. "And the Bratva? Are you any further forward with your investigations?"

Leaning back in my chair, I run a hand through my hair. "I am. I was going to set up a meeting with you. I have found out who the other traitors are. Turns out, Federico was working with two of our other soldiers to feed information to Vadim Mikhailov." I tell him, the information I just learned earlier today.

He watches me, his eyes turning to slits. "And why wasn't I informed of this?"

"Because, like I said, I was calling a meeting. I only found out myself, just hours ago. I have the rats, strung up in one of our safe houses in Brooklyn and being guarded by trusted men. We need to make a stand. Make a show of killing them in front of all our soldiers so they know not to step out of line. They need to fear us. Understand what will happen if they turn against us." I reply, my voice calm.

Leaning forward, he stubs out his cigar in the ashtray, his dark eyes coming to mine. "I have taught you well. You will make a good *Don* one day Nico." The compliment should make me feel good, but coming from a man like Lorenzo Marchetti, I know by now not to take it to heart. "Have an arena set up in one of our warehouses. Spread the word, I want every man in the *famiglia* present when we kill those rat motherfuckers. Make the arrangements."

I nod. "Consider it done. Now why don't you go downstairs and relax? I will have Leo set up the best seat in the house."

He chuckles, running a hand down his tie as he pushes out of his chair. "Do that, but in a private room. And have a half dozen of your best girls in there to entertain me and my men." He licks his lips as my stomach turns, knowing full well what he is saying. He wants a girl or two, to fuck for the night.

I grit my teeth, biting back what I really want to say to him. "Head on down. I will arrange it for you."

***

"Christ, your papà is an animal." Dante whistles when he saunters into my office. I grit my teeth, annoyed that my observing of Ocean has been disturbed for the second time this evening.

I glance up at him. "Do I even want to know?"

"Probably not, but you're gonna." He shakes his head, disgust curving his lips. "I don't know why he would want any other woman when he has your mamma at home, but he is in the Diamond room, with Dana riding his dick, Elmenia straddling his face, while Sasha has his foot in her cunt and Delila has his fingers in hers."

Revulsion rolls through me at the mental image that has just formed in my head. How the man hasn't died from all his sexual proclivities yet, I don't know. I mean, I like fucking as much as anyone, but my papà is next level.

"Jesus," I murmur, shaking my head in disgust. "How many men does he have with him?"

"Two guards standing outside the room. Giuseppe and Marco inside, each have a girl of their own."

"Make sure Leo knows to have the cleaners deep clean that room. I will pay them extra." I drawl.

"Done. What are you doing anyway?" he asks, his gaze on me.

I shrug. "Just catching up on some business." Dante doesn't know about me moving Ocean into one of my apartments. And not that I have to tell him anything, but I will. We spend too much time together for me to hide it from him. "I moved her into an apartment in the Barbizon building."

His brows furrow in confusion, before understanding crosses his face. He throws his head back, laughing. "Ocean? You moved her in? Christ Nico, I didn't know you were that serious about her. I just thought you wanted to fuck her."

Glowering, because quite frankly, I don't want anyone thinking about her in any kind of sexual capacity, I snarl out. "Don't fucking talk about her like that."

He sobers, searching my face. "Fuck, man, you do know it can't go any further than what you are already doing with her, don't you?"

"I can do what the fuck I want. She is *mine*." I bark, knowing full well what Dante says is true, but also knowing I

Dancing In Sin

have no intention of giving Ocean up, no matter what comes next.

He scrubs a palm over his face, shaking his head. "Look, you are my best friend Nico, and I am not going to tell you what to do. You wouldn't listen anyway. But I can see it in your eyes, hear it in your words. You are already in deep with this girl, and I want you to think about it, like really fucking think about it. This can only end one way. I doubt a girl like that will be happy to be a–"

I cut him off. "I know what I'm doing. And you're right. When it comes to *her,* I won't listen to you. She is off-limits. Now if that's all?" I know I'm being an asshole but fuck it. I will not have anyone telling me what I can and can't do with *my* woman.

He nods. "Yeah. That's it." Pushing out of his chair, he looks at me. "I'm only looking out for you, man." I hear the honesty of his voice, but I am past caring what he or anyone thinks when it comes to what's mine. With one last look in my direction, he leaves my office.

Sighing, I glance down at my computer screen, to find Ocean fast asleep in bed. A grin curves my lips as I log off and shut down my laptop. There is only one place I want to be right now.

And that's buried in my perfect piece of heaven.

***

Flashing my fob at the panel on the wall next to the door a click sounds, signaling that the door has unlocked. Smirking, I push it open, stepping into the apartment. My gaze moves around the spacious area, before moving to the door of her bedroom. Blood pumps through my body, moving down to my swelling cock. Fuck, I want her so much.

Making my way to the bedroom, I am quiet in my movements, not wanting to wake her up – not yet anyway. She is sure to rouse when I get my cock in her though, and I can't wait to see the fear on her face when she realizes what is happening. Sees that she is completely at my mercy.

Fucking someone while they sleep has never really been my kink. If I'm honest, I've never really thought about it. But when I shoved my cock inside her last week while she was still sleeping, it awakened something inside of me. My body came alive, my dick harder than it had ever been. The most primal part of me was awoken and a need so feral took over. I had to have her whether she was awake or not and no one was going to stop me. Not even Ocean herself. There is something to be said about fucking her when she was in such a vulnerable state. I have never come so hard in my life. My vision had blurred, and I swear I nearly blacked out from the pleasure. And the emotions on her beautiful face as she stirred from her sleep. Confusion turning to fear. Fear turning to pure lust. Fuck. It makes me rock hard just thinking about it. Maybe I'm an asshole for doing that to her, especially since she is still so new to sex, but I don't care.

Ocean is mine.

Mine to do with as I please.

Stepping into the bedroom, my gaze lands on her prone body, hidden beneath the sheets. The moonlight, that shines through the gap in the drapes, hits her face. She is so flawless, so beautiful. My chest tightens.

What am I going to do with her?

Shoving that thought aside and getting back to what I came here for, I make quick work of removing my loafers, and then stripping out of my clothes. Moving to the bed, I lift the comforter and slide in beside her. She wears a little tank and matching sleep shorts. Hmm, that won't do.

Careful not to wake her, I grip the hem of her top, lifting it slowly over her body. Then gripping the waistband of her bottoms, I pull them gently over the curve of her hips and down her legs until she is completely bare for me. Eyes locking on her pussy, my mouth waters when I find her already slick. Is she dreaming of me? I bite back a growl. She better fucking be. If another man crosses her mind – whether it is in her dreams or not – I will kill him.

Logically, I know my thoughts are borderline insane, but I am going to submit to them. I fucked her virgin pussy, was the first man to be inside her. I claimed her, made her mine and I will go to war with anyone if they try to take her from me. I scrub a palm down my face, sighing.

Christ. Dante was *wrong*. I'm not just in deep with this girl. I'm *Mariana Trench* fucking deep. Buried so far down in something – that I can't even comprehend in my own head, let alone explain to anyone else - I don't know which way is up. I grit my teeth, anger slithering through me that a woman has managed to make me feel this way. And then because she has angered me, I want to punish her.

Reaching down, I run a finger through her wet pussy. "Nico," she mumbles. I pause, eyes darting to her face to check that she is still asleep. She is. And she said my name. *My. Name.* Satisfaction rumbles in my chest. Good. I wouldn't want to have to leave this bed, get dressed, and hunt down another man, had she called out a different name.

"That's it, *Tesoro*. Even in sleep you know who owns you," I murmur, moving down her body and running my tongue across her cunt as I stroke myself. I'm rock-hard. I could thrust into her right now, but as much as I am pissed, I don't want to hurt her. She is still so tight, so small, and I'm big and thick. I will tear her up if I get too rough. The nasty, wild fucking I am used to will come eventually, just not tonight.

Sliding my tongue up and down her slit, her juices leak onto me. Jesus, she tastes so fucking good. Carrying on with my ministrations, she begins to soak my face and the sheets with her arousal. Smirking, I stop what I am doing and crawl up her body. She is wet enough now that my cock will slide right into her with no resistance.

Glancing at her face, I find that she is still in a deep slumber. Frowning, I briefly wonder if she has taken something to help her sleep. Had someone even stepped through the door and into my penthouse, I would be awake. Yet apart from her saying my name that once, she hasn't so much as stirred. *It's exactly how you wanted her*, that sick part in my head, that wants to fuck her like this, taunts. I grin. That's right. I did.

Rubbing my dick against her ready pussy, I lean down, my tongue darting out and running up her cheek. "So fucking beautiful *la mia piccola ballerina*," I groan, pushing inside her tight cunt. She tenses slightly, brows furrowing. Her thick lashes flutter against her high cheekbones, her face screwing up. She looks so fucking stunning like this.

Slowly, I pump into her. In and out. In and out. Her pussy grips me like a vise, holding onto me like it never wants me to leave. Drawing in a breath, I start to thrust harder and it's only then that her eyes snap open. Fear and shock stare back at me, exactly the look I wanted. Thrusting harder, I grin down at her. Her mouth parts. Then she is screaming and not in the way I like. I slap a palm over her mouth to shut her up, dropping mine to her ear as I whisper.

"Sshh, baby. It's only me. Look at you taking my cock, even when you're asleep. You fucking love it. You're so wet your pussy is weeping for me, begging for me to fuck you raw. You know who owns you, don't you, *Tesoro*, hmmm? Know my dick owns your little cunt." I murmur the dirty words before pulling back to look at her. She blinks those big doe eyes before her frightened gaze locks on mine. My cock turns to steel. Reaching down, my hand wraps around her throat, I squeeze, not enough to hurt her but enough to let her know that I am in control. That I will always be in control. Ocean doesn't know it but controlling her is a necessity if she wants to survive in my world. A world she has no clue about, but she will submit all the same. There is no other way. Her eyes bug out of her head, and I see the clear panic on her face, but I don't stop. "Yeah. You fucking love it when I take what I want, don't you, baby. You love being at my mercy," I growl, pounding into her harder. Her back arches, hot air hits my palm when her mouth opens, and I feel rather than hear her breathy moan. Smirking, I release her throat, reaching down to rub her plump clit. It only takes a few strokes of my finger, and she is coming all over my dick. Her cunt soaks me, clamping down around me so hard she draws out my own release. I still, groaning, as ecstasy courses through my veins. My eyes roll to the back of my head, cock pulsing my release, as I empty inside her.

"Fuck," I curse, my vision blurring from the intensity of my orgasm.

A question that I have asked myself before filters into my brain. Why is it so good with her? I've fucked loads of women, but it has never been like this with anyone else. I don't understand it, but I'm also past caring about the whys and what's of the situation.

Movement beneath me drags me from my thoughts and has my gaze locking on Ocean. Shit. I'm still covering her mouth. Removing my hand, I revel in the way she sucks in much-needed air.

"Nico?" she gasps out.

"Yeah, baby?" I hum.

"Wh-What are you doing?" she stutters.

Pushing up on my elbows, I make sure to keep my cock in her warm cunt so that none of my seed can leak out. Grabbing her hips, I roll us so she is on top of me, but am careful not to slip out of her. She stares down at me, waiting for an answer.

Reaching up, I run a finger down her cheek. "Fucking what's mine."

Her brow furrows in confusion, a range of emotions flickering in her eyes. "But I was asleep?" It's a question, one I don't answer because she is stating the obvious. Yes. Yes, she was sleeping when I stuck my dick in her. And to be completely transparent, this won't be the last time this happens. I like fucking her while she is sleeping, so she better get used to it. Nonetheless, I don't want to freak her out further, so I don't tell her that.

"And now you are awake." Pressing a kiss to her head, I wrap my arms around her, holding her tight to my body. "Sleep, *Tesoro*."

"I can't sleep now." She whispers, her body tense.

I sigh, pulling out of her and rolling her to her back. She blinks up at me, her blue eyes sparkling in the little bit of light shining through the drapes. Gripping my semi-hard cock, I stroke it up and down her slit, then around her clit in a soft soothing motion.

She moans softly, her eyes flickering shut, heavy with sleep and desire. I lean in, dropping my mouth to her ear. "Sleep, *Tesoro*. I am going to rub your little clit and pussy with my cock until you go to sleep," I whisper, continuing with my ministrations.

I lick a wet trail up her neck, running my tongue around her ear and nibbling on the lobe. She doesn't speak, just lets out little gasps of pleasure. Her cunt leaks, soaking me with every caress of her pussy, and her legs widen. I smirk. She thinks that I am going to fuck her again, but I'm not. I want her to sleep. And she will. It's just a matter of time.

"Nico," she mumbles, the lids of her eyes growing heavier.

She sighs, her body turning lax as she melts into the mattress. I smile. I knew my baby was tired. She was just fighting it because of what she found me doing to her when she woke.

With my free hand, I run small circles on her hip. She exhales, her eyes fluttering shut. The strokes of my cock, my fingers, and the feel of my mouth on her soft flesh all lulled her to sleep. Her breathing evens out, a small gush of air leaving her parted lips and I know my job is done. She is asleep.

Smirking, I climb off her body, falling on the mattress beside her. Throwing my arm over her, I pull her into me, cocooning her in my body like the little precious treasure she is.

Pressing a kiss to her hair, I whisper. "You are unlocking things inside me I never knew existed. I will never let you go, *Tesoro*. You are mine in this life and every life that comes after."

Chapter 26
Ocean

My eyes flutter open, then snap shut when I see how bright the room is. Groaning, I wince at the way my whole body aches. Rolling onto my side, I startle as I hit a hard body. My eyes snap open in panic, mouth opening, ready to scream, only to close when I see Nico sleeping beside me. Blowing out a breath I relax at the sight of him. A smile curves my lips, my gaze raking over his handsome face. And then it all comes flooding back to me. Memories of last night. I frown.

He fucked me.

While I was sleeping.

Again.

And I didn't even wake until I came all over his cock.

While that should concern me, for some reason I like it. I like that he dominates my body and owns me even when I am asleep. My brows furrow. What the fuck is wrong with me? There is obviously something missing in my brain for me to get off on shit like that. I have gone from being a virgin to having some weird kink with being fucked while sleeping in a matter of a couple of weeks. It's messed up.

Last night, I swallowed down a melatonin tablet. I haven't been sleeping well and knew it would help. What I didn't anticipate was it giving Nico an in to fuck me in that sleepy state. And how did he even get in here? I roll my eyes at that thought. Of course, he got in here. He owns the apartment. It was naïve of me to think he wouldn't be able to get in here anytime he wants.

He mumbles something, drawing my attention back to him. His face scrunches up and he is so gorgeous, it's almost hard to look at him. With his chiseled features, and a jawline you could cut glass with, he is God-like. Perfect.

Mine?

Snorting under my breath, I shake the thought away. No. There is no way I could keep a man like Nico Marchetti forever, even if I wanted to. He could have any woman in this city. I know whatever we have has an expiration date. His interest in me will soon wane. And I should be happy about that. We can't be together. Eventually, I will have to move on and so will he. There is no other way. I'm just the girl trying to make it on her own and he is... well, him. A deity among men.

"Instead of staring at me like a creeper, why don't you put that mouth to use and wrap those pretty lips around my cock?" he murmurs, making me jump. His eyes are still closed but he has a smirk tipping his lips. Lips that bring me so much pleasure...

I grin, cocking a brow down at him even though he can't see it. "I'm not a creeper. I was just wondering what you are doing in my bed. I don't remember going to sleep with you."

His eyes snap open, and before I can blink, he is grabbing me. I squeal as he drags me on top of him, positioning me so that I am straddling his waist. "You didn't. But what you did get was me fucking your pussy and a nice orgasm."

I narrow my gaze down at him. "About that? That is the

second time you have..." I trail off my cheeks heating. He grins. I suck in a breath then start again. "You know. Had sex with me while I was sleeping." I drop my voice to a whisper. I don't know why. It's not like anyone can hear us.

His smile grows wider. "And it won't be the last time either. There is something to be said about fucking your tight pussy while you are asleep, vulnerable. It turns my cock to steel, knowing I could do anything to you, and you wouldn't be able to stop me. I came so hard, filling you with my cum. And you loved it. I know you did. Your cunt clung to my dick like it never wanted it to leave."

His dirty words have me panting when I know I should be mad. I'm obviously a very sick, sick girl. "Isn't it... weird? Doing things like that, I mean?" I ask, dropping my eyes to his chest.

Wrapping a finger around my chin, he lifts it until my gaze meets his. Pinning me with a look, he says. "No. What we do in private is nobody's business but ours. I liked it. And I know you did, too, even if your mind is trying to tell you it's fucked up. Set yourself free and own who you are, Ocean. It will make things easier for both of us." He reaches up, pressing a kiss to my lips. "Because I won't stop. I will fuck what's mine, when and how I want, no matter if society tells us it's right or wrong. Fuck them. You belong to me. If I want to stick my cock inside your tight cunt while you sleep, then who the hell is going to stop me? No. One." He enunciates, drilling the words into me. "I will fucking kill them if they try." He says all this so confidently, as if his words are law. And maybe they are. Who knows? All I know is he is right. People will judge you no matter what. Our private life is just that. Private. It's not like I'm going to tell anyone what we get up to and I doubt Nico is the type to share information about his sex life either.

"Okay," I whisper.

He grins. "It wasn't a question, Ocean. This is your life now.

Get used to it." He thrusts up, his hard cock pressing against my thigh as his eyes narrow. "Now, my dick won't suck itself. Wrap those beautiful lips around me. I want to fuck your mouth until I blow my load down your throat and flood your insides with my cum." My tummy flutters, moisture dripping between my thighs. But I don't move. I can't. He looks pointedly to his cock, which is now tenting the sheet and back to me. "What's wrong?"

My cheeks heat in embarrassment. I don't know why. This man has seen every part of my body in ways no one else ever has. "I-I've never done it before." I blurt.

Something a lot like satisfaction flashes in his blue orbs, a smirk curving his lips. Reaching up, he runs a finger down my face. "I love that I'm the first man to have you. And the only man." He adds in a growl. "I will talk you through it, *Tesoro*. Always. Now scoot down and take me in your mouth. I'm big so you won't fit me all in - not on your first time anyway – but you can wrap your hand around the base and jerk me while you work the head with your mouth. Just think of it as a popsicle, suck me nice and hard until I shoot my load down your throat. I will tell you when I'm going to come."

I pause, taking in all the information. Exhaling a breath, I nod. I can do this. Give him pleasure with my mouth, just like he has given me. Shuffling down, I swallow when I come face to face with his dick. It's bigger up close. I marvel at the size of his veiny, thick, length, briefly wondering how it fit inside me. Pushing that thought aside, I focus on the task at hand.

Parting my lips, my tongue darts out, swiping up the tip. Nico releases a pleasure-filled groan. My gaze shifts to him, finding his hooded eyes already on me. Smiling, I open my mouth wider, taking him inside and wrapping my lips around his hard cock. My hand shifts to the base, and I wrap my fingers around it just like Nico told me to. *It's like sucking a popsicle*, I remind myself of Nico's words. Not that it is a useful comparison. Growing up, I wasn't allowed things like sweets and candy in my diet - but still, how hard can it be?

Taking him down as far as I can go, I pump the rest in my hand. I want to give him the best blow job he has ever had. Better than any woman that came before me. One he will never forget.

Out of my peripheral, I see his hand dart up, landing in my hair. He strokes down the strands before gripping it with force and shoving me down on his length. My eyes widen, turning watery as he hits the back of my throat. I gag, slapping at his thigh for him to release me. Just when I think that I am going to pass out, he pulls me off of him. Jerking up, I cough, splutter and suck in air, as I glare at him.

He smirks. "That's it, *Tesoro*. Just like that. But remember to breathe through your nose. It will stop you from blacking out." He tries to push me back down, but I knock his hand away.

"I couldn't breathe." I seethe.

He chuckles. "Baby, you could breathe, you just panicked. Trust me, this is going easy on you. I can always hold you down and fuck your mouth as I please..." he trails off, the threat hanging in the air between us. I shake my head. "Now, hollow out your cheeks. Lay your tongue flat. And remember to breathe through your nose."

Guiding my head back down to his groin, I suck in a breath before taking him in my mouth. He talks me through it, his voice soothing, gentle and in total contrast to how he is currently using my mouth. Hard. Rough. As if I am his personal fuck toy.

Relinquishing all control, I submit to his dominance and the brutal way he is thrusting into me. If my wet pussy is anything to go by, then some part of me must like it. Tears stream down my face, saliva runs down my chin. I gag and choke, but he doesn't let up. And I don't put a stop to it. No. I let him thrust harder, succumbing to his sexual proclivities.

"Rub your clit," he hisses, dragging me from my thoughts. I bring my free hand between my legs, shocked to find that I'm not only wet, but I'm soaked. Circling my clit, my eyes flutter closed as pleasure shoots through my veins. I rub harder, and I don't think I have ever been so turned on.

"I'm going to cum." Nico groans, thrusting into my mouth so hard, he lodges himself in my throat. My hand falls from my pussy as I try to suck in a much-needed breath but come up empty. I try to inhale through my nose, but it doesn't work. Panic hits me full force and I claw at his thighs so hard that I draw blood. But he doesn't let me go. Holding me in place, I feel it as his cock begins to pulse. Black spots dot my vision and the last thing I feel is warm, salty liquid coating my throat before everything goes black.

Laughing.

Someone is laughing.

A deep, throaty laugh.

My eyes peel open, to find Nico hovering over me. It's him. He sits against the headboard, laughing with not a care in the world as he watches me. Blinking up at him, I cast my mind back for any memory of what just happened, but I come up empty.

Disorientated and confused, I croak out through my sore throat. "What happened?"

Cupping my cheeks, he presses a soft kiss to my lips. "You passed out baby."

I gasp, pushing up off the bed. "Wh-what? Why?"

Reaching for me, he pulls me onto his lap. "Let's just say, I think sucking my dick got to be a little too much," he drawls, amusement lacing his tone.

And then it hits me. He choked me with his cock.

Nico. Choked. Me. With. His. Big. Dick.

I remember smacking and clawing at his legs, trying to get him to stop, but he didn't. My eyes narrow in on him.

"Asshole. You did that on purpose." I accuse.

He laughs harder. "I didn't, *Tesoro*. You ignored my instructions and didn't breathe through your nose like I told you to. So you blacked out. Next time will be better, if you just listen to me."

"Next time?" I shriek. "There won't be a next time. I'm not putting that thing in my mouth ever again."

His face turns serious, arms tensing around me. Leaning in, his hot breath hits my ear. "Oh, trust me, there will be many more times, baby. Don't worry though, you will get used to it *and* you will like it." He pulls back, the look in his eyes daring me to argue.

I shake my head, not wanting to right now. I feel exhausted and need some time away from him so I can think. Wriggling out of his hold, I climb off the bed and head for the shower. "I need to get to work."

Chapter 27
Nico

Pulling up to the warehouse, I push all thoughts of Ocean away. Right now, I need to focus on business. The need to exact revenge slithers through my veins, pumping adrenaline through my body and making me unhinged. I don't know what I am capable of in this moment and for that reason alone, Ocean has no place here. Not in this vehicle or in what is about to happen. I don't want my darkness to taint the perfect piece of innocence and purity that I have found. She is my light in the dark. The angel to my devil. And that is how it will stay.

Christopher hops out of the vehicle, breaking me from my thoughts. Within seconds, my door is pulled open just as Dante slides out the other side. I inhale the cold, frigid air, breathing it in and hoping it will settle some of the frenzied energy coursing through me. It's no use, the need for blood and violence runs through my veins and it will stay that way until I expend some of this pent-up retribution. Tonight, the rats will die in the most brutal way possible. And we will show every soldier in our organization that we are not to be fucked with. Death. Blood.

Revenge. And I will deliver it all like the fucking Grim Reaper himself.

"Fuck, it's a good night for traitors to die," Dante drawls, stepping up beside me. He rubs his hands together, a manic gleam in his eyes. He is a bloodthirsty motherfucker just like me. We are both going to enjoy this. The savages in us, reveling in the kill.

"Come on. Let's get this over with. I have somewhere I need to be." I start towards the building, noting all the vehicles in the lot and the guards situated around the perimeter.

Dante chuckles. "I'm sure you have."

He keeps his response short, not mentioning any names just in case there is anyone around to overhear our conversation. "Yeah," I grunt, pulling open the door and entering. The stench of cologne, along with sweat, assaults my nostrils. A multitude of loud voices hits my ears. "Jesus," I mutter under my breath, my gaze bouncing around at all the men gathered here, waiting for blood to spill.

My papà's deep drawl sounds above everyone else. Obnoxious and arrogant per usual. My eyes shift to where some leather couches have been set up and there he is. Lorenzo Marchetti. Sitting like a king, as Giuseppe and a couple other of his closest men surround him.

Dante whistles under his breath, a curse leaving his mouth and I follow his line of sight to the makeshift ring set up in the middle of the warehouse. There is a table in the center, filled with a selection of tools, and a chair, much like what is used to kill death row inmates, beside it. Instead of straps, this one has barbed wire chains.

"Nico," my father calls, drawing my attention to him. The room falls silent, and I feel the heat of everyone's stares on me. With a blank face, I stride toward him like the royalty I am, with Dante by my side.

"Papà," I greet, stepping up to him.

He grins, pulling a cigar from his suit jacket pocket and jerking his head to the place where men are about to die. "Figlio, I trust you are going to give us all a show tonight?"

I smirk, "Of course. By the time I'm done, no one will dare step out of line."

Satisfaction and, if I'm not mistaken, a hint of pride flashes in his eye before he covers it and his expression turns cold. "Very good. Now can we hurry this along? Your mamma expects me home at a decent hour. Your sister is being handed some award at her school in the morning." His eyes narrow. "You will be there." It's not a question, more of a demand.

"I wouldn't miss it." I drawl, irritated I will have to leave Ocean's bed earlier than expected.

"Good. I have something to discuss with you about…" he trails off. "That thing we talked about." I tense as does Dante. His words are cryptic, but I know exactly what he is talking about. The arrangement with the Romanos.

My jaw clenches as I try to tamp down my anger, and I swallow down a scathing retort. Now is not the time. It will be my death sentence – son or not – if I embarrass him in front of his men. Instead, I nod curtly, confirming my agreement.

Turning, my gaze shifts around the warehouse, finally landing on the guards watching the room where the traitors are being held. Giving them the signal, they nod and begin to drag them out of a side door. Their muffled screams are the only sound to be heard in the large space and as they get closer, I notice the sweat, blood and bruising from the beatings they have already taken. I grin, cracking my neck from side to side. And then stepping inside the ring, I move to the table to do what I came here to do.

I am going to enjoy every second of this.

***

Blood coats my hands, face, hair, and clothes.

My body shakes with the intense adrenaline running through me.

I want to go to Ocean, bury myself in her pussy and forget all about the brutality that just happened. But I can't. Not like this. Not when bloodlust and vengeance still run through my veins.

She is freaked out enough about me fucking her in her sleep. If I show up covered in blood and damn near feral, I get the feeling she will try to run, and I can't allow that. Not that she would get far. I would find her. I just don't really have the time to hunt her down right now, so it's easier to stay away when I am like this. I also just don't want her asking questions. She thinks that I'm just some rich businessman and that is how it will stay.

Though, shockingly, I am surprised no one has said anything to her. I know the rumors that surround me, and it's a miracle she hasn't heard said rumors. I smirk. People know better than that. They know she is mine, which is why they have probably kept their mouths shut.

"Drink?" Dante asks, as he slides into the backseat beside me.

"Yeah," I grunt.

"You heard the man, Christopher. Take us to The Executive Club," my second-in-command barks at my driver, knowing full well that I am about to crash.

My head falls back on the seat, eyes closing. It always happens. The rush. Then the crash. No matter how many men I kill, the reaction is the same. Not because I feel guilty or anything. I don't. My guess is the adrenaline is so extreme that when it leaves my body, the comedown is even more severe.

Hence why my limbs go weak, and I feel like I could sleep for a week.

"Text Leo. Have him set up a private room," I order.

"Done," Dante responds only seconds later, having done exactly what I asked.

Peeling my eyes open, I roll my head to look at him. "And have Hansen get the chopper ready. I want to be in The Hamptons by midnight." I tell him.

He tenses before nodding. "I will come with you."

My eyes narrow. "Why? Is there something you're not telling me?"

"What? No. I just..." he trails off. Blowing out a breath, he shakes his head. "I just care about Allegra. I want to see her get her award."

Searching his face, it only takes seconds before I see the answers to every single question I haven't yet asked. Fuck. I scrub a palm down my face, concern sitting heavy in my gut, for both Dante and my sister. Pinning him with a knowing look, I speak, my voice serious but also holding a little empathy for my best friend. "Man, you aren't hiding shit from me. You know he will never allow it to happen right?"

Straightening in his seat, he meets my stare head-on. "And what about you, Nic? Would you? Allow it to happen, I mean?"

I mull over his words. Truthfully, I don't like the idea of my best friend fucking my little sister, but I know he would at least love and respect her. I'm not stupid. I have seen the way they look at each other. And honestly, it's better than the alternative. At this point, I would do anything to keep her away from Riccardo Romano.

I sigh. "I mean, I don't really want to imagine your fucking dick anywhere near my sister. The thought alone makes me want to gag. But I think you would be good for Allegra. Would be good for each other and *to* each other." And even as I say it, I know it's true. I know I could trust him to look after her. I wouldn't have to worry about him putting his hands on her. This is the case with most mafia men and arranged marriages.

His eyes roam my face, for what I'm not sure. A hint that I might be lying, maybe. With one last look, he slumps back against the seat. Shaking his head, he glances at Christopher, no doubt worried he has said too much. He hasn't. My driver knows how to be discreet, hence why I allow him to drive Ocean around.

"Fuck. What am I going to do, Nic? This is killing me. I want to steal her away, and hide her, so that no one can touch her. I know what her fate is, and what is expected of her, and I can't handle it. I *won't* be able to handle it."

This is the first time I have ever seen Dante so desperate. So frantic. It's unsettling to say the least. And though he doesn't know about the Romano deal, I am not about to tell him right now. Not until I know more. There is no point. If I have my way, it won't get that far anyway.

Reaching out, I clamp a hand down on his shoulder. "I want you to keep quiet about this. Papà will put a bounty on your head if he knows about your feelings. He will also speed up any arrangement he has in the works for Allegra. I can't or won't have you risking that because you caught feelings." My face is passive but my lips twitch with a smile. All this time, he was giving me shit about Ocean and he had his own secret.

"Fuck you man." He grumbles, his eyes dropping to his cell when it beeps. His gaze comes back to me. "Everything is set."

I nod, my head falling back on the headrest once again.

If I can't fuck this feeling of unrest itching under my skin, I will drink it away.

Chapter 28
Ocean

Nico never showed last night. After saying he would, he never turned up or even sent me a quick message to tell me why.

I don't want to be the clingy girl who freaks out or feels insecure. I never want to become one of *those* women, who is fully reliant and dependent on a man, only to break every time he messes up. I watched my mother do it for long enough and promised myself I would be different. But somewhere along the line and in the limited amount of time that I've known Nico, he has me feeling this way. On edge. Anxious. It's frustrating. He came into my life like a whirlwind and has turned me into someone I don't want to be. He has me second guessing everything and screwing up my carefully laid plans.

Ugh. I'm my mom.

I would laugh if it wasn't so pathetic.

Shaking my head, I focus on my dancing, moving into *demi plie* before forming a *Glissade* position. Gliding my working foot from the fifth position and in the required direction, I extend and glide. Extend and glide. When I feel like I have done enough, I move into a *Grand Jete*, working my body harder than I have done in a long time. It's just past six thirty in the morning and I've been in here nearly an hour already.

Thankfully, Elenore, the lady who owns and runs the studio, is an early riser and opens at five thirty every morning. It suits me perfectly and means I can get a workout in before my shift at *Bellissima*. It's much needed today, perfect for me to work out my pent-up frustrations.

"Wow, you're an incredible dancer, Ocean." The soft voice distracts me, making me stumble.

Righting myself, I turn to face Elenore, my chest heaving with exertion. I smile. "Thank you."

She waves me off. "Sorry for distracting you. I just couldn't walk away without telling you. You're captivating. You should be with the New York Ballet, traveling the world, not in my little studio."

My chest tightens. "That's very kind of you, but I don't think that's in the cards for me," I tell her. And maybe in another life, I would be. After years of practice, I know I'm good. I had no choice but to be. My mother enrolled me in ballet school as soon as I could walk. Had things been different and my father not… I shake the thought away before it can form. Anyway, it's not like I don't get to dance. It's just not at the level I wish it could be.

Her eyes light up. "You know, I've danced most my life, too. I didn't quite make it to the level I would have liked, but that's because I wasn't as talented as you are. I have some friends. They know people. Maybe I could have them come and assess you?" I'm shaking my head before she even finishes. She pins me with a glare, not one bit perturbed by me cutting her off. "If it's the money you're worried about, there are scholarships, Ocean. A girl with pure talent like you, well, that shouldn't go to waste. From what I've seen, you are a very gifted and unique dancer. Something most people could only dream of possessing.

Don't let whatever is scaring you, hold you back. You only get one life, Ocean, take what you can before it's too late." She shoots me a contemplative look, before turning on her heels and disappearing back through the door.

Sighing, I grab my bottle of water, mulling over Elenore's words. She is right. I know she is. There just isn't a single thing I can do about it. I can't risk being seen.

My priority is staying hidden and if that means sacrificing my dreams, then so be it.

***

Instead of being even more pitiful than I already am, and spending the day thinking about Nico, I keep myself busy at *Bellissima*. I go out of my way to help anyone who needs it. When Monica, one of the hair stylists, asks me to bring coffee to one of her clients, I do. When Sian asks me to go to the tea shop down the street and purchase the special herbal tea that one of her ladies' drinks, I do it without hesitation. I figured, if I keep busy, then it will stop any and all thoughts about Nico. It does. To an extent.

Though we haven't talked about what we are doing or whether we are even exclusive, I really hope he wasn't with another woman last night. The thought alone has my chest tightening painfully. I pause what I'm doing. Oh my God. Is that why he didn't come to see me? My heart beats erratically in my chest. I clench my jaw. He said I was his. Surely that same notion applies to him. I huff a laugh. You only have to look at him to know that isn't the case. Rich, successful and so handsome it hurts to look at him. He could have anyone he wanted. While I believe I'm just... average at best.

I hate my self-depreciating thoughts, but until recently I lived in a hostel and took off my clothes to make a living. Nico should be with an actress or a model, someone on his level. Not little Ocean Embers, who is not only a nobody but also has a whole closet full of secrets and skeletons. And no matter how much I want to, I could never tell him, for fear of what would happen to both him and me. I groan inwardly, so caught up in my negative thoughts that I don't hear the door open or see the person stepping up to the front desk.

"Ocean?"

I startle at the masculine voice, my gaze snapping up and landing on Leo. He wears a frown on his face as he looks at me, but just seeing him brings a smile to mine. He gave me a chance. Was a friend. And I'm the shitty person who hasn't made time to see him since I left The Executive Club.

"Leo." I beam, stepping around the counter and giving him a hug.

He wraps me up in his arms and I didn't realize until this moment how much I needed a hug. "Whoa, how ya doing girl?" he chuckles, pushing me back some so he can look at me.

I shake my head, stepping out of his hold. "I'm good. I miss seeing you and Selena at the club but I'm doing alright here. Everyone is so nice here, so there's that."

He laughs. "Way to be subtle, Ocean. It was no secret that all the girls hated you apart from Selena."

"Yeah." I sigh my agreement.

"What time do you get off? I thought we could grab a drink before I have to get over to the club. Grant is opening up tonight, so I have a little time before I need to be there."

I check the clock on the wall, smiling when I see it's just before seven. "In five minutes actually. And yeah, a drink would be great."

His brow raises. "Bad day?"

"You could say that," I grumble. I don't know what Leo knows about me and Nico, or if he knows anything at all. But

I'm not about to tell him. Not only is Nico his boss but they are friends. I'm not going to get in between that with my drama.

He searches my face for a long beat before blowing out a breath. "Come on, get finished up and I will get you that drink."

***

"So, how's it going at *Bellissima*?" Leo asks, as he sits across from me at a high-top table.

After saying goodbye to Macy, we came to a bar a couple of doors down from my place of work. Though it would have been nice to go somewhere else in the city. It's perfect, staying in this area, if only for the fact that it's close to my new apartment and I won't need to flag down a taxi or book an Uber to get home.

I shrug, taking a sip of my soda. "It's good. I like it more than I thought I would."

He nods, worry flashing on his kind face. He runs a nervous hand through his hair. I frown and wait for him to speak. Exhaling a harsh breath, he pins me with a pensive look. "I knew Nico was going to stop you from working at the club. I'm sorry I didn't warn you." I see the apology in his eyes, but he doesn't need to give me one.

Reaching across the table, I squeeze his hand. Did Nico go about things in the right way? No. But I am here now, and I don't think I would change it. "It's fine, honestly. It all worked out for the best."

He sips his drink, his gaze on me as if contemplating how to say his next words. "And Nico, is he treating you okay?"

I get the feeling there is more to the question. Does he know about us?

Dropping my eyes to my drink, I twist my straw as I nibble my bottom lip. "Nico... can be intense." I shrug.

Leo chuckles and I raise my gaze in time to see him shaking

his head. "Yes, he is. But I can honestly say, I've never seen him act like this over a woman before." My stomach dips at his words and it's all the confirmation I need. Leo knows about us. "I would know. We basically grew up together."

I sag in my chair, voicing my insecurities. "I don't understand, though. He could have anyone."

He cocks his head, shrugging. "Yeah, he could. But he wants you. You don't even see it, do you?"

"See what? And why are you telling me this? Did he ask you to take me for a drink and talk to me?"

Leo laughs. "Nah. He will probably kill me if he knows that I'm having a drink with you alone." he cocks his head, searching my face with an intensity that makes me squirm under his scrutiny. "And how can you not see how gorgeous you are. Had Nico not made a move on you, I would have made you mine."

The honesty of his words makes my cheeks heat in embarrassment. What the hell? I like Leo but only as a friend. I've never looked at him in any other way. Sure, he is attractive, in that boy next-door kind of way. But I just don't see him as more than he already is. When a long moment of uncomfortable silence passes, I open my mouth to respond, but am cut off by an angry, feral growl.

"No *probably* about it. I will kill you, you motherfucker. Friend or not. Now what the fuck are you doing with *my* girl." My head snaps to a fuming, snarling Nico.

I jerk back, nearly falling off my stool. Nico stands beside me, a cold, calculated look in his eyes as he glowers at Leo. "Nico," I gasp, then frown. How did he know where we were?

My head whips back to face Leo when he chuckles. He holds his hands up in surrender, a big grin on his face. Nonetheless, I don't miss the hint of fear in his eyes. Pushing off his stool, he steps toward him, shoving his hands in his pockets.

"Hey man, I just thought I would take your girl here for a

drink. She had a bad day and I wanted to cheer her up." His gaze shifts to me briefly before moving back to Nico. He jerks his finger to the door. "I better get to the club."

Nico's jaw clenches. I feel the power and darkness radiating from him. A shiver runs up my spine. I have seen him mad, but this seems... more.

"You do that." Nico barks. Leo nods, taking a step toward the door only to freeze when Nico adds. "And Leo? I will be discussing this with you later."

"Noted." He mumbles, defeatedly. And then without another word, he leaves.

My eyes snap back to Nico. I glower.

What the hell just happened?

Chapter 29

Nico

She glares at me. I glare back.

I'm so fucking angry right now.

As soon as Gio texted me to tell me that she had left work, with Leo of all people, and was in a bar, I saw red. Within five minutes, I was in my SUV, making my way here. It was the last thing I needed after the meeting with my papà earlier.

This morning we all – Dante included – attended Allegra's awards ceremony at her private school. After that, we headed back to the house where Papà took me aside and told me that not only do the Romano's want to go ahead with the arranged marriage to my sister, but they want to do it as soon as she finishes school. In just five short months and at only eighteen, my papà wants to marry Allegra off to Riccardo Romano. I had already hit my anger limit with that information, but then I find out that Leo is trying to sneak around with my girl.

I heard exactly what he said to her. How he would have made her his, had I not swooped in. Friend or not. He will be fucking punished. He should know better than to mess with what's mine. I knew the asshole liked her, and for him to go behind my back has me seething with something so much worse than rage. I'm fucking murderous.

"Nico, that was rude." She scolds, but I am so full of fury that even the cute way she says it does nothing to calm me.

Gripping her bicep, I pull her off the stool. "Let's go." I hiss.

She swats at my arm, shooting me daggers with her blue orbs. "Ow. You're hurting me."

"Trust me, *Tesoro*, this is nothing compared to what I'm going to do to you when I get you home." My voice is cold despite the heat running through my veins.

"What? Why? I didn't do anything wrong. I can go for a drink with a friend. You don't own me."

I laugh but it's humorless. Shoving through the door, I pull her to a stop on the sidewalk, bending so that I'm eye level with my little firecracker. "You. Do. Not. Go. On. Dates. With. Other. Men." She opens her mouth to cut me off, but I stop her, not giving a fuck that people are looking. "In fact, you don't so much as look at other men. You are mine. I. Do. Own. You. And if I catch you looking at any other man that is not me, I will keep you chained in that apartment of yours."

Her eyes widen. In shock or fear, I'm not sure, neither do I care. "Jesus, you are crazy. It wasn't a date. Leo is a friend." She argues, but I am done.

"No, he is not. Date or not, you were with a man that wasn't me, in a bar having a drink. I won't tolerate that, so don't test me on this. You're lucky I didn't kill him then and there."

She gasps, a tremor in her voice when she speaks. "But-but he is your friend."

I shrug. "And you are *my* girl. I will kill anyone who tries to tell me otherwise."

Done with the conversation for now, I grab her hand and haul her into my waiting vehicle. Ocean huffs, blowing her long blonde hair out of the way and I bite back a smile at how comical it looks. Now is not the time for humor, though, and I can't have her knowing that she is getting to me.

"Where to sir?" Christopher asks.

"Ocean's apartment," I grunt, my gaze never leaving the infuriating blonde beside me.

"You're not coming in." She crosses her arms defiantly.

I chuckle sardonically. "Oh baby, I most definitely am. I'm coming in and then *coming* inside your cunt, just to remind you who you belong to."

She inhales, her head whipping to my driver and then back to me. "Stop being so vulgar." She whisper-hisses.

Leaning back against the seat, I grin. "You haven't seen anything yet."

***

"Kneel," I bark out as I strip out of my suit pants and white dress shirt.

We are in Ocean's bedroom. At an impasse. But she will submit. I will make sure of it.

She stares at me from across the room, the defiance, laced with a hint of fear, flashing in her eyes has my cock hardening to steel. I should leave her alone when I'm feeling this way, but I am past caring. She has awoken the beast inside of me that won't stop until it shows her exactly who owns her ass.

"No," she snaps, arms crossing over her chest.

I chuckle but it's not a nice sound. "So help me God, *Tesoro*, you will kneel. You will submit. If you don't, I will take you over to The Executive Club right now and make you watch as I kill Leo. And then, I will make you kneel in *his* blood as I fuck your mouth, then your cunt, then finally your ass. Your choice." It's a low blow - and to be honest I still might kill him - but I know it will get her to do as I ask.

Her lips tremble, and tears leak down her face. I want to go to her, and lick them up. But this is a punishment, and she needs to be reminded of just who she belongs to. That she might not know it yet but there are rules in place, and she just broke a cardinal one. I'm going to fuck her throat so hard, that by the time I am done with her, she will feel and taste me every time she swallows. I might even choke her out again, then tie her up and do it all over again.

Hmm. Now there's a thought.

"Why are you doing this?" she whispers, defeat laying heavy on her shoulders as she finally submits and drops to her knees.

Pulling my boxer briefs off, my cock springs free, hitting me in my abs. Her eyes shift to my length, and she licks those pouty lips. She may hate me right now, but the look of hunger on her face tells me she wants this as much as I do.

"You know why. Because you're mine and I don't share what's mine." I growl, closing the distance between us. "Shove your hand inside your panties. I want you to touch *my* little cunt while I fuck your mouth." She pauses for a second, indecision on her beautiful face. She swallows harshly, her throat bobbing with the movement as she comes to terms with her fate. Reaching down, she pushes a hand under the waistband of her yoga pants. My mouth waters. Fuck, I want to eat her pussy. I want to saturate myself in her juices while I make her come repeatedly. But we are not here for that. Had she not gone on a fucking *date* with Leo, then I would be doing just that, but she did, so now here we are.

"Open your mouth. Wide. Stick your tongue out and flatten it. You will take all of me."

She shifts nervously, her lips parting when she whispers. "I don't want to black out again."

I chuckle. "Baby, right now you don't have a choice in what

happens. If you do as I say, I might go a little easier on you." I pause, pinning her with a smirk. "Then again, I might not. You fucked up. You will pay the price."

Fire flashes in her eyes and I know she is about to argue. I shoot her a look, daring her to challenge me. She pales, obviously thinking better of whatever retort she was going to throw at me and keeps her smart words to herself. Blowing out a breath, her tongue pokes out coming to rest on her bottom lip. Satisfaction courses through me at her submission.

Cupping her cheek with one hand, I stroke my length with the other. "Such a good little girl. So fucking perfect. So *mine*. You've never looked more beautiful than you do at this moment, waiting to take my cock. You are going to swallow every drop of me and then thank me for it. Okay baby?" My voice is soft despite my words. She blinks, then nods. "Good girl." I praise, smirking when I see the desire flicking in her eyes. My girl has a praise kink, and she doesn't even know it.

Straightening, I bring my dick to her lips. Pushing inside, I groan at the feel of her hot, wet, mouth. "Fuck," I curse when I hit the back of her throat, and she gags. "That's it, breathe through your nose and rub your clit. This is going to be hard and quick." I rasp, sliding inside until I am down her throat. She heaves, hollowing out her cheeks. Tears stream down her face and saliva pools down her chin. The sight alone nearly has me exploding.

Smirking, I fist her hair in my hands, holding her exactly where I want her as I fuck into her mouth, faster, harder. Shoving my cock so far down, you can see me in her throat. Her free hand slams onto my thighs, silently asking me to ease up but I don't. "Use that hand on my balls and keep rubbing your juicy clit. Don't stop until I say. I want you to make yourself come with your fingers while you make me come with your mouth." I bark, gripping her head tighter and using her as my own personal fuck toy.

Pleasure sparks inside me, igniting my veins as I punish her. And despite her messy state and the way she glares at me, I know she is enjoying the roughness of this moment as much as I am. I'm proved right when in the next second, Ocean cries out around my dick when her climax hits. Her moan is so loud, the sound vibrates on my cock, setting off my own release. My balls tighten, a feral snarl on my lips when I shoot my seed down her throat.

"Christ," I growl, pulling out of her and running a finger up her soft cheek.

Coughing and sputtering, she knocks my hand away, looking up at me with tear filled eyes. "You, asshole." She spits, her voice raspy out of her abused mouth.

I grin, grabbing her under the arms and pulling her up against my body. "I may be an asshole, but you liked it. You came so hard your whole body shook and your fucking mouth vibrated around my cock. Seeing you at my mercy, taking me how I wanted you to? It was a sight that will stay with me until the day I die." I press a soft kiss to her lips, because I'm not a complete asshole and want her to feel a little comfort after the brutal way I just fucked her throat. "Now, why don't you take a nice bath." It's not a question, but an expectation. "I have some business to attend to. I will be back later to take care of *my* pussy."

Her eyes widen, fear clear on her face. "Where are you going?"

I kiss her nose. "Nowhere that concerns you, *Tesoro*. Get yourself cleaned up and I will see you in a couple of hours."

Dropping her to the bed, I quickly redress, and then head out of the room without another word. My girl has been dealt with.

Now it's time to deal with Leo.

***

"Nico, I swear I wasn't trying anything. I just..." he trails off, blood dripping down his nose. "She looked sad, I wanted to do something nice for her."

"She isn't yours to do something *nice* for." I seethe, my voice low, deadly. I've used his pretty face as my punching bag for the last five minutes. Yes, Leo is my friend. But that doesn't mean shit. He crossed a fucking line and messed with what's mine. I can't or won't tolerate that. No matter how long I've known him.

He shakes his head, defeat in his eyes. "I know. I know. I meant no harm."

Eying him, I say. "I cut a man's fingers off for touching her, Leo. Give me one good reason why I shouldn't do worse to you. Hmm?" The feral way I'm feeling right now and just the memory of how I found them, of what he said to her, makes me want to slit his fucking throat.

"We go back a long way Nico. I fucked up. It shouldn't have happened. It *won't* happen again. Ocean is yours. I know that now." The asshole is slumped on the floor, but I see it in his eyes. The honesty. He means every word of what he just said.

Sighing, I reach down, taking his hand and enjoying it when he flinches away. He's scared. He knows he fucked up. "Go and get yourself cleaned up." Déjà vu hits me at saying that for the second time tonight. He nods, before slowly staggering to his feet. With a solemn, apologetic look on his face he turns to leave but not before I deliver my last threat. "I don't give second chances, Leo. I don't give a fuck how long I have known you. Go near Ocean again and I will fucking kill you. That's a promise."

Chapter 30
Ocean

My throat is sore.

Nearly a week later, it still throbs after the brutal way Nico took my mouth. I should be horrified, repulsed at what he did to me, but some part of me, some sick and twisted part...liked it. The way he dominated me, fucked my mouth with abandon – like he hated me. It turned me on, even though logically, I know it was wrong.

Scrubbing a palm down my face, I shake my head. "Jesus, what is wrong with me and who have I become?" I whisper to myself, my gaze shifting to the mirror above the sink in the *Bellissima's* staff bathroom. I'm hiding out in here. Macy hasn't left me alone all morning, her inquisitive stare and her questions putting me on edge.

Can she hear the thoughts in my head?

Does she know the sick, depraved, things I want Nico to do to me?

How did I get here?

I ran away from my old life so that I could be free. I wanted to live a simple life, hidden in the shadows. Maybe marry a blue-collared man, have a couple of kids, and live in a little house with a white picket fence in a small town. But all I have managed to do is run from my father, a monster, and into the arms of a devil in a designer suit. And Nico is the devil himself. I saw exactly what he was capable of the other night. It was written all over his face, flashing like a warning beacon in his cold blue eyes. Yet, for some reason, it draws me in more. I want him. There is no debating that. I must be crazy, wanting to stick around, especially after his threats to kill Leo. Yet the thought of leaving this city, leaving Nico... it makes me feel physically sick. What is it about him and his darkness that draws me in? And why can't I quit him?

"Ugh," I groan, turning on the faucet and splashing my clammy face with cold water.

"Ocean, honey, are you okay?" Macy's voice startles me out of my thoughts.

Straightening, I clear my throat. "Yes. Fine, thank you. I'll be right out."

Grabbing some paper towels, I pat my face dry before taking a deep breath and stepping outside. Macy stands in the hallway, concern marring her features. "You okay honey? You look a bit pale."

I smile. "I'm fine. I just needed a five-minute breather."

She nods. "Well, if you ever want to talk about it, I've been told that I'm a very good listener."

Laughing, I wave her off. "Noted. But honestly, I'm okay. I'm a little overwhelmed with things..." I trail off, as I think of how to phrase my next words. Something tells me not to discuss Nico with his employees. "All I mean is, I have some things going on, and it's making me feel a little exhausted trying to keep up with it all. But I will be okay. Promise." I smile, hoping my words sound genuine.

A worried expression appears on her face. She searches mine. "I know it's none of my business, and I would never overstep, but just be careful with Nico. He's..." she trails off. "Well, let's just say, that he is a very powerful man. I don't want to see you get hurt."

I nod, though her words spike a little fear inside me. "Thank you for looking out for me Macy," I say honestly, not wanting to delve into any more conversation with her.

Shooting me a sincere smile, she turns on her heels and sashays back down the hallway to the reception area.

I watch as she disappears, and then, sagging against the wall, I blow out a breath. If I were a smarter girl, I would take note of Macy's warning, but something tells me it's already too late.

I'm in too deep and at this point, I don't think there is any way out.

***

My body spins as I move into a pirouette. I turn, moving to the music before slowing down to my ending position. My eyes are closed, a smile gracing my lips when I come to a complete stop. This. This is what I needed to clear out the chaos in my head.

Slow clapping sounds make me startle. My eyes snap open to find Nico leaning against the wall, so big and powerful as he watches me, like a predator about to devour his prey. Chest heaving, I stare at him. "What are you doing here?" I frown when something else hits me. "And how the hell did you know where I was?" Just like how he found me at that bar with Leo. My eyes widen. "Do you have someone following me?" Nico can't be doing it himself. He is much too busy for that.

Pushing off the wall, he stalks toward me. My breaths come

in thick and fast, waiting for his answer and wanting to know what he is going to do next. He comes to a stop in front of me. My gaze meets his chest, taking in the way the white dress shirt stretches across his pecs, molding to him perfectly. I lick my lips. Why does he have to be so hot? Raising my chin, my eyes clash with his. Blue on blue.

"Yes." He admits without shame.

"What? Why?" I snap, shooting him a glower.

Gripping my chin, he lowers his head until it's level with mine. "To keep you safe. To keep *my* sanity. I need to know where you are at all times."

I gasp at his honesty, trying to take a step back from him but he doesn't allow it. Of course, he doesn't. If there's one thing Nico Marchetti does with confidence most can only dream of, it is step over every boundary in his way as if it never existed. Nothing will stand in the way of him getting what he wants and right now that's me.

"Nico," I shake my head, stunned by his frankness. "Why me?" I blurt, unable to hold back the question that's been driving my insecurity.

Cocking his head, he stares at me intently for a long beat. His gaze rakes over my face, taking me all in and making me feel exposed. And then he speaks, stealing all the air from my lungs. "From the moment I saw you, I knew you were mine. You don't even realize the effect you have on men, do you? You are innocence and sex all rolled into one. And you are so exquisite it fucking hurts to look at you. Your beauty alone makes me lose my goddamn mind. You're the most breathtaking woman I have ever laid eyes on, and you are *mine*. I was the first man to be inside *my* pussy," he cups my sex as if to prove his point. "And I will be the last. The only." He finishes, his lips brushing mine.

My heart pounds at his words. That something so honest,

raw and vulnerable could come from a man like Nico. And what's even more shocking is that it's all aimed at me.

"You could have anyone," I say weakly.

His lips tip up in a smirk and he leans in. "But I want you." His hot breath hits my ear, making me shiver. Pulling back, he lifts me into his arms. My breath hitches, my legs circling his trim waist on their own volition. He smirks, turning and striding toward the bar that sits against the far side of the studio. "I've had enough of your insecurities, Ocean. I won't discuss this again. All you need to know is that you are mine and I will never let you go. Not ever."

Dropping me onto the bar, he reaches down, pulling my leotard to the side. I gasp when he grips my tights, tearing a hole in them. Panic slithers through my veins when I realize his intentions and I slam my palms on his chest, trying to shove him away. "No Nico. Elenore is still here." I hiss.

Gripping my hands in one of his, with his free hand, he releases his cock before pulling my panties to the side. "Don't care. Now be a good girl and watch as I own your perfect cunt." With that he slams into me. I cry out, my back arching at the intrusion. Though looking at Nico alone arouses me, I need to be prepped properly to take him with ease.

"Fuck," he grits out through clenched teeth. "So fucking tight."

"Oh my God." I whimper, nails clawing at his back.

His expression darkens. Leaning in, his lips brush my ear. "No, baby. *Oh, my Nico.* I am your god. Your *fucking* religion. Your everything. And the only man you will ever worship, pray to, or get on your knees for. I own you, *Tesoro.* Every inch of you." He growls out, his thrusts picking up speed. I swallow, holding on for dear life as his words sink in. His gaze drops to where we are joined. I follow his line of sight, staring in awe as he thrusts in and out of my body, stretching me, *owning me.*

"Look at your tight little cunt taking my cock so good. You and this pussy were made for me, *Tesoro,* and only me."

Succumbing to the desire that courses through me, my legs wrap tighter around his lean torso, while my arms snake around his neck. A satisfied gleam enters his eyes, no doubt at my easy submission. He fucks me harder, thrusting in and out of me so brutally my back hits the mirror and I hear a cracking sound.

Just as I am about to check the damage, a loud gasp echoes around the room. For a second, I think it's come from me but when I look up and my gaze clashes with a horrified-looking Elenore, I know I'm wrong. Oh God. No. No way. Embarrassment and absolute humiliation flood my body at the way Elenore is staring at me in complete horror. I try to push Nico away, but he doesn't stop. Grabbing my hands in one of his, he holds them tight, restraining me.

His eyes connect with Elenore in the mirror, his lips turning up in a snarl. "Get the fuck out of here." He roars making her jump out of her shock and scurry away.

"Nico," I plead, but he cuts me off by slamming his lips to mine and rubbing circles on my clit. My eyes squeeze shut, intense pleasure consuming me. Within seconds my pussy spasms around his length, my orgasm hitting with an intensity so strong, I nearly black out. A loud moan bursts from me and I can only be thankful that Nico swallows it down.

Tearing his lips from mine, he smirks. "That's my girl, soak my fucking cock." He pumps faster, harder, his gaze never leaving mine. Satisfaction sparks in his and with one last pump of his hips, he stills, his cock pulsing when he releases inside me.

"Christ," he rumbles, his forehead dropping to mine. His chest heaves, the material of his shirt rubbing my breasts with every breath he takes. Slowly, he pulls out of me. My gaze drops to the space between my legs, and I watch as a thick cloudy white fluid drips down my thighs. Nico frowns, dropping to his knees and moving his head between my legs. I try to close then but he slaps them apart. "Open," he growls, and I do. Of course, I do, because there is no doubt in my mind that I am completely gone for this man.

His tongue licks a trail up my pussy, collecting all his seed leaking from me. I squirm. "Wh-What are you doing." I stutter as he pushes his tongue, now covered in his come, inside me and thrusts his release back into me slowly.

His gaze comes to mine, satisfaction shining in his blue eyes when he pulls away. "Baby, what have I told you about letting my come leave your pussy? Don't make me plug you." he warns, pushing to a stand and pinning me with a look.

I open my mouth to tell him that he is crazy, but I have bigger things to deal with. Like the nice lady who owns this studio. Pushing him away, my feet fall to the floor. "Oh my God. Elenore." I whisper, my heart rate spiking rapidly as blood rushes to my ears.

Nico looks at me, tucking himself back into his pants. "Is nothing for you to worry about. I will take care of it. Now go and get yourself cleaned up." He orders.

I glare at him. "You are not God, Nico, no matter how much you believe that you are. She…" I trail off, my cheeks heating in embarrassment. "She caught us. Having sex in her studio. She teaches children in here." I whisper, horrified at what just transpired now that the ecstasy of my orgasm has passed.

Nico glowers at me. "I'm Nico fucking Marchetti, I can do whatever the fuck I like. Now, I told you I would take care of it. And I will. Go clean up and get dressed. We're leaving." Shooting me a *don't fight with me right now and just do as you're fucking told look*, he turns and walks out of the studio, no doubt to talk with Elenore.

I sigh, scrubbing a hand down my face and debating whether to follow his orders. I almost snort that I am even questioning myself. Of course, I will do as he asked like the good girl he tells me I am.

Huffing under my breath and hating the fact that I am so easily letting another man control me, I rearrange my underwear as best I can and make my way to the changing area.

Chapter 31
Nico

Sitting at the dining room table of my childhood home, I ignore the conversation going on around me, my mind going back to two weeks ago and the moment I fucked Ocean in her ballet studio. Hands down, it was the best sex of my life. Fucking her in front of that mirror, watching as she took everything I gave... Christ. It was the hottest thing I've ever seen.

After paying Elenore a hefty amount of money, I threatened her to keep her mouth shut and never mention what she saw if Ocean visited the studio again. My girl has no reason to feel embarrassed about what we did, and no way would I let anyone make her feel uncomfortable about it. Least of all some prissy, prudish, dance studio owner. By the terrified look on her face and the fear in her eyes, I know I got my point across. Not wasting any more time, I grabbed Ocean and took her out for dinner. She argued that she needed to go home, shower, and change but I didn't allow it. There is something to be said about her smelling like me, full of me... It brings out the most primal side of me, makes me crazy and threatens my control. I both hate and love it.

I shouldn't feel this way over a woman. My whole life has been dedicated to the *famiglia*. To learning everything there is to know about the business for when I eventually take over as *Don*. But right now, all I can seem to focus on is Ocean. She has filled my mind, leaving no space for anything else–which is unacceptable. I don't know how she has managed to do the unthinkable, something no other woman has before. But she did and now she is under my skin, so deep I will never get her out.

Hmm, running my finger across my lip, I make a mental note to punish her for making me feel this way.

"Nico?" My papà snaps, dragging me from my thoughts. Case in point. I should be in the moment. Not letting *her* occupy my mind so much that it distracts me from being present.

My gaze shifts to him. His face is angry. Red. He is about to completely lose his shit if I don't get my act together. I clear my throat. "Sorry. I missed what you said Papà." I'm not sorry, not one bit. But not only is he my father but my *Don,* too, and I need to show him respect.

His eyes narrow into slits, his jaw clenching. He wants to say more, but he won't, not at the dinner table. "I said, was everything okay with the latest shipment? Everything accounted for?"

I nod, my mouth watering when I smell garlic, basil, and oregano. "Yes. It was fine. I think after our...show, the soldiers are taking us more seriously. As of now, reports from our Capo's tell me everything is in order. I intend for it to stay that way. People know not to fuck with us."

"Good." He murmurs, taking a sip of his amber liquid just as Mamma places her homemade lasagna on the table. My sister follows with a basket of fresh garlic bread and a bowl of mixed salad. I don't miss the way her eyes dart to Dante. Or how my best friend's whole body relaxes when Allegra enters the room.

"It smells delicious, darling," Papà praises, with a genuine smile which Mamma returns. She smiles at the bastard like he hung the damn moon. My chest tightens. If only she knew. Mamma takes her seat beside Papà, and he takes her hand, kissing it. My jaw clenches. Even though he fucks a different whore most nights, I know he loves her in his own way. It's not good enough, not by a long shot, but there is nothing I can do to change it. No man in the *famiglia* can interfere in another man's marriage – son or not.

"It really does, Mrs. Marchetti." Dante pipes up, his eyes darting to me. He no doubt sees the anger roiling through me and is trying to get dinner back on track.

Mamma rolls her eyes. "I'm not going to tell you again, Dante. Please call me Valentina." She looks at my father. "And your daughter helped some."

His eyes gleam when he looks to my sister, and I know what's coming before he even says it. "You will make someone a perfect wife one day, Allegra."

I tense. As do Dante and my sister. The atmosphere in the room turns thick and wanting to change the subject, to ease the tension so as not to ruin the meal Mamma has made, I speak. "You made the lasagna yourself, right?" I'm teasing her, trying to lighten the mood. I know without a doubt she made it.

She shakes her head, a small smile on her lips. "Don't insult me, *mio figlio*. Of course, I did."

"You should know by now; your mamma is the perfect example of a good Italian woman and only prepares meals from scratch." Papà drawls, transferring some of the meat, cheese, and pasta combination from the dish to his plate.

Glancing at my sister, I relax when I see Allegra looking slightly less tense. She shoots me a grateful smile. I return it, knowing that I achieved what I set out to do. The conversation successfully changes and with everyone more relaxed, we fall into light conversation and eat the delicious food Mamma made.

**

"Are we heading back into the city tonight?" Dante asks from his seat in what my papà calls the 'gentleman's lounge'. It's a room a couple of doors down from his home office. With plush leather Chesterfield chairs, a bar cart, and a poker table, it's everything you expect for a *Don's* entertainment room. The only time the space is really used is when I'm home or when Papà wants to have a guy's night with Giuseppe and some of his other higher-ups. It's a shame, really. I glance around, imagining it through Ocean's eyes. Would she like this space? Would she like this house?

I shake the thoughts away, knowing that it's stupid to even imagine because Ocean will never be allowed on this estate, let alone in this room. And for more reasons than one. Anger slithers across my skin and I inhale the thick smoke into my lungs, releasing it before answering. "Nah. Its late."

He waggles his brows. "You don't fancy seeing your woman tonight?"

My eyes narrow in on him. He knew I was lying with my reply. Truth is, I want to exert some control around Ocean before it gets out of hand. I need to prove to myself that I can spend a night without being buried in the tightest, wettest, most perfect pussy I have ever had. Plus, I have Gio following her every move and giving me updates. There is also the small matter of the cameras I have set up in her apartment, that make me feel more comfortable about staying away tonight. With one click of the app on my cell, I can have my eyes on her. I know she is there – Gio told me – so I have stopped myself from looking, just to prove that I can have some control where she is concerned. Only just though. The need to see her with my own eyes itches beneath my skin, begging me to open up my cell and take a peek. I won't though. I've always practiced constraint and I am not about to completely lose it over Ocean.

"I think you have your own shit to worry about, Dante." My voice is cool as I shoot him a smirk.

He glowers, pointing his glass of whiskey at me. "Fuck you, man."

I snort. "If you don't want me to come at you, stop trying to start shit with me."

He eyes me with a smirk before shaking his head. "God, we're both so screwed."

"Speak for yourself," I grunt.

"You forget who you're talking to, Nic. I know you. I see–" he is cut off by the door being shoved open and my papà entering the room.

"Ahh, I thought I would find you both in here." He moves to the bar cart, where he pours his own glass of thirty-year-old Macallan. Spinning to face us, he takes a sip, before moving to his leather chair. The one no one else would dare to sit in. His gaze bounces from me to Dante then back to me, a contemplative look on his face. I know he is preparing to speak so I wait him out. It doesn't take long.

"I've been talking with Giuseppe." He starts and all the hairs on the back of my neck stand to attention. Whatever he is going to say won't be good. I am proved right by his next words. "What are your thoughts on selling women?"

I nearly spit my drink out, my whole body stiffening at his words. My lips curl in disgust. "Human trafficking? No. The *famiglia* has never dealt in trafficking humans. So why now? It's a bad move, Papà." I'm shaking my head, unable to hide the revulsion on my face. "No," I repeat.

He chuckles, the sound making my skin crawl. "I thought

that would be your answer figlio. It was just a thought. You know, to branch into other avenues of income."

My jaw clenched, I say, "We have enough *avenues*. Enough money to last ten lifetimes. We don't need to *branch* into that sick shit. We despise the organizations that do it, and that's one of our issues with the Bratva, so why would you even think about doing something like that?"

He waves me off, a devilish look on his face. "Alright. Alright. No humans."

"No humans." I reiterate through gritted teeth, my gaze shifting to a silent Dante. He knows better than to speak up to my papà. It won't do him any favors to do so.

"I need to come to your club again. Jesus, your dancers are something else." he hums his approval, the quick change of subject giving me whiplash. "Give them enough money and they let me fuck them in any way I wanted." He smirks lasciviously, his tongue coming out and running against his bottom lip.

Disdain washes over me. Christ. When did Papà get so... gross? I run a hand over my mouth, to hide my aversion toward him. "Yeah. I heard you had fun." I deadpan.

He chuckles heartily. "That I did son. That I did." His face sobers and he pins me with a look I can't decipher but I definitely don't like it. "What about you? Any... girls taken your fancy?"

I stiffen at his question. It has never come up before because I knew any woman would be decided for me. So why is he asking this now? I search his face, keeping my own blank mask in place. Does he know about Ocean? I inwardly shake my head. No. There is no way. I have been careful and he would have dealt with the situation already. I take a sip of my own drink, trying to calm my racing heart and avoiding Dante's gaze, which I can feel burning into the side of my head. Clearing my throat, I plaster on a fake smile. "Nah. Still the same Nico. Fuck women and discard them. I don't do feelings. I fuck. You know that, Papà."

He grins, happy with my response. "It's the best way, son. You will be tied down soon enough. Not that a wife will stop you. You are a fucking Marchetti, you can do what the hell you please. You can have a wife and a hundred *puttana's* if that is what you wish." He chuckles and I force myself to laugh along with him.

His cell rings, drawing his attention away from me. I glance at Dante to find a look of concern on his face that I'm sure matches my own. After the conversation about selling women, and that question, I fear Papà is losing his damn mind. It's making him dangerous. Unpredictable.

It's in this moment, I know one thing for certain.

Lorenzo Marchetti must go before he ruins us all.

Chapter 32
Ocean

The weeks pass in a blur of working at *Bellissima*, dance, and Nico... so much Nico.

It took two weeks before I went back to Elenore's studio, too embarrassed to face her. When I finally did, I tried to apologize but she waved me off and told me that she didn't know what I was talking about. I know it had nothing to do with sudden memory loss and everything to do with the overbearing, possessive man who has turned my life upside down. Nico said something to her. I know he did. Instead of pushing the subject, I let it be. It saved any further embarrassment for me, and bonus, I wasn't banned from the studio, so I couldn't be too mad at Nico for whatever he said to Elenore.

Strolling into the lobby of my apartment building, I move toward the elevator, flashing a smile at the security guards and concierge as I pass. Hitting the button, the doors open almost instantly. Stepping inside, I exhale a weary breath. It's been a long day of back-to-back clients, and I barely had the chance to have a lunch break. I didn't realize how exhausting it is to wear a smile and be polite for ten hours a day. I can't wait to get inside the comfort of my apartment and relax. I am going to draw a nice hot bath to soak in and then set up the gift Nico brought me. A Kindle. I always loved reading and it's something I haven't done in a long time. I mentioned it to Nico the other night after he made love to me. and the next day I found a Kindle waiting for me when I returned home from work. After my bath, I am going to snuggle up in bed and download a good book.

It's the perfect evening to distract myself from not seeing Nico tonight. He told me he has business to take care of at the club and honestly, I'm grateful for the reprieve. The man has an insatiable appetite when it comes to sex, and my vagina could do with a break after the savage way he took me repeatedly last night, not letting up even for a moment. A shudder wracks through my body just thinking about how he sat me in front of the long mirror, legs spread, Nico forcing me to watch as he played with me. Then what came after...

"*Watch, Tesoro. Watch how your pussy grips my fingers like it never wants me to leave.*"

My gaze never leaves the mirror as he thrusts his fingers into my saturated pussy. He plays with me, toys with me, his thumb coming up to circle my clit. My eyes threaten to close and seeing this, his free hand comes up to wrap around my throat. It's a silent warning. I swallow, forcing my eyes to stay locked on the spot in the mirror where Nico is playing with me.

"*Good girl.*" *He praises, his hot breath hitting my ear. I shiver, my stomach tightening, pussy contracting with the praise. I love being his good girl. Love how he plays my body, makes it sing like he is the conductor, and I am his own personal choir. How my whole body comes alive under his skilful ministrations. He has trained me to respond to his every little touch, just like he said he would.*

"*Nico,*" *I whimper when he hits that spot that has me seeing stars.*

"*Come on, baby. Come for me. Watch yourself as your pussy contracts and you soak my fingers.*" He growls, thrusting into me harder. My back arches, an intense orgasm taking hold of me. My gaze shifts to Nico's face. He smirks. "*Eyes on your pussy, Tesoro, and keep them there. Look at your pulsing cunt. It's an exquisite sight.*"

I moan, riding his fingers harder until my climax wracks through my body. I cry out his name, my gaze never leaving the mirror as I watch Nico take me over the edge. Watch my pussy throb. Pure ecstasy, thrums in my veins and from the mixture of satisfaction, awe and lust on Nico's face. I have never felt so desired. So sexy.

The elevator stops with a ding, snapping me from my sensual thoughts and my body heats just remembering it. I'm aroused. Horny. And I really wish Nico didn't have to work tonight. Shaking my head, I sigh, moving into the hallway. My cell chimes in my purse and I reach to grab it. Making my way to the door, I fish it out, grinning when I see the name on the screen. Flashing the fob at the screen beside the door, that grants me access to my apartment, I wait for the lock to click, pushing it open and stepping inside.

Swiping the screen to answer, I bring the phone to my ear. "Hey," I greet.

"Don't hey me girl, I haven't heard from you since you moved out of the hostel." Selena scolds.

I chuckle, dropping my bag to the counter and making my way to my bedroom. "I know. I'm sorry, I've been busy. What's up? How have you been?" I ask, padding into the attached bathroom. Holding my cell between my shoulder and ear, I plug the tub, turn on the faucet and pour in a healthy amount of bubbles and bath salts.

"Yeah. Yeah. I will forgive you. This time," she adds with a dramatic sigh. I chuckle, reaching up and pulling the cell from my ear when she squeals down the line. "I moved in with Eric."

"That's no surprise. I knew it would happen." I state.

The line goes silent, and I almost think the call has disconnected but then her unsure whisper hits me. "He wants me to quit dancing at The Executive Club."

I pause, straightening. I hear the uncertainty in her voice, and without thinking about it, I blurt. "And is that what you want?" I could tell her not to, that it's controlling behavior and a red flag, but then that would make me a hypocrite. After all, Nico demanded I stop dancing at the club, and I didn't put up much of a fight about it. Honestly, I'm the last person qualified to give Selena any advice.

Without even seeing her, I know she is chewing her lip, contemplating my question. "I mean, I want to be with Eric, and I love dancing. But is it where I see myself in another year? No. The money is good, but I don't want to take my clothes off forever." She laughs but I hear the honesty in her voice.

"You have your answer then", I say with a nod of my head, even though she can't see me.

She sighs wearily. "Not really. I don't have anything else lined up and I don't want to rely on Eric for money. I'm not that girl. I want to make my own way, you know."

My chest tightens. This is why Selena, and I are friends. We are similar in that way. "Only you can make the decision, Selena. I'm sure you already have a nice stack of cash adding up. Even if you only stay there for another couple of months, you can make enough to give you some breathing room to find something else. Enough so that you don't have to rely on Eric."

She is silent for a long beat, no doubt mulling over my advice. "I guess. How did you feel? When you left The Executive Club, I mean?" she clarifies.

I consider her words, but it doesn't take long before I give her an honest answer. "I didn't strip because I wanted to, Selena. It was a means to an end. I made more money doing that than I would working in a diner. Yes, I love to dance. I've been doing ballet even before I could walk. But even though it was a high-end club, and yes, sometimes it made me feel powerful, there was a tiny part of me that felt dirty. Taking my clothes off. Exposing my body to men. Men who had more money than they knew what to do with, thinking they could treat you however they wanted. You saw how that guy man-handled me on my last night there. It scared me, Selena. His hands on me, touching me like he had a right to."

My brows furrow. Until I just said those words, I didn't realize it was how I really felt about working at The Executive Club. Maybe I suppressed my real feelings because it was my only way of survival. Though at the time, I hated Nico for making me quit. I can admit now, I'm grateful he did.

Glancing down, I notice the tub already halfway full and the bathroom filling with steam. Reaching over, I turn off the faucet and move back to my bedroom.

"I guess I have a lot to think about then." She blows out a breath. "Anyway, changing the subject. When can I come over for girls' night and to see your new place?"

"Whenever you want." I laugh, though I doubt Nico will be pleased with my offer. I know he likes me all to himself. As much as I like him all to myself.

Selena shrieks. "I have some time off next week. Let's do something then."

"Okay," I agree, climbing on my bed and lying back. We talk for around another five minutes before promising to catch up soon and saying our goodbyes.

Dropping my cell beside me, I throw my legs over the side of the bed, strip out of my clothes, grab my Kindle from the nightstand and hop in the bath.

Dancing In Sin

***

I'm startled awake by something.

Glancing at the clock, I see it's just past four a.m. My body tenses, the hairs on my body standing on end, and my heart races at the feeling of being watched. Pushing up to a sitting position, I pull the sheet up over my body, my gaze darting around the room, looking for something, though what that something is, I'm not sure.

Finding the room empty, I relax back into my pillows only to jackknife up at the sound of footsteps on the marble tiles in the living area. My heart rate picks up to an unnatural speed, and I feel like I'm going to pass out.

Who is out there?

It can't be Nico, he said he wasn't seeing me tonight.

Did *he* find me?

My whole body shudders at the thought and the steps grow closer. Sucking in a breath, I stare at the door in anticipation only for all the air to leave my lungs when Nico appears, like the devil himself. He pauses when he sees me awake, his blue eyes intense as they roam over me.

"Jesus, Nico. I thought you were an intruder." I wheeze, trying to suck air back into my lungs.

His brow cocks, a sardonic smirk curving his lips. "*Tesoro*, no one would get past the front desk alive, let alone up to this apartment."

I shake my head at his nonchalance, though I feel like my heart is going to beat out of my chest. "I thought you weren't coming tonight. You can't just show up when you want. You scared me."

Closing the distance between us in just a couple of strides, he takes my chin between his fingers. Leaning down, his hot breath fans over my face, the smell the whiskey making my nostrils scrunch up. Pressing a kiss to my lips, a groan rumbles in his chest before he pulls back. "I can show up when I want baby. I don't need yours or anybody's permission to be here."

Tearing myself out of his grip, I stare at him and repeat. "You scared me."

He shoots me a droll stare as he starts to undress. "Nothing to be scared of. I told you. No one can get up here but me. And I will come and go as I please."

I glower at his arrogance, but instead of arguing my case, I lay down. "You aren't touching me tonight."

He laughs, sliding into the bed beside me. Throwing an arm around my waist he pulls me against his hard body and whispers. "Oh, baby. You really don't have a choice whether I touch you or not. Fortunately for you though, I'm tired, so I won't. But come daylight, my cock will be buried so deep in your pussy you will feel me in your throat."

My breath hitches at his dirty promise and wetness seeps into my panties. I might be sore, but I can't deny the effect this man has on me.

"Where were you tonight?" I know he was at The Executive Club, but something seems off with him. He seems distant, even colder than usual. The darkness, that I know he tries to keep at bay around me, shines through clearly.

His body stills. If I wasn't so close to him, I would have missed it. Dropping his mouth to my ear, his voice turns low. "Working." He says cryptically, his tone suggesting I ask no more questions. His eyes close and I stare at him, wondering what thoughts are in his head. Does he think of me? Is it other women? Business? I know he won't tell me even if I ask but, whatever it is, it's obviously exhausted him. It's not even minutes later that his breathing evens out and he falls asleep.

Sighing, and suddenly feeling very tired, I cuddle into him and eventually sleep pulls me under.

Chapter 33

Nico

I wake to the sunrise shining in through the open drapes and Ocean wrapped around my body like a spider monkey. I could get used to this. But after last night and the events that transpired, I know that I'm going to have to fight like hell to keep her by my side.

I scrub a palm down my face, staring at her. The girl who somehow weaved her way into my whole being and made herself a home. Long lashes fan high cheekbones. Her pouty lips are slightly parted. She is magnificent. Stunning. *Mine*. And I need to be inside her tight cunt, right now.

Slipping the sheet off her body, I slowly shift her onto her back, my lips curving into a smirk. Perfect. Moving down the bed, I grip the waistband of her sleep shorts, pulling them down. My mouth salivates when I find her pussy already soaked, just begging for me to touch, eat, fill it. Groaning, my tongue darts out, running up the length of her slit. She moans, her body jerking. My eyes snap up, landing on her now open ones. I grin.

"Morning, *Tesoro*," I murmur, desire laced heavy in my voice. I dive back in, wanting, no *needing*, to have more of her taste on my tongue.

"Nico," she whimpers, her hands darting out, threading through my hair and pulling me closer as she chases her pleasure.

Shoving my tongue inside her, my eyes roll to the back of my head when her unique, sweet taste hits me and I turn feral. "Fuck." I curse, withdrawing. Ocean mewls, lifting her hips as if to try and keep me there. I chuckle. "The only place you are going to come this morning, *Tesoro*, is on my cock."

Her eyes fill with lust. She licks those pouty lips of hers, her voice trembling as she says, "I need you."

Something cracks in my chest. I don't know whether it's the vulnerability in her voice or the fact that I need her, too. Instead of dwelling on it, I move up her body, line myself up with her pussy and thrust inside. Her back bows and I grit my teeth at the feel of her. "Fuck. Always so fucking tight."

"Oh, *Nico*," she cries out when I fill her to the hilt.

"Yeah, baby. That's right. You say my name when I'm fucking you."

Satisfaction thrums in my veins at the range of emotions flickering over her beautiful face. Pleasure. Awe. Need. Though I see it clearly, I blink at the most dominant emotion I witness in her eyes. Love. She is in love with me, and she doesn't even know what she has gotten herself into. I want to keep her love, keep her, but with my papà and his unpredictable nature, I don't know whether I can. Shaking the thoughts away, I focus on the way she is gripping my cock.

"That's it, *Tesoro*, take every inch of me. I own this pussy, don't I? You don't need to answer, I already know I do. You belong to me. This is *my* cunt. You are mine." I growl animalistically. I don't know what overcomes me. I just know that I can't get enough of Ocean Embers. I want her. All of her. Heart, body, and soul and it's in this moment that I know; that no matter my obligations or what Papà says, I won't give her up. Not willingly. I will die before I let someone take her from me. And if they do manage to pry her from my fingers, I would burn the world down just to get her back. There is no Ocean without Nico. She belongs to me. In every sense of the word.

From the minute she let me inside her body – and if I'm being honest, even before that – she belonged to me. And she will be mine for the rest of time. Even in death, I will keep hold of her. No one, not even the devil himself will take away my little piece of purity. That's a promise. In a world that is filled with darkness she is my light – *I* deserve my light.

"Nico," she moans, snapping me from my reverie.

I look down at her, the way her eyes roll shut. How her pussy clamps down around me like a vise when her orgasm hits. Screaming out my name, her voice echoes around the room as she soaks my cock. "That's it baby, milk my dick. Take what's yours." I say, pounding into her so hard, I know I'm going to tear her up, make her bleed. I'm past caring though. The untamed, primal side of me has taken over, and is claiming her however it sees fit.

Besides, I will draw her a nice bath and take care of her once I have had my fill. My brows furrow. Fuck, when did I turn into such a pussy? I almost laugh that I am even questioning when. I know when and it's only specific to one person. The woman beneath me. Goddamn her.

Fury pulses in my veins that she is making me weak but before I can take it out on her body further, all the blood rushes to my cock and my balls tighten. My chest heaves, and I stare down at her, groaning when my cock jerks my release inside of her. Coating her cunt with my cum and marking my territory. "Christ," I mutter, dropping my forehead to hers and breathing her in.

She runs her delicate fingers through my hair, the gentle

move calming me in a way I've never felt before. I huff out a quiet laugh. Jesus, I really am screwed.

"I think that's the hardest you've ever taken me," she whispers tiredly.

Lifting my head, I glance down at her. "Was I too rough?"

She shakes her head, a small smile on her lips. "No. I mean, I will probably be sore for a couple of days but that's not new. I liked it." She adds and I hear the honesty in her voice. She did like it. Can handle the animal I become when I'm with her.

I smirk. "Good. Because I liked fucking you like I was trying to kill you."

She sighs, nibbling her bottom lip. I see the indecision in her eyes and the moment she decides that she is going to speak her truth. "I love you," she blurts out. I stiffen at her declaration. The love that I saw in her eyes now said aloud and drifting between us. A love I *definitely* don't deserve and one I can't return. Not right now.

I try to loosen my tight muscles, but it's no use, the words are out there, the sound of her voice as she said them pulsing in my head. Pressing a kiss to her lips, I say. "I will run you a bath."

I glance down at where we are still joined, just so I can avoid seeing the hurt on her face. Hurt that I caused by not acknowledging or returning her words. Pulling out of her, I frown when I see the cum and a hint of blood on my cock. I shift my gaze up to find her cunt, bloody and swollen from the brutal way I took her. The monster in me puffs up in pride that I made her bleed. It reminds me of the night I took her virginity. But the side of me that wants to protect her with everything that I am, hates that I drew blood.

"You're bleeding," I state.

She glances down, snapping out. "I'll live Nico."

Sighing, I climb off the bed – this time not bothering to shove my cum back inside her, because one, it's just not hygienic with the mixed blood and two, I need to get away from her – and move to the attached bathroom where I plug the tub and turn on the faucets.

Moving to the shower, I step inside, turning the water to cold and hoping it will wash away all my sins. I can't. My hands will never be clean. And there is more sinning to come.

I just hope I can protect Ocean from the fallout.

***

"So, last night was interesting." Dante drawls, eying me cautiously from where he sits in front of my desk.

Leaning back in my chair, I exhale. "Interesting is putting it mildly."

"You were so pissed. I thought you were going to kill your papà then and there."

Hmm, though that is a nice thought... "I have more control than that Dante. You know that."

He laughs. "Forever the calculated, tactical one, Nic."

"I have to be. Everything is..." I trail off as the memories of last night come back to me and clench my jaw. "Fuck. I wish I'd never met Ocean. I had a fucking plan, Dante. She is ruining everything. I should have left her alone. Never touched her." I know I don't mean what I am saying. I'm just frustrated with all that has happened in the last twenty-four hours.

"You don't mean that," Dante calls me on my shit.

I shake my head. "If Leo had never..." I can't even finish the sentence because had Leo never taken a chance on Ocean, we would never have met. And I never want to imagine a life where she doesn't exist. I eye my friend, my face serious. "It's fucked man. But I have a duty. The family above all else. You took the same damn oath."

His jaw clenches as do his fists. "I would give it all up for *her.*" He doesn't have to say the name of the 'her' he is talking about because I know full well that he means my sister. "Look where being loyal has gotten us. I can't even be with the woman I love." My brows shoot up at his admission and he shakes his head. "And you? Well, you know what is expected of you, Nic."

"You love Allegra?" I ask, slightly shocked. I knew he had feelings for her. But love?

He huffs a humorless laugh, running a hand over his face. "More than anything. And your fucking papà is selling her off to the highest bidder. I will kill Romano before she ever becomes his wife." He vows and I believe him. He would. Not only did my life come crumbling down last night but so did Dante's. He finally found out about the arrangement my father has made for my sister.

I nod. "Agreed. The marriage to Romano will not happen."

Dante eyes me. "And what about you?"

"I will do what's expected of me. That doesn't mean I will let Ocean go. I can't. I just need to make sure she stays in the dark about *everything*."

Chapter 34
Ocean

There is an ominous feeling in the air.
Like something big is about to happen. I just don't know what.

Maybe it's because of the way it started?

I told Nico that I loved him.

He didn't return the sentiment.

Stupid, naïve me, I thought he might feel the same.

But how could he? He is rich, successful, powerful and I'm just... me. Running from something, I can't ever tell Nico about and just trying to survive day to day.

I groan in embarrassment. I'm still that same little girl from years ago, begging for attention and wanting to be seen, and loved, but instead of craving it from my parents, I want it from Nico. I shake my head. Why the hell did I say those three little words?

Yes, I meant them. I do love Nico. But I was so caught up in my post-orgasmic bliss, that it made me say things that I would have usually kept to myself.

I slap a palm to my forehead, whispering under my breath. "I'm such an idiot."

"Everything okay?" Macy's soft voice has my head snapping up. She smiles and I return it. Though I try to keep to myself, Macy has become a mother figure of sorts. She is always watching out for me.

"Yeah. I'm just being stupid."

She eyes me. "I know that I've said it before, but if you ever want to talk, I'm here."

My chest tightens and I shoot her a grateful look "Thanks Macy. You've been a great boss. From the moment that I stepped foot in here you have looked after me."

She chuckles. "And you've been the perfect employee." Her face turns serious. "Now, I mean it. You need anything you know where my office is."

"Thank you," I say around the lump in my throat. Macy doesn't have to be nice to me. In fact, she should hate me for all the special treatment I get because of my *situationship* with Nico but, ever the nice person she is, she doesn't penalize me for it. She nods before sashaying away and back down the hall that leads to her office.

Blowing out a breath, I focus on the laptop in front of me and the clients that we are expecting. The next booking is not due in for another forty minutes which gives me time to go grab a sandwich from the deli across the street. I'm just about to step away from the front desk to tell Macy my plan when the door dings, announcing someone's arrival.

Glancing up with a smile, I say. "Welcome to–" I trail off, swallowing as I spot the threatening presence entering with a sardonic smile on his face. He is surrounded by two other men, and I know that whoever this man is, he is not someone to be messed with. Clearing my throat, I plaster on a fake smile. "Welcome to *Bellissima*. How can we help you today?"

He grins, taking a step toward me. "You must be the lovely Ocean." It's not a question but a statement. By the devilish gleam in his eyes and the way they rake over my body, he knows exactly who I am.

My smile falters, heart pounding in my chest. Does this man know my family? Oh god. They have found me. Sweat drips down my spine and my body begins to tremble in fear. I clear my throat, hoping that I can convey confidence even when I feel like I am about to black out. "I'm sorry, do I know you?"

His predatory eyes spark, and I know full well he caught the tremor in my voice. He is terrifying in a way that I've never experienced before. I want the ground to open up and swallow me, just so I don't have his gaze focused on me. I thought Nico was scary but whoever this man is, he is next level. Darkness coats him, sucking all the air out of the room. His stare, cold and calculated, never leaves me, sending a shudder through my body. A voice in my head screams to get as far away from him as I can, but I am rooted to the spot by the fear thrumming through my veins.

"Ocean, I heard–" Macy starts as she steps into the reception area, only to cut off when her gaze lands on the man whose name I still haven't learned.

"Loren–" her mouth snaps shut when he speaks.

"Leave." His timber is deep and terrifying, leaving no room for argument.

My eyes widen when with that one word, Macy does exactly as he asked without even sparing me another glance. His dark eyes shift back to me, an evil smirk curving his lips.

Closing the distance between us, he steps up to the counter. All the air leaves my lungs, my body stiffening with his proximity. I try to take a step back - put as much space between us as I can – but am stopped when I hit the wall. Now all that separates me and this... well whoever he is, is the front desk and a couple of feet. "As Macy just confirmed, you are Ocean. I must say, my son has excellent taste. You are even more beautiful than I imagined. Exquisite even."

My body shakes and no matter how much I try to force myself still, it's no use. I am terrified. He is *terrifying*. I blink, a shuttered breath leaving me as I stare at him. This is Nico's father? I let my gaze travel over him and now that he has confirmed who he is, I can see the small similarities. The dark hair and chiseled features. The curve of his nose and masculine jaw. I exhale, trying to calm my racing heart and the pounding of blood in my ears.

"It's nice to meet you," I finally say, though I don't mean any word of it. It's not nice to meet him. In fact, I don't think a man has intimidated me like this man does, since I last saw my father.

He laughs, the sound sending a shiver down my spine and raising all the hairs on the back of my neck. "Oh, I'm sure you will change your mind about that within the next ten minutes or so."

My blood turns to ice in my veins. And needing to do something, *anything*, I clasp my hands together, trying to find some purchase. "Wh-why do you say that?" I stutter out.

He searches my face, for what, I'm not sure, before pulling something out of his suit jacket pocket and holding it out to me. Glancing down, I notice it's a thick manilla envelope. My brows furrow in confusion. I shift my gaze back to him. "I want you to take this money and leave the city."

My stomach drops, nervous laughter bursting out of me. "What?" I blurt out, not sure I am hearing him correctly.

Anger and impatience roll off him. He pins me with a look that nearly has my knees buckling. "You will leave the city. Take this money and go. I don't want to see your face again and if I do? Well, let's just say our next interaction will be a lot less... friendly. I can assure you that if you do not follow my orders, it won't end well for you. We can do it the easy way or the hard

Dancing In Sin

way. I would prefer easy. I don't want to have to add another body to my count."

I swallow, not sure what he means by that, but hearing the threat in his voice all the same. But still, I have questions and I want answers. "But why? I don't even know you. You don't know me." I shouldn't be antagonizing this man, but I want to know the reasoning behind his demand.

Dropping the envelope to the counter, he pins me to the spot with a deadly look. "I don't need to know you. From what I do know, you have my son distracted and I can't have that." A sick smile forms over his face. "Nico thought he had hidden you well, that I didn't know about you, but I have known for a while now. I was going to let whatever he was doing with you run its course and let him discard you as he has done with every woman that came before you." I flinch at his vile words. "Seems that I underestimated his obsession with you and now I need to take things into my own hands. Get rid of his mess. My son has not been honest with you, but I won't lie to you. Nico is the heir to one of the most powerful organizations on The East Coast. The Marchetti *famiglia*. The Mafia." I freeze, shock hitting me in every part of my body. I knew Nico was dangerous. Powerful. But mafia? Fuck. His father doesn't stop there, though. No. With his next words, he puts the final nail in my coffin. "You do know you are nothing but a side piece to him? A hole to fuck? Nico is engaged to be married to another woman." My heart cracks in my chest, splintering me with every word he is saying. "A good *Italian* woman, that belongs in our world. You will never be more than a whore to him. *La sua puttana.*" He spits, laughing derisively as everything I thought I knew is torn apart in an instant. "You are nothing. No. One." He enunciates to get his point across and filling me with even more self-doubt. I was right to have my insecurities when it came to Nico and now, I know why.

Clicking his fingers, his gaze never leaves me as one of his goons steps forward, handing him what looks like a paper. Slamming it next to the envelope, he points a finger.

Despite my apprehension to see what he is pointing at; something tells me I have to look. Stepping forward, I glance down. What is left of my heart completely fractures at the sight. Nico. His arm wrapped around the waist of a beautiful dark-haired woman. He smiles down at her as she beams up at him. Nausea churns in my gut and I think I'm going to be sick.

"No," I whisper, shaking my head.

He laughs. "Yes. Now be the good little *whore* that you are and take the money. You are young and gorgeous. I'm sure there is a man out there for you. One that you will have a future with. It's just not my son."

Tears blur my vision, my whole body shaking with the weight of the truth. Looking up at the man who has just destroyed me in less than ten minutes, I choke out. "I need to get some things." I shouldn't be agreeing to his demands. I should be finding or calling Nico and confronting him about his betrayal. But I just don't have it in me to fight. I'm tired. So damn tired. I have spent the better part of six months running from a monster and the irony is, I ran straight into the arms of an even bigger one. Nico is the devil. I saw the red flags like a beacon of light flashing at me. I just chose to ignore them. I thought Nico cared about me, but he was only using me. His father is right. I'm his whore. He made me a fucking side piece without me even knowing.

A broken laugh bubbles out of me and I shake my head. I fucking told him that I loved him and now his silence makes sense. He doesn't love me. He is in love with some other women. Someone so much better suited to him than I would ever be. Every insecurity I had was warranted. I meant nothing to him but a fuck. None of it was real. I gave him everything, my fucking virginity, and all the while he was engaged. God, I really am stupid.

"Not necessary. My men took the liberty of collecting some things from the apartment my son had you holed up in."

Fury heats my veins, anger rising in me, and I don't care if I provoke him. These fuckers went into my apartment, went through my stuff. My underwear. My jaw clenches. "You invaded my privacy." I snap.

He smirks as a look of...pride crosses his face. I frown. "Feisty little thing, aren't you? I bet you are a tiger in the bedroom. No wonder Nico couldn't quit fucking your pussy." He winks lasciviously. Bile rises in my throat. "Take the money and go now. Nico is in The Hamptons with my wife, his sister and fiancée. My men will drop you at the bus or train station or whatever means of transport you need to get out of New York." He pins me with a sinister look. "There will be consequences for your disobedience, *Ocean*, and you won't like them." he leans in, his voice dropping. "I don't want to have to put a bullet in your pretty little head." His words are honest. He will kill me. "Now get your shit and get gone." He turns on his heel only to stop. "And hand me your cell. I don't want you to be able to contact my son. In your duffle bag, you will find a new cellphone along with your fake and *real* documents that my men found hidden in the apartment." He smirks. I freeze. Fuck. He knows who I am. "Don't worry. I won't tell my son that you have been deceiving him the whole time, as long as you do as you are told. But be warned, I don't know your story, but it is clear you are running from something. Your family if I were to guess." He grins, while I'm sure that I've turned an abnormal shade of white. "Your reaction just confirmed what I already knew. You are scared. Which means, I won't have to threaten you with putting a bullet in your head. I will just let your family know exactly where you are, and they can deal with you however they see fit."

Tears stream down my face and defeated, I nod. I've shown him my hand and he ran with it. He knows he has me. Going back to my family would be a worse fate than him killing me. Reaching down, I grab my purse from under the counter, thankful, that I didn't put it in my locker today. I don't want to have to go back there and face any of the other staff that work here.

"Okay." I agree.

He stares at me. "Okay. Now get gone. I need to take care of some things here."

He doesn't need to ask me twice. With one last look around the place I have called my job for the last couple of months, I grab the envelope full of money and rush outside.

Tears prick my eyes and I try to suck much-needed air into my lungs. A man steps up beside me, making me jump. "Where do you want to go?"

"Port Authority."

He nods, opening the door of the black SUV. I should be wary of climbing in this vehicle with a strange man, but right now it's the least of my worries.

Sliding inside, he shuts the door behind me. I notice my duffle on the seat next to me and open it, wanting to know what's inside. Nico's father wasn't lying. My real passport and birth certificate sit on top of a pile of clothes, the name I ran away from staring right back at me. The tears come harder now and with a weary sigh, I zip the bag back up, not wanting to see my past.

Falling back in my seat, I squeeze my eyes closed, my thoughts going to Nico and all that I found out. Anger slithers through my veins and before I let anything form in my mind, I quickly shove them away.

Fuck him.

Fuck his father too.

As the car pulls away from the curb, a sense of calm washes over me and I mentally go over what I'm going to do next.

I don't really have a plan in place. I just know that no matter what happens, I will be okay.

I disappeared once before. I can do it again.

I just need to make sure Nico can never find me.

To be continued...

✳✳✳

Quick Note from The Author

Wow, what a ride. Thank you so much for reading, your support means so much to me!

Dancing in Sin has been a long time coming and something that was due to release in August last year. Unfortunately, things didn't go to plan and a case of writer's block hit, preventing me from giving you something that I could be proud of. After a couple of months of not writing, I finally snapped out of it and Nico and Ocean's story was completed. As you now know, this ended on a cliffhanger but don't worry, you can continue their story in Twisted in Obsession, coming in just two short weeks.

I want to say a big thank Kalie who pushed me and helped in so many ways. Without you cheerleading me on from the sidelines, I don't know if this duet would have happened.

I also want to thank Gabriella and my pa Kerri, both of whom have been superstars and to Andrea for all your help with getting the correct Italian words and phrases. And finally, last but definitely not least, you, my readers. Without you all, I couldn't do any of this, so I thank you.

To find out what happens next, you can preorder Twisted In Obsession here: **https://books2read.com/u/br9Mpk**

kelly Kelsey

To keep up to date with all things Kelly Kelsey, you can follow me on social media.

Facebook Readers Group - Kelly Kelsey Readers Group
    Instagram – Authorkellykelsey
    Goodreads – KellyKelsey
    Tiktok – Kellykelseyauthor
    Newsletter – https://authorkellykelsey.myflodesk.com/wp2aquzed8

About the Author

Kelly Kelsey is a UK-based author who started her writing journey during the pandemic when her career in events came to a complete stop. The more she read the more she wanted to try her hand at writing and eventually self-published her debut novel Sweet Temptation in July 2021. She now has ten books published and has been involved in several anthologies.

Books

The Sweet Collection
 Student/Teacher Standalones
 Sweet Temptation
 Sweet Possession
 Sweet Addiction

The Maxwell Family
 Jump Series – Thalia and Theo
 Elimination
 Checkmate
 Unconditional
 Inevitable – Aria and Bishop

Beautiful Beaumont
 The Secrets We Keep

Novellas
 Wrong Desires

Jingle All the Way

Marchetti Family
Dancing in Sin – Nico and Ocean
Twisted in Obsession – Nico and Ocean. Pre order here:
https://books2read.com/u/br9Mpk

The Jump Series
Elimination

Thalia Maxwell has it all. Daughter of one of the richest men in the world and a movie star mother. Except all she dreamed of is for the chance to make a career in showjumping. Thalia manages to convince her father to send her to train with world number one showjumper Theodore Rhodes after she finishes school.

Arriving in Wellington Thalia expects hard work and dedication. What she doesn't expect is the tension, the push and pull between a man she should never have. A man that is in a relationship. A man that could ruin her. As they get to know each other and feelings develop, will she be able to stay away from him or will she jump in headfirst?

Theodore Rhodes is at the top of his sport. His results and reputation in the world of show jumping are yet to be beaten. When he gets asked to train Thalia Maxwell, he jumps at the chance. Not because he wants to but having a big name like hers will bring him even more into the spotlight than he already is.

But when Thalia arrives, he expects a spoiled little princess that wants to play my little pony. What he doesn't expect is a girl so determined and beautiful he can't help but be drawn to her. The more time they spend together the further he falls. Will he risk everything for the one girl he should never have?

ELIMINATION is a new series and book 1 in the series with a cliff-hanger. It does contain tropes that some may find triggering such as cheating. However, the series will end in a happily ever after... eventually!

Thalia

Excitement courses through me as I spot the imposing sign on the brick wall.
Rhodes Farms.

The place I have wanted to train ever since I watched Mr. Theodore Rhodes, himself, compete at the Global tour in New York a few years back. I was mesmerized by him. The way he rode. The way he was at one with his horse. His riding was an art form. He won the whole competition, and I knew then I wanted to be just like him.

Theodore Rhodes is the number one show jumper in the world and the one person who can help me achieve my show jumping dreams. He won individual and team gold at the last Olympics - his third time competing for Team USA.

After much discussion—and begging on my behalf—my parents agreed to let me train with him, with the stipulation that I finish high school first. Of course, I agreed, and I graduated from St. Constantine's private all-girls school a couple weeks ago. Now my journey can really start. I will be a showjumper. I will prove to my parents that this is what I want.

We pull through the wrought iron gates. I scan the area

through the blacked-out SUV windows, taking in the lush green grass and palm tree lined drive before the barn comes into view. I smile knowing I am going to see my horses in just a couple more minutes.

Zeus and Lolly.

I have had them for a couple years now, competing on the East Coast whenever I had the chance between modelling, filming, and school. I want to take the next step now and that can only happen if I get the right trainer.

Coming to a stop, I open the door before the driver gets the chance to do it for me and hop out. I hear my father's stern voice but that doesn't stop me as I race toward the stalls. I have never gone this long without seeing my horses, so the excitement is real. Spotting a woman, I come to a halt.

"Hey, do you know where my horses are? Zeus and Lolly?" Her eyes widen before she composes herself.

"You're Thalia Maxwell?" I nod in confirmation. It's only when her mouth gapes that I remember what my name means.

Thalia Maxwell, daughter to the owner of the world's biggest diamond and jewelry corporation, Christian Maxwell III, and America's sweetheart, movie star, Elena Maxwell. She straightens, clears her throat. I frown. I don't want to be treated any differently from anyone else here.

"Uhh, yeah. Follow me." She spins on her heel, and I follow her lead. "I'm Tessa by the way. Barn manager at Rhodes Farms."

"Hey," I reply. She glances over her shoulder with a small smile then carries on to my horses' stalls. She comes to a stop at a door. I peek over, smiling when I see Zeus. He is gray in color and around 16.2 hands, big compared to my five-foot six height. Spotting me, he neighs. I open the door, strolling in and wrapping my arms around his neck.

Dancing In Sin

"Hey boy. Did you miss me?" I ask even though he can't reply.

"Zeus and Lolly have been very well looked after," Tessa says. I glance over at her and smile.

"Thank you. This is the longest I have gone without seeing them," I tell her. Both my horses were transported from New York to Florida over a month ago. I know it sounds cliché, but I have been lost without them.

"Lolly is next door," Tessa adds. I release Zeus and make my way to Lolly. I grin at my girl. She is around 16 hands and brown in color with a black mane and tail. She is beautiful. Opening the stall door, I walk in and wrap my arms around her just the same as I did with Zeus. I breathe her in, breathe in the smell of horses.

It feels like home.

I hear footsteps approach and I know it is my father. My mom couldn't make it today, as she is on location for a new movie she is filming.

"Thalia?" I release Lolly, stepping out of the stall to find my father with his cell in hand and a frown marring his face.

"Here, Daddy." He glances up at me with a smile.

"Come. Mr. Rhodes is in his office." I swallow down my nerves as I follow my father. I have never met Theodore Rhodes in person, but I have seen pictures. He is known as the hottest guy in show jumping and it is not hard to see why. With his dark hair, striking blue eyes, and chiseled features, he is a god. Beautiful. I have been around good-looking men, worked with them on several modelling campaigns, but Theodore Rhodes beats them all. Unfortunately for all women that covet him, he isn't single. He has been with his girlfriend for six years and as far as I know, there has never been any rumors of him being unfaithful. Not like you would be if you were dating British socialite,

Melody Whitworth. With her blond hair and brown eyes, she is gorgeous and together, they look like the picture-perfect couple.

Coming to a stop at a big oak door, my father knocks. A few seconds later a deep male voice responds, sending a shiver down my spine.

"Come in." My father pushes the door open before stepping through. I follow behind him only to come to a stop when I spot the man behind the desk. My breath hitches. I swallow.

Hard.

Jesus. Pictures do not do this man justice. In person, he is even more god-like. Noticing my stare, he clears his throat and holds out his hand for me to take. "You must be Thalia?" My cheeks heat in embarrassment at being caught ogling him. I take his hand.

"Yes," I breathe. He smirks. A smirk I feel right down to my...pussy? I frown, stunned by my reaction. This never happens to me. I have never been interested in men, choosing to focus on my horses, yet for some reason, this stranger has my stomach in knots with lust.

This is bad. Really bad.

The guy is not only in a long-term relationship but is twelve years older than me. I glance at my father who would, for sure, have me back on our jet and back to the East Coast if he heard my thoughts right now. Being the baby of the family, I am my father's little princess. The good girl. Never had a boyfriend and I am sure he would like to keep it that way. My father takes a seat, dragging me out of my thoughts.

"Nice to meet you, Thalia. I'm Theo, but I am sure you already knew that," He says smugly, releasing my hand. The instant loss leaves me cold. I shake my head trying to compose myself.

"Nice to meet you, Theo," I say in a voice I don't quite

recognize. I need to get it together before my dad realizes something is wrong. And anyway, Theo is way out of my league. A grown man with a girlfriend who I am sure has no interest in me other than training. I am a paying trainee. He is my trainer. I chant the words silently to myself, reminding myself to keep my head in the game and off this glorious specimen in front of me. He smiles once more before rounding his desk and taking a seat.

"So, Mr. Maxwell—" My father holds his hand up to stop him.

"Please, call me Christian." He nods before carrying on.

"Christian, I know we spoke in detail before about Thalia's ambitions and what she is looking to achieve from training with me. We discussed her accomplishments so far and that she is now looking to step up a level, move up the ranks." Theo's gaze moves to me. I blush at the intensity in his blue eyes. "Is that correct Thalia?"

Clearing my throat, I nod. "Yes. I have followed your career for a long time now, Mr. Rhode's..." I trail off at the look on Theo's face.

"Please call me Theo. If you are going to be training with me, I would rather we be informal with each other. Mr. Rhodes is far too formal when we will be working closely."

I nod. "Like I was saying, I have been following your career for a long time now, Theo. Your performance at the Beijing Olympics was extraordinary. It is what inspired me to want to do more. To be better. I have wanted to train with you for a long time, but I needed to finish school."

Theo's eyes light up at my hero worship and my tummy flutters with excitement that I have pleased him. "I want to compete at a higher level. Do the tours in Europe. Maybe make the nations cup teams. I understand I have a long way to go but I am willing to do what it takes." I feel my father's stare at my speech, but my eyes stay locked on Theo's. My gaze drops to his lips when I see them twitch.

"You are passionate, Thalia; I will give you that. But I need you to understand the work that will go into getting you to that level. It does not and will not happen overnight. Show jumping is one of the toughest sports." I frown at his words, but he continues. "But with your parents' backing, I think you have as good a chance as any. Show jumping is also a money sport, you have that. Your father has already informed me that you will have your parents full support in whatever we need to do to get you to where you want to be."

"Whatever it takes," my father cuts in. Theo nods.

"I have schooled both your horses and studied videos of you competing. While they are both nice horses, they are average at best. They need to be exceptional to compete at the level you want to." My jaw clenches, fists ball at the audacity of this man. How dare he speak about my horses this way. Before I can stop myself, the words tumble out of me.

"My horses are just fine. They may not be competing at top level yet, but they can," I hiss. I feel my dad's eyes on me, but I don't move my gaze from Theo. Something flashes in his eyes, his lips curving into a smirk.

"Thalia," my father warns. Being childish, I shoot Theo an indignant look before he carries on like the arrogant asshole he apparently is.

"As I was saying. While they are both nice animals, I feel that to compete at top level, you need a top-level horse. Fortunately for you, I do have one in mind and although the owners aren't desperate to sell, I have it on good authority from the current rider that they are willing to allow you the chance to view and purchase him. We will need to be discreet, but I think it will be the perfect horse for what you are looking to do." Theo glances at my father then back to me.

"You know my position, Theo; I am willing to spend the money to get my princess," I cringe at my dad calling me that in front of this man, "to where she wants to be. What sort of figures are we looking at?"

Theo clears his throat. "I have been told he is going to be in the high six figure numbers. That being said, it will be worth it if it gets Thalia the results and exposure she wants. He is competing at top level in Europe and is on all the Dutch Nation Cup teams with very good results. I think it would be the perfect fit." I frown at his words. Although it would be exciting to have a new horse, I don't want to sell my current ones.

"I don't want to sell Zeus or Lolly. I won't." I look at my dad, shaking my head as if to drive the point home. My father's eyes soften.

"Princess, we won't be selling them. I just think that if you want this as much as you say you do, you are going to have to take Theo's advice. He knows what he is talking about and if that means buying a better horse then that is what we will do." I smile before my gaze moves to Theo. Something passes in his eyes that I can't quite decipher before he speaks.

"I think this is the right move, Thalia. Of course, we will spend a couple of weeks getting to know one another, so I can see the level you are at with both horses. But ultimately, I think buying a horse or even a couple of horses that have good records competing at top level is the best way forward."

I nod, feeling my anger at his earlier words dissipate. "Of course. I want this and I trust your advice. I wouldn't be here otherwise." He eyes me for a long beat before he nods.

"Good. I am glad we cleared that up. Now onto the next thing. You will have two assigned grooms and one stable hand which are included in the price of your monthly fees. I will introduce you to them later today. You will also meet my whole team. I have three other students here training with me and they all live on site, as do the staff. Your father mentioned you will be living off-site in a condo purchased for you." My father cuts in.

"Yes, that is correct. It is around ten minutes from here and Thalia has a vehicle to travel back and forth."

"Good. I also understand you will be taking college courses online so I will take this into account when working out your schedule."

"This is important," my father says in a tone that leaves no room for argument. "Thalia knows that it is part of the condition of being here, so she knows to take her studying seriously." My father shoots me a stern look to remind me that I promised to continue my studies. The fact I can study online is a bonus. I don't want to go to a classroom.

"I am sure we can come up with something that suits us all. With two horses, Thalia will only need lessons four or five times a week. The rest will be trail rides, flatwork, or the horse exerciser." The way Theo says my name has my core clenching. I didn't know my name could sound so sexy on someone's tongue.

"That is what I want to hear. Studying is important and although I know Thalia is determined to make a career in show jumping, I still want her to continue her studies. She is a very bright girl." My father beams at me while my eyes slide to Theo to find him watching me intently. Something in his stare makes goosebumps break out all over my body and wetness seeps between my thighs. What the hell? That's new. I squirm and as if he knows what he is doing to me, Theo grins before his eyes move back to my father.

"Theo, I would also like to discuss the NDA. As you know, my wife is a very high-profile actress. But not only that, Maxwell is one of the biggest names in the US and while I trust you to be discreet during Thalia's training with you, it is something I insist on being signed by yourself and the people who will be working closely with my daughter." Annoyance flashes in Theo's eyes before he schools his features.

"That won't be a problem, Christian. Consider it done." I don't miss the bite in his tone. I grimace that he is having to do this, but it comes with the territory. When you are the daughter of a world-famous actress and one of the richest men in the world, it is something that must happen.

"Good. Now that the formalities are over, I would like to take Thalia to her condo and then tomorrow, she is all yours." My father pushes to a stand, holding his hand out for Theo to shake. "It was nice to meet you in person, Theo. I trust you will make sure my daughter gets settled once I leave." It's not a question. My father expects Theo to take care of his 'princess'.

"Of course, Christian. I will make sure she feels at home here at Rhodes Farms." Theo's eyes slide to me before going back to my father. I push out of my chair, my gaze on Theo as I flash him a small smile. He smiles back causing my stomach to twist. Ignoring it, I rush out of his office and back to the waiting car that will take me to my condo.

Sweet Addiction

Knox: Being the star quarterback of the NFL, I had it all. Women, money and a life most could only dream of. I thought I was invincible. Then I made a mistake, then another and it all came crashing down. I was suspended from the NFL and forced into a relationship and job I didn't want. But then i met her—my fiancee's sweet innocent daughter. She stirs something inside of me that I never knew existed. I know I should stay away. I know it's reckless to want to touch her, to want to make her mine. But I am Knox McCabe and living life on the edge is what I do best. So why change now?

Madison: Being Madison Devereux, people think I have it all. Popular. Rich. Beautiful. What more could I want, right? Wrong. All I want is to be able to follow my dreams but doing that means hurting my mother. Then suddenly she gets engaged to NFL bad boy Knox McCabe. He is mysterious, gorgeous and the new coach at my school. What starts out as a game of lust and desire soon turns into something neither of us can stop. It's reckless, wrong but it feels so right. I should walk away. Stop the madness. But Knox has other plans, ones that include me. Everything I have ever wanted is within reach, will I risk it all for a man that belongs to the one person I never want to hurt?

Knox

"You have got to be shitting me?" I glare at my agent before my gaze moves to my publicist Clarissa. The latter's mouth forms a tight line, and she shakes her head.

"I'm afraid not. You really messed up this time. There are online petitions calling for you to be removed from the NFL permanently." She sighs, rubbing her temples as if trying to find the strength to deal with me. "Listen to me Knox and listen good. I know this all seems far-fetched but it's the only strategy we have come up with that we think will make you look human and not like the above-the-law god you seem to think yourself to be. Scarlett Grisham is a fading actress. She needs the publicity as much as you do. She is a good choice for this—"

I hold my hand up to stop her. "Scarlett is one of your clients, isn't she Clarissa?" It's not a question but she answers anyway.

"Yes," she admits although I knew what her response would be. "But that is not why I am doing this. We need to transform your image. Right now, you are seen as a playboy, the bad boy of the NFL. I will arrange for you and Scarlett to meet to get to know each other. If all goes well—and I think it will—we can move on to the next stage in your *fauxationship*." I pin her with a look that says, I have no idea what that is. "Like a relationship but fake," she explains before continuing. "You will be pictured out at restaurants, doing the grocery shopping, and other normal couply shit. You will be in the tabloids, seen in loving embraces, kissing, cuddling, and in a couple of months we will announce your engagement. I know it's not what you want, and I am not asking you to marry Scarlett, but you will be engaged. The world will think that the twenty-nine-year-old lothario Knox McCabe has finally settled down and become a one-woman man. When the dust has settled, we can slowly start the breakup rumors if that's what you want. You never know. You might fall for her for real." Clarissa smirks.

I shake my head. I know of Scarlett Grisham. Yes, she is a beautiful woman, but there is also talk that she is crazy. At seventeen she seduced and became pregnant by the director of her hit show, Girl Talk. Peter Devereux was ten years her senior and a married man at the time. The press went wild over the news and still to this day—eighteen years later—they talk about it. The only reason Peter never went to prison was because they were living in New York City and the age of consent for sex is seventeen. There was also the fact that Scarlett publicly admitted to seducing him. After taking a few years out to raise her daughter and only accepting small roles, she finally got back into the world of showbiz and became a huge star. You would have thought the opposite after going after another woman's man and being very open with not caring about his poor wife but no, both of their careers hit superstardom. He was a director in demand, and she was the actress offered role after role. Until now. At thirty-six, her career has all but dried up. I guess that's where I come in.

"Scarlett Grisham is hardly the right choice. She has as many skeletons in her closet as I do mine," I point out.

"That may well be. But at the height of her fame, she was the golden girl of Hollywood. People saw her as the sweetheart single mother, doing her charity work and keeping her nose clean. She has had no bad articles written about her in the last fifteen years. Yes, there will forever be the reminder of her less-than-good deeds—her teenage daughter is proof of that, but I can control it to fit a good narrative. Let me do it for you. Just think about the headlines. The bad boy NFL player and the ex-darling of Hollywood. People will go wild for it. And more than anything it will make you look good." She sighs in exasperation. "Look Knox. Do it. Don't do it. But I am going to be frank with you. It's the only way I can save your reputation. It's not bad enough that you were caught driving while you had a goddamn Victoria's Secret model sucking your dick, but then you proceeded to tell the female officer to join you and the male one to fuck off. You now have public indecency on your record. Plus, the whole bullshit with that quarterback you fucked up in your last game. People don't like you right now. Even your loyal fans are questioning their devotion to you. Let's kill two birds with one stone. Over the next few months, we will present you as remorseful for your actions. To the world you will be the devoted boyfriend and then fiancé to Scarlett Grisham. You will live together and act like a model citizen and while you are doing that you will also complete your community service."

I stare at her, waiting for whatever bullshit she is going to tell me now. I knew I had to do it. It was part of my agreement when I went to court. But I was never involved in what that service would be. "Which is?" I prompt.

Clarissa keeps a straight face, but I see the amusement in her eyes. "You will be teaching physical education at Scarlett's daughter's private school. For a year," she adds.

My head swivels to my agent, who has stayed quiet this whole time. Now I know why. He knew what Clarissa would offer me, knew about the teaching. "What the fuck? I am not a PE teacher," I spit, pinning accusing eyes on Brett. "Get me out of it," I demand.

Brett shakes his head. "Can't. Your lawyer negotiated to get you the best deal. That was it. It's better than picking up litter off the side of the road and the only reason the judge agreed to it is because she didn't want a circus of paparazzi following you while doing it." He exhales. "This is the best option for you right now, Knox. My advice? Take it. You don't even have to fuck Scarlett, just live with her and take her out for the occasional dinner for all we care. But it needs to be for a year. By then the negative stories should have all died down. The Rams have suspended you and will only talk to me about contracts if you can prove yourself over the next year. Take the teaching position. Be the doting boyfriend. This will be good for you Knox. It will give you time to grow the hell up and be a better person. I don't want to hear one bad thing about you in the press. If I do, I will have no choice but to think about ending our working relationship. I don't want to do that, man. I've been with you since the beginning, but I can't be seen supporting someone who self-sabotages and is constantly making bad headlines. I have already had two clients drop me because I am sticking by you. Don't make me regret standing by you Knox."

I scrub a palm down my face. I didn't realize my bad choices were affecting other people. People I care about. And I do care about Brett. He took a chance on me when I was just a college kid with a dream. I owe him this. I owe him to be better.

Mind made up, I look from Brett to Clarissa. "Fine. Set up a meeting."

Madison

Two months later...

"What the fuck?" I mutter to myself as I flick through the article on my cell. My mom, engaged? To someone she supposedly only started dating two months ago. I only spoke to her a couple days ago and she never mentioned it. When I ask her about her relationship, she always brushes it off which makes me think that all is not as it seems.

Her dating NFL bad boy Knox McCabe came out of the blue, the timing was also very convenient. He was on the front of every tabloid and for all the wrong reasons. Then suddenly, he is the doting boyfriend with only eyes for my mother? Yeah. No. I don't buy it.

Call me a skeptic but there is also the fact that I know my mom. She never dates younger men—daddy issues or something—and Knox is seven years her junior. I could be wrong about all this, they could be hopelessly in love, but something tells me that my instincts are right.

I haven't met Knox in person yet. I am on summer break and decided to spend it in New York with my father and his wife. It's been perfect and given me the chance to pursue what I want most in life—to become a wildlife photographer. My dad's wife is the editor in chief for the most successful nature magazine in the world—Wildlife World. Vanessa Devereaux not only bought me my first camera, but she encourages me to chase my dreams. Much to my mother's disgust. Mom wants me to follow in her footsteps, to be an actress. I can think of nothing worse.

Growing up she was your typical stage mom and at eight years old she started pushing me to audition for different roles in acting and modeling. After a few years of playing parts I thought I wanted, I realized I wasn't doing it for me but to make my mother happy. I hated acting. I hated modeling. When I told her all this she was horrified. The daughter of actress Scarlett Grisham hating the very industry that she loved. Unacceptable.

She continued to push me but the more she pressed the more I refused. Not wanting me to embarrass her she agreed to let me live a normal childhood but only if I did acting and modeling when I finished school. I accepted her terms—emotional guilt will do that to you—but I have no intention of being an actress. I want to be a photographer. I just need to find a way of telling my mother that.

Flicking to my call log, I press down on my mother's number and bring my phone to my ear. The call rings out and I don't think she is going to answer but then her voice sounds down the line. "Hey sweetie. How's my baby?"

I grit my teeth at her nonchalant attitude. She knows damn well I would have seen the article. "Don't 'hey sweetie' me, Mom. What the hell. You're engaged?"

She sighs and I know without seeing her that she is rolling

her eyes so hard right now. "Don't be so dramatic Madi." She chuckles. "Although it will come in handy when we get you back into acting."

I pinch the bridge of my nose, praying for patience I don't feel. At eighteen, I sometimes feel like the adult in our relationship. Which is no surprise. Mom got pregnant and had me when she was only seventeen. It was a whole scandal at the time and not only because my mother was a teenager but because my father, the director of the series she starred in, was a married man and ten years her senior. Case in point. Scarlett Grisham loves and has always dated older men. As much as she would never admit to it, she is still hopelessly in love with my father. He is the love of her life while she is probably his biggest mistake. Don't get me wrong, my dad loves me, but I think deep down he wishes he had never gotten involved with my mother.

"Mom, what is going on? Is this for real or is it just another PR stunt?" I ask, wanting to know what the hell is happening and why she is messing around with someone like Knox McCabe.

"Jesus Christ Madison. Don't sugarcoat it," she barks. "I will discuss this with you when you get back, which is in two days right?"

She is evading the question which means my suspicions might just be right. "Yeah." I exhale already feeling drained at the thought of going back to LA. "I will send you my flight details."

She squeals like a best friend rather than a mother. But I guess that describes our relationship perfectly. Since the moment I was old enough to understand things, Mom always treated me like more of a friend than a daughter. I remember when I was fourteen and she was drunk. I spent four hours with her while she rambled on about my father, how much she loved him, and how *he* lost the best thing that ever happened to him by letting her go. The sad thing is she genuinely believes that. But the truth is, Dad never loved Mom. It was a fling that turned into me. I know that no matter how much time passes, no matter that he is married to Vanessa—the real love of his life—Mom will never get over Peter Devereux. She loves him. Always has. Always will.

"Perfect. I can't wait to see you, baby. You will love Knox. He is the best."

I roll my eyes at her over enthusiasm. "Okay Mom. I will talk to you later."

"Bye sweetie," she sings before hanging up.

Dropping my cell on the bed, I shake my head. What the hell has my mother gotten herself into now? Before I can think about it further a knock sounds at my bedroom door. My head snaps up just as Vanessa appears. She smiles. "Hi honey, do you have a few minutes? I wanted to talk to you about something."

"Of course. What's up?" I pat the empty space beside me silently asking her to sit.

Moving further into the room, she drops down next to me and takes my hand. Her eyes meet mine, so kind, so full of love. "We will miss you when you head back to LA," she says thickly, the emotion in her voice clear.

"I will miss the both of you too. I always feel more settled here in New York," I admit.

Vanessa nods. "You know you are always welcome here Madison." She sighs. "Look, I know that you are still deciding what you want to do after school and although I don't want what I say next to sway your decision, I want to put it on the table. Wildlife World would like to offer you an internship."

My eyes widen in shock, and I gasp. "W-what? Are you serious?"

She smiles. "I am. I discussed it with your father and again, he doesn't want you to feel pressured into it or like we are pushing you to do this. We both want you to be happy and do whatever it is you love. However, after our discussions over the years, we both know that photography is a passion of yours, especially nature and wildlife. If you want the internship, it's yours. If you decide to do something else..." She shrugs. "Well, we will support you in whatever you do."

My heart constricts. I hit the jackpot when it came to a stepparent. Throwing my arms around her, I say, "Thank you, Vanessa. I would love to intern at your magazine."

She chuckles. "Take some time to think about it, honey. The offer stands for as long as you need."

I open my mouth to tell her I have already decided when my dad's voice sounds. "There you both are." My gaze shifts to him and he frowns before smiling. "So, you told her about the internship?"

"I did," Vanessa replies before climbing off the bed. "I hope you don't mind?"

He shakes his head. "Of course not." He smiles down at her, kissing her temple quickly before his eyes shift back to me. "I know it's what you want baby but take some time to think about it. I know your mother has plans for you and I know how much you hate to let her down."

I frown. He's right, I do but that doesn't mean I am going to give up an opportunity like this. "I don't need to think about it. And don't worry about Mom; I will talk to her when I get back to LA."

He nods. "Okay then. Dinner's ready. Let's go and eat before it gets cold."

Climbing off the bed, I follow them down to the dining room feeling more excited than I ever have in my life. All my dreams of becoming a photographer can come true.

I just need to have a talk with my mom.

Sweet Possession

Asher: They say everything happens for a reason even if you don't know that reason at the time. Being screwed over by the two people closest to me, I thought I lost everything. I thought that statement was the truth until I saw my angel and at that moment, I knew she was my reason. I can't take my eyes off her and I will do anything to make her mine. Even stalk and manipulate situations if I need to. Everything starts to fall into place but things out of my control want to interfere and try to change my plan. They can try all they like but they don't know how far I will go to keep my Angel in my sights.

Remi: They say everything happens for a reason even if you don't know that reason at the time. What a load of rubbish that statement is. Life seems to want to break me at every turn. But I won't let it. I've been through hell and won't be beaten. Everything I want is within reach and then I meet him. A mysterious, gorgeous man. He wants to turn my world upside down and it's tempting... but then secrets are revealed, and people want to break us apart. How far will they go to succeed? How far will Asher go to keep me as his?

Asher

The smell of sweat and cheap liquor permeates the air, making me want to gag. I stare at the stage but focus on nothing.

This run-down shithole of a strip club is not the type of establishment I would normally frequent, but it's been a rough day.

A bad two weeks, for that matter.

I laugh at the memory of that day, but it's humorless. Walking in on your fiancée fucking your best friend since first grade is not funny.

The devastation of that day plays in my head like a movie, hitting me right in the chest. I don't know which is worse, losing Calista or Brody.

All I know is that it hurts so bad, I feel the pain in my now dead heart.

It's what brought me to this seedy place on the wrong side of town. I needed to get away. Needed to forget.

If only for one night.

Taking a sip of my bourbon, my head snaps up when catcalls break out all around me, and my gaze lands on the stage.

A woman walks out in a lacy black bra and thong; not unusual in a strip club, but there is something about her. The way her head is held high, and although she screams confidence, I can see the vulnerability in her eyes.

I stare at her and, in that moment, something strange happens. Something that hasn't happened since that day two weeks ago. My cock hardens in my pants. Shifting in my seat, my eyes trace every inch of her body from head to toe. Shiny, chocolate-brown hair that reaches her small waist. Chocolate eyes. Perfect, pert tits that bounce with every sway of her hips. Long, tan legs that would look so good wrapped around me. Flawless skin. Heart-shaped face with plump lips and a button nose.

Jesus.

No wonder the crowd perked up. The girl is fucking gorgeous.

I watch as she dances to a song, though I'm not sure what it is. My gaze is fixed on the stage in front of me, captivated by the woman moving her body like a temptress. Taking my eyes from her, I glance around, and sure enough, all eyes are fixated on her, like I knew they would be. A sliver of possessiveness and a whole lot of jealousy course through me. I pause. What the fuck? I never once felt like that towards Calista, so why am I feeling these emotions right now?

The song comes to an end, and the girl drops down, grabbing at all the bills on the stage. Its only then that I notice she didn't strip. No. The angel is still in her underwear, yet she is by far the most popular girl that has danced so far. With a handful of money, she pushes up, straightens her spine, turns, and sashays away, only to stop when a drunk asshole grabs at her leg. I growl in anger as she slightly stumbles. It takes everything in me to stay in my seat, to not beat the living shit out of the fucker.

But I don't need to. Security is there in a second, pulling the man away and out the door.

The beauty on stage stares after him, her lips slightly parted. It's then I see the innocence in her eyes, on her face. She looks young. Fresh faced compared to the other dancers. Blinking, she snaps out of wherever she just went and continues off the stage and through the curtain so I can no longer see her.

I watch the space she disappeared into long after she has gone and briefly wonder if she's coming back out. This incessant need takes over me. The need to go back there, find her, and make her tell me everything about her. But I don't. I stay seated, my eyes never leaving that black drape that has hidden the angel from my view. I sit there until the last girl comes on stage, until the lights come on, signaling the bar is closing.

I never see my angel again.

But that doesn't mean I won't be back.

I need to know her.

And I have every intention of doing just that.

* * *

The next evening, I find myself pulling up to Legs Eleven, the rundown strip club where I saw my angel last night. A woman like her should be nowhere near a place like this, let alone on the stage in her underwear while creepy dudes salivate over her. That may be hypocritical of me to say, being as I was one of those men last night, but I am not some weirdo. I just happened to be in the right place at the right time.

Hopping out of my car, I make my way to the entrance, pay the cover charge, and then find a free table near the stage. Not a minute later, a topless waitress appears, her eyes lighting up as her gaze rakes over my body.

"Hey sugar, what can I get you to drink?" she purrs, her

finger darting out and running down my arm. I grab her hand, pushing her away. She frowns like she can't quite believe I'm not interested.

"A water is fine," I say coolly, my eyes back on the stage. She huffs, spins on her stripper heels, and makes her way to what I assume is the bar to get my drink. I watch as a naked girl wraps herself around the pole. She isn't half bad. Just not my type, with her surgically enhanced breasts and cheap, dyed, bleach-blonde hair.

A half hour passes, and there is still no sign of my angel *or* my water. I am just about to turn to signal a waitress when the music starts. The lights dim even more, and the girl who I am here to see walks onto the stage. I watch as she takes a harsh breath, then looks up to the ceiling as if she is praying to someone who won't answer her. Then, like she remembers where she is – as if you could ever forget – she starts moving her body in such a sensual way, my cock hardens in my pants.

Fuck me.

That has never happened before. Not until yesterday, at least.

If she can make me hard by just moving her body side to side, then I'm pretty sure that most of the men in here are in the same state. Anger courses through me at the thought. I glance around, and it's the wrong thing to do because I suddenly want to rip every eye out of every socket in here. I want to get on that stage and cover her with my body so no one else can look at her.

"Here's your water." A feminine purr startles me out of my thoughts as she slams it down in front of me. As she turns to leave, without apologizing for taking so fucking long, I grab her wrist. She yelps, then scowls down at me. "Let go of me. No touching the ladies," she hisses.

I jerk my head to the stage. "Who is that?"

She looks to the stage and back to me, a look of jealousy and disgust crossing her face. "Oh, that's Crystal. I wouldn't bother with her though. She's a frigid, moody bitch. Thinks she is too good for this place, yet here she is, doing exactly what we all are. Stripping." She yanks her arm out of my grip and sashays away.

The song comes to an end, and, just like last night, the angel grabs up the bills and walks away without entertaining any of the catcalls being thrown her way. I am up and out of my chair, making my way to the small booth in the corner. It has a flashing neon sign saying *Book a Private Dance*. I push my way in front of the two men in the queue, ignoring their disgruntled words.

"I want a private with Crystal," I say impatiently, grabbing some notes out of my pants.

The lady, who must be pushing fifty, if not more, stares at me, her lips pursed. "Back of the line, asshole. You cut in."

Slapping the bills on the counter, I make her jump. "I want a private with Crystal. Now how much will it cost me to have that?" I grit.

Her eyes narrow before her lips curve into a grin that screams that she's about to make me pay extra. "One hundred dollars for the dance." I start to count it out, stopping when she speaks again. "And a hundred for me. Just because you're a jerk." She flashes a look that dares me to argue. I won't. I just want to get the angel to myself.

And I don't care what it costs me.

Remi

"Crystal, you're up. Room twelve," Jason, the owner, shouts at me as I stuff money in my duffle. Slamming my locker closed, I look at him. He knows that I hate private dances. That I hate to be touched, even if he doesn't know the reasoning behind it. As long as he's earning his fifty-percent cut, he doesn't care. It's not like I can say no; it was a condition of working here, and there is no way he'll give me special treatment. Even if I am his highest-earning girl.

I glance around the room and remind myself why the hell I am doing this, dancing in some shitty bar when it makes my skin crawl.

I'm all alone.

And I need the money since my mom left me alone with all the bills to pay. Plus, I now have school to pay for after taking a year off from my old one to work. I even got lucky, for once, and managed to win a scholarship at a prestigious school. And that shit does not come cheap. There is no way I'll give it up after all the work I put in to win it, and if that means strutting myself on stage in front of a bunch of pervy old men or in the private rooms, then I'll do it. I just need to keep my wits about me. Any sign that they are going to touch me or cause trouble, I'm out. No person would like a stranger touching them, but mine stems from something much more sinister. Men my mother would bring home with no regard for me. A couple of them touched me in ways they shouldn't have. I was fortunate it didn't go further, it could have been so much worse, but I still have the mental scars. No young girl should have to worry about grown men touching them inappropriately.

Sighing, I check my makeup in the mirror then stride out the door to the private rooms, all the while ignoring the bitchy stares from the other girls. They don't like me, and they've made that clear. I am the youngest - not that they know how old I really am - and I make the most money. It's made me a target for all their vile insults. I don't care though. I'm here to earn money, to pay my bills, to be able to afford to eat. Nothing more, nothing less. If they have a problem with that, then that's on them.

Stepping up outside the back entrance to room twelve, I take a breath. I can do this. Get in. Earn money. Get out. Pushing the door open, I stride in with a confidence I don't feel, only to falter when I see the man waiting for me. My jaw slacks, eyes widen.

He is gorgeous. A god. The kind of man you see on the cover of GQ magazine with his dirty blonde hair and piercing blue eyes. He looks like a better-looking, leaner Chris Hemsworth.

I swallow. What the hell does he want with me? Why is a guy like him in a place like this?

Instead of speaking, or even moving, he sits there in his chair like a king as he runs a thumb across his bottom lip. I shuffle on my feet, nervously.

"Hey," I greet but he doesn't respond, just watches me. "What would you like?"

Dancing In Sin

He cocks his head, his hungry eyes raking down my lingerie-covered body. I shiver under his intense gaze. I mean, I know I look hot. It's how I got this job and why I am the top earner in this place. But with the way this man is staring at me, it makes me feel... powerful.

"Dance for me." The rasp of his voice goes straight between my legs, making my pussy clench with need. Jesus. If I have that reaction from just the sound of him, I hate to think what he could do if he touched me.

Nodding, I move to the corner of the room where an iPod sits in a docking station. Settling on one of my favorites, Little Bird by Annie Lennox, I hit play and make my way to the raised platform with a pole in the middle. Never taking my eyes from him, I let the music consume me as I move around the pole, my hips swaying and moving sensually to the music. His gaze never leaves me as he leans back in his chair, relaxing like this is an everyday occurrence for him. Maybe it is. I frown. This place doesn't suit him.

When the song comes to an end, I drop to my knees, my back to him as I arch it up. My long, dark hair hits my feet as I lean back and get a look at him from this angle. His eyes narrow in on me, and I scramble to my feet when he pushes out of his chair and moves towards me.

"Wh-what are you doing?" I stutter as he steps up in front of me. Again, he doesn't respond, he just reaches out and runs a finger down my cheek. I pull away. "No touching the girls," I hiss, ignoring the shiver of arousal he elicits from me.

He smirks. "I think you like me touching you."

I step away from him and scowl. "I don't think so." Spinning, I make my way to the dancer's entrance and grab the handle to pull the door open, but I'm stopped in my tracks when he speaks again.

"What's your name?"

I glance over my shoulder at him. His hands are shoved in his pants pockets, and I have never seen such a good-looking man in my whole life. He really is stunning. My eyes drop of their own accord as I take in his body. I can't see him fully with his clothes on, but by the way his shirt clings to his abs, I can tell he is the whole package. Hot and a good body. The kind of man women would drop to their knees for without him even asking.

My eyes snap to his when he chuckles, and an arrogant grin curves his lips. I roll my eyes. "Crystal. The name's Crystal." With that, I step outside and slam the door behind me.

***

The next night goes pretty much the same way. I do my set, grab my money, and head backstage to get ready to leave, only to be stopped when Jason shouts out my name.

"Crystal, room twelve. You're in there for an hour tonight," he barks out, leaving no room for argument. Excitement and a sliver of fear courses through me at the thought of it being the same man from last night. And if it is, why is someone like him, someone who could surely have anyone he wants, paying to watch me dance for an hour?

Unless he wants something else. I shake my head to myself. No matter how hot I think he is, he is not having that. If the other girls want to earn extra by having sex with clients, that's fine. But it's not for me. I may be a stripper, but I am not selling my body. I draw the line at that.

Quickly checking that my makeup is in place, I straighten my spine and make my way to room twelve. I feel a sense of déjà vu as anticipation runs through me at who I might find behind the door. On the one hand, I hope it's the guy from last night, but on the other, I hope it's not. Because that means I've caught his attention. And I don't need anyone's attention on me right now.

Pushing through the door, I step through, only to stop when I find him sitting in the same position, thumb running across his bottom lip, eyes on me. I shudder at the intensity he exudes and almost run back the way I came. But then I remember I need this job and being in here for an hour means extra money.

"Hey," I chirp confidently as I make my way inside the dimly lit room. When he doesn't reply, I shake my head and move to the corner where the music sits. I go to hit play, guessing he wants the same as last night. But then he speaks.

"Don't." The command in his tone makes me pause.

Spinning, I face him, and suddenly I feel very insecure under his attention. I'm wearing lingerie, but I may as well be naked with the way his hungry eyes devour me.

"What do you want tonight?" I ask, confused.

He stares at me for a long beat before pushing out of his chair. My eyes widen as he stalks towards me, and panic takes hold. My eyes dart to the cameras in the room, praying that whoever is in security sees this and rescues me. "Stop," I blurt. "You can't touch me. It's not allowed. I don't do extra."

He pauses a step away from me and frowns. His head cocks to the side as his eyes drill into me. Letting out an amused breath, he says. "I'm not going to hurt you, angel. I just don't want you to dance tonight."

It's my turn to frown. "Then what do you want with me?"

He smirks. "I just want to talk."

Shaking my head, I shuffle sideways towards the door. No man ever just wants to talk. There is always an ulterior motive, and I'm not about to wait around to find out what his is. No matter how gorgeous he is.

My eyes snap to his, and I stop when his deep drawl shatters the silence. "Please. I don't beg Crystal, but I'm willing to beg you. Just give me an hour of your time. I paid good money for that hour, and I will pay more if that's what it takes to get you to stay." The plea in his tone gives me pause.

"Why do you want to talk to me? You don't even know me," I murmur.

He smiles. "Exactly. I want to get to know you."

My brows furrow in confusion. It doesn't make sense. "Look, you seem like a nice guy and not some weird, hot serial killer." He smirks, no doubt at the fact I called him hot. "I just don't understand why someone that looks like you," I wave my hand at him as if to prove a point. "Is paying *me* to talk to them. You probably have women throwing themselves at you, so why are you here wasting money on me?"

He steps closer, his hand comes up and a finger runs down my cheek, making me flinch. He frowns, softly stroking me. I shiver at his touch, my body coming alive at just that small contact. He knows it, too, if his smug grin is anything to go by. "You're right, women do throw themselves at me. But it's you that I am captivated by. One look at you on that stage last night, and I knew I had to know you."

I suck in a breath. What the hell? Is this for real? The words are out before I can stop myself. "Why me?"

He shrugs. "Why not you?"

I chew my bottom lip in contemplation, but I know my mind is made up. "Okay," I blurt.

His lips curve into a triumphant smile. He steps away from me, his hand dropping from my cheek. The loss of contact makes me feel empty. With that thought, I know I should walk away, I don't need any distractions. Especially not the male kind. Before I have the chance to change my mind, his hand connects with my lower back, and he pushes me towards the sofa that sits to the right of the stage.

Dropping down, I shift until I am against the arm, making

sure to put space between us. He notices but doesn't make any move to close the distance. Instead, he reaches to the ice bucket beside him and pulls out two bottles of water, handing one to me.

"Thank you," I mumble.

Nodding, he leans back to get comfortable, those piercing eyes never leaving me. I twist the cap on the bottle and take a long sip, trying to wet my now dry throat. The atmosphere in here is almost stifling, suffocating me as I wait for him to speak.

"What's your name?" he repeats his question from last night, but I won't give in and tell him. Rule number one: don't reveal your identity. I don't need anyone finding out who I really am.

"Crystal." I give him the same answer as before.

With a shake of his head, he smiles. "Your *real* name."

"No," I snap, my eyes narrowing in on him, daring him to argue.

"Fine, I will leave that question for now, *Crystal,* but mark my words, you will tell me. Now, how old are you?"

I scoff at his arrogance. "None of your damn business. What is this? An interrogation?"

He growls, making my spine stiffen. As if sensing that I've tensed, he softens his features. "I just want to know you." His voice is soft, making me relax some.

"Twenty-one." The lie rolls from my mouth easily.

He nods. "Now, what is a girl like you doing in a place like this?"

I groan as I rub at my tired eyes. I've had this question asked a couple of times. People don't seem to understand that when you're desperate, you will do almost anything. "I need to eat, pay my bills. It pays better than working in a diner or a grocery store."

He seems to mull over my words for a long beat before speaking again. "Did you not go to school?"

My heart pounds in my chest as my whole body turns rigid with his question. It's a basic question, sure, but one I could easily trip up on if I don't think carefully. "Of course, I did. I just didn't have the money to go to college. That's why I'm here. I applied for community college and figured I could make good money here while studying."

His thumb runs across his full bottom lip, drawing my attention. I lick my lips at the thought of him kissing me, of those lips running over my body, and I shiver. "Mmm," he hums, and I bring my eyes back to his. My cheeks heat as he smirks, and I drop my eyes to the couch. We sit in silence for a while which makes me anxious. Is this all he really wants? To talk? It seems weird to me, if so.

"What are you going to study at college?" he asks, breaking the quiet.

I shrug. "I'm not sure. Maybe something like business or accounting."

"But that's not what you want to do, right?" Jesus this man is intuitive. "I mean it seems such a boring, mundane choice for a girl that could have anything she wants."

I snort. Does he really believe that? I am not a girl that can have anything she wants. I'm a girl struggling to make ends meet. A girl that would love nothing more than to be a professional artist but knows, deep down, it's a pipe dream, and I'm better off sticking with the *boring* and *mundane,* as he put it. "What's your name? And what do you do?" I ask, ignoring what he said. The question reminds me that I know nothing about this man and that maybe I should have asked his name when he was pushing to know mine.

He smiles like he was waiting for me to ask. "I'm a teacher… amongst other things. And my name is Asher."

Dancing In Sin

The name somehow suits him, but as for being a teacher, I can't see that. He's just too hot. I briefly wonder what school he teaches at but push that aside for now. "Asher?" I repeat his name in a whisper, tasting it on my tongue.

His eyes squeeze shut, and I swear he groans a little before they snap open. "Now, what's your name?"

I push off the couch with a smile, and stride to the door, pulling it open in the next second. "Crystal," I say before I walk out.

Sweet Temptation

Eden: They say a moment can change your life.

I shouldn't want him. But I do.
I should stay away. But I can't.
He's off-limits.
But that won't stop me.
After all, rules are meant to be broken.

Nate: They say a moment can change your life.

I shouldn't want her. But I do.
I should stay away. But I can't.
She's forbidden. Off-limits.
A sweet temptation, one I should never have.
But that won't stop me.
After all, rules are meant to be broken.

Prologue

Eden – Age 14

I shove the key in my front door, wondering what state I will find my mom in today. Yesterday was a bad day when I got home....... I found her passed out on the kitchen floor surrounded by empty liquor bottles and Xanax.

Please be okay today, Momma, please, I chant over and over in my head. I take a deep breath and push the door open, stepping in I call out to her, "Mom?" No reply. "Mom?" I call again while still chanting a silent prayer in my head.

I check the kitchen first, there is no sign of her. I head back toward the entryway calling out for her. "Mom!" I call again, the worry in my voice evident. Still, I get no reply. My pulse picks up as I start to panic, my heart beats against my ribs as I make my way to the living room. I freeze just inside the door, scrunching my nose up in disgust. The smell hits me first... vomit.

Tears prick my eyes as my gaze lands on my mom, laid out

on the couch, an empty vodka bottle beside her. I rush to her prone form - avoiding the puddle of vomit by the couch - relaxing a little when I see her chest rising and falling. *At least she isn't dead—this time.* I think to myself bitterly. Grabbing her hand, I gently shake her.

"Mom. Mom. Mom." I repeat. She doesn't respond, too passed out from the liquor and God knows whatever else she took. I shake my head.

I shouldn't have to deal with this at fourteen years old, but I do. Living with an addict for a parent, I've had to grow up quickly. To be there for my mom. When I look at other kids my age, I see the difference between me and them. But scenes like this have become a regular occurrence over the last few years.

Ever since my *father* left, I have had to step up. I hate *him*. I hate that he just left us. Left me. He gave up on us for a younger woman, moved to another state. I resent *him* for leaving me to clear up the mess he created. I resent my mom for not being stronger. For constantly putting me through this. I resent her for losing her nursing job due to addiction. Leaving us to depend on the monthly maintenance *checks he* sends. Fortunately, our two-bedroom house on the outskirts of Seattle is paid off, otherwise that would have been another thing to worry about. Although it's small, it suits us just fine and is in a nice neighborhood.

Mom stirs, dragging me out of my thoughts.

"Honey is that you?" she croaks, her voice barely audible, weak like the person she's become. I hate that she has made me feel so bitter towards her. I shouldn't blame her. She was so in love with my dad. That all-consuming type love. He was her life. Then one day he decided he didn't love her anymore, Leaving mom heartbroken.

Anger courses through me at the thought, I take a deep breath to calm myself. "Yeah, Mom, it's me. Let's get you a shower, then into bed." She mumbles something unintelligible, as I help her sit up. It takes her a few seconds to steady her swaying body as I hold her. She opens her eyes, tears fall from them, down her face, my chest tightens at the sight.

"I'm sorry for being this way, baby." she sobs, and it breaks another little piece of me, making me feel guilty for my earlier thoughts. I rub her back in a soothing motion, trying to calm her.

"Ssshhh, it's okay, Momma. Everything will be okay." But even as I say the words, I know I am lying to myself. Things have not been okay for a long time now and I cannot see that changing.

My cell vibrates in my pocket. Pulling my hand from my mom's back, I fish it out. My best friend Piper's name flashes on the screen—she is the only person who knows what I am going through with my mom. The only person who knows everything and I have for support. I don't think I would have been able to cope if it weren't for her. I decline the call, dropping my cell on the coffee table and make a mental note to call her later.

"Come on, let's get you cleaned up." I pull her to a stand, holding her fragile, unstable body as if she is going to break. Tears prick my eyes thinking about who my mom once was. She was beautiful - still is in a broken way.

Back when she was eighteen, she became Miss California, had everything going for her. But ever *since he* left....... Well let's just say, there is barely anything left of her, thanks to the alcohol and pills. Her appearance is haggard, skin sallow, hair brittle and unkempt.

I clench my jaw in frustration. I wish she would get better; wish she would realize that *he* is not worth all this. More than anything I wish she could be there for me in the way she is supposed to. Glancing at my broken mom, I instantly hate my selfish thoughts. But then I remember it's my truth and sometimes the truth is ugly.

A few minutes later, I manage to get her up the stairs and in the bathroom. I'm not a big girl by any means, but mom is now pretty much skin and bones, so I don't struggle to much getting her up the stairs. I strip her out of her clothes while she drunkenly mumbles - bits I hear, bits I miss- but what I do hear has my blood boiling.

"I will get better, honey. It's just hard right now with your dad leaving," she slurs the same thing she tells me every time this happens. I resist shouting at her, but all I want to do is scream *that he* has been gone for two years, and she is worse. Not better. It wouldn't do me any good though, so I leave it.

Twenty minutes later, I have her showered, changed and in her bed. She passes out as soon as I lay her down. I sigh as I leave her room, exhausted and hungry. Heading downstairs, I tidy up the mess my mother left behind. If I didn't, it would be left, and I refuse to live in a shit hole.

After I finish the cleaning, I search through the cupboards, finding some ramen noodles for my dinner, which I quickly prepare and eat. I will need to go shopping tomorrow, get some decent food in but for now these will have to do.

When I'm done, I make my way to my room. Hopping on my bed, I lay down and stare at the ceiling. Thoughts race through my mind. How did we get here? Why did he leave? Were we not good enough? It's a vicious cycle. One that's left me with an addict mother who cannot let go of a man who no longer wants her.

My thoughts drift to *him*. He was a good father up until he left. We were a family. A happy one at that. I was a bit of a daddy's girl. Mom worked shifts at the hospital, so my time was spent with my father. When I told him I wanted to dance, *He* was the one who found me a dance school and took me to classes. When I knew I loved cupcakes, *He* would make sure we had them every Friday.

And now? Now, I cannot remember the last *time he* called

to check in on me. *He* thinks sending a monthly check is enough, thinks by doing that it makes him a father. I wonder *how he* would feel if he knew how things had turned out, knew I was failing school. Would he come back and help?

I snort bitterly. He can't even call because he is too busy, so I doubt he gives a second thought about me or my life. *He* is too caught up in his trophy girlfriend, his new life in California.

A stray tear rolls down my cheek. I swipe at it furiously. *He* doesn't deserve my tears. Closing my eyes, I pray.

Pray for the day things change, for mom to get better and for that day to come sooner rather than later.

Eden – Age 18

So much for praying for things to get better.
 To say things got worse would be an understatement. And now I am alone in a bar, doing the one thing I swore I wouldn't do. Getting drunk. I sit glaring at my drink as anger from the whole situation threatens to consume me. A laugh bubbles out of me, but its humorless. I pick up my drink, necking the entire thing just to help me forget.

I glance around taking in my surroundings. The bar is chic, it overlooks the pretty California beaches and Pacific Ocean. Any other time, I would appreciate the beauty of this spot, but as I sit here, underage with my fake ID, I can't help but hate the place. Hate Orange County and that I was forced to come here.

I don't usually drink. Have never been drunk. But I was now on my third vodka cranberry, and I didn't even care. Today I need it. Need to forget all the shit, the life I left behind and everything I have known for the last eighteen years. There is a silver lining though, one that makes it a bit easier to relocate. My best friend Piper accepted into Beaumont College, and would be living only an hour away.

My mom was a good mom, once upon a time. Before my

father left and everything went to shit, at least. Ironically, he is no longer with the women he left mom for. Traded her in for an *even* younger model. I would laugh at what a living, breathing cliché the man is if he hadn't turned my world upside down.

He decided to come visit me for the first time in six years. Visit is a little farfetched. What *he* came for was to announce his engagement to a woman he had been dating for the last eight months. I say woman, but she is closer to my age than his.

During his visit, he found out I wouldn't be graduating high school. He wasn't happy.

You see, dear old Dad is the Dean of a prestigious private high school in California. The embarrassment of people finding out his only daughter would not be getting her high school diploma is something he didn't want to suffer. It took him all of a few hours to realize something was up and a few minutes to start throwing his weight around. I frown as I replay his words from that day in my head.

"Jesus, Eden, why didn't you tell me it had gotten this bad? She is not capable of looking after herself, let alone you," he had boomed. *"And to let you miss so much school. What about college? It won't be an option without a high school diploma? I'm so angry. It is preposterous. Humiliating."* I had let out a humorless laugh at his audacity and then let loose.

"If you actually checked in more than once every couple of years, then maybe I would have been able to talk to you. You left us. We are fine without you. I can take care of the both of us just fine." I screamed back at him.

"Like hell you can." was his response.

After calming down, we all talked. For the first time in six years, all of us sat down and spoke. He wanted mom to attend rehab and would pay for it on the condition I would agree to attend his school to repeat my senior year. I laughed at his ulterior motive. Daddy dearest would never do anything out of the goodness of his heart. Even for his daughter. My traitorous mother was quick to agree to this, much to my annoyance.

Now mom is in a rehab facility in Arizona, to complete a three-month treatment program. And me? I'm in sunny Orange County living with *daddy* and his real-life real housewife, about to repeat my senior year at Regis Saints Academy.

I have done my research on the place. From what I can tell, it is a place for trust-fund brats. Spoiled kids who thought they were special with their designer outfits and latest gadgets that had probably never known hardship. Maybe I was being judgmental, and these kids would be different, but I am bitter and angry about my whole situation. I just need to focus on why I am doing this. Mom is finally getting the help she needs. I can do this. For her. It can't be that hard, can it?

I am basically living the real OC life. With the big mansion, the step ford looking wives and the rich men. Declan earns good money as the Dean of Regis Saints, but it's not what made him rich. No. That is the app he designed and developed for use in schools and sold for millions.

Honestly, as much as it pains me to admit this, I have seen it and even used it. Its good. I asked him why he continued his work at Regis Saints when he obviously didn't have to. His response?

"*Work is in our blood, Eden, whether I have ten-thousand dollars, or ten-million dollars, it doesn't matter, I will still work.*"

I didn't know what to say to that, so I said nothing. His young, gold-digging fiancée doesn't work. Eyeroll. So, I guess she does enough *not working* for both of them. I am only going off what I have seen but it is obvious why she is with him, he isn't a bad looking man by any means, but he must be twenty years older than her.

A deep, sexy, masculine voice pulls me from my thoughts, sending a shiver up my spine.

"You look like you could use another drink?"

My head whips round, eyes connecting with his face, they widen before all the air leaves my lungs. I have never seen such a beautiful looking man in my life. I blink to make sure he is real and not an apparition I have conjured up in my drunk mind. Yep, still there. As if he can read my thoughts, he flashes me a smirk. A smirk so sexy, I swallow just to wet my dry mouth. My eyes rake over his face shamelessly, drinking in every inch of him. He looks like a god. Face chiseled and defined. Sparkling emerald, green eyes full of mischief. Tousled dark hair that is begging to have my hands run through it. My gaze drops down his body, mouthwatering at what I find. He wears a simple black t-shirt that showcases every bit of muscle, although they are covered, I can see the outline of his abs. I count them in my head. One, two, three, four.... is that an eight pack? I think it is.

My eyes drop further south of their own volition. He wears navy khakis which showcases the prominent bulge. His cock. I gulp. I may not have much experience with men but even through his pants I can tell he is big. My gaze snaps up when a throat clears. When I find the sexy strangers' eyes on me, my cheeks heat in embarrassment. His lips curve, eyes sparkle with amusement. I glare before turning my gaze on my empty glass. Bastard knows I was checking him out. His arm brushes mine as he takes a seat on the stool beside me. My eyes flick back to him, he raises an expectant brow and I realize I haven't yet spoken.

"What makes you say that?"

He smiles knowingly. "Because you look how I feel." He signals the bartender with a wave of his hand. Do I look that bad?

I know I'm attractive and that's not me being conceited; I have been told enough times. I was even model scouted last year at my local mall in Seattle but never pursued it. With my dancer's legs, long blond hair, and blue eyes. I can easily be mistake for your typical Californian girl. I got mom's looks and *his* eyes. For a long time, I hated looking in the mirror and seeing *him* staring back at me.

My eyes dart to the mirror behind the bar where I slyly check myself out. I internally scold myself at the sight that stares back at me. Messy hair, face free of make-up. As for my outfit? I glance down at my ripped denim shorts, black tank top, and Chucks. I never usually care what I look like but right now I do, especially when I look at the man beside me. All attractive, nicely dressed, and put together.

"So, what can I get you to drink?" he asks, flashing his perfect white teeth.

I turn my whole body to face him, ready to decline his offer.

"Look, I'm sure you are a really nice guy. But I am not really in the mood to be hit on, and I am not a one-night type of girl… so you can leave." I turn back to face my empty glass, hoping he will get the message. As hot as he is, I don't need any distractions. I just need to finish my senior year and get the hell out of Orange County.

"Tell me," He drawls so sexy it makes my core clench. That's new. I turn to face him again, this time with a cocked brow urging him to speak. "How is a woman who looks like you……" he trails off, his lips twisting as if he is searching for the right words. He clears his throat. "I mean, you are exquisitely beautiful, but I'm sure you know that." He pauses waiting for my reaction. I don't give him one. "Anyway, why are you on your own? Looking like the world has ended? A girl as pretty as you should never be without a smile." My heart flutters at his compliment, but I still don't give in. Like I said, I don't need the distraction, no matter how hot he is.

"Look, you can probably have any woman in this place. Probably most of the men too," I add, with a wave of my arms. "Why don't you go and hit on someone you actually have a chance with? An easy fuck which is more than likely what you are looking for. I'm not that girl, you are wasting your time. I just want to sit and drink in peace." His eyes narrow before his lips tip up in breathtaking smile, that leaves me momentarily stunned. There are no words to explain how attractive this man is.

"Beautiful and funny…just my type," He smirks, leaning in so close his hot breath fans my face. My breath hitches at his close proximity. "You're right. I could probably have any woman in here. It's not like I didn't notice the come fuck me eyes when I walked in. I don't do desperate. I can smell their desperation from here," A snort bursts from me on its own volition. Jesus, he may be gorgeous, but he's an arrogant bastard. "But you? You didn't so much as look at me until I approached you. Even then you barely spared me a glance," His emerald eyes bore into me making me squirm in my seat. Noticing he smirks. "I do like a challenge. I think I will take my chances and join you." He finishes, leaning back in his stool getting comfortable, he shoots me a wink. I roll my eyes, acting nonchalant even though I can feel my arousal in my panties. They are embarrassingly wet; I was sure by the time I leave here my shorts will be too. Not that I will ever admit it…something tells me this man doesn't need anything else to inflate his already oversized ego.

I eye him. Feeling confident, I cock my head with a smirk. "Beautiful, huh? Quite the charmer, aren't you?" He flashes an arrogant smirk not deterred by my words. "Maybe if I were a few more drinks in, I would have fallen for what I am sure is normally a bulletproof way to get a woman into bed. Unfortunately for you, I'm not. And I definitely will not fall for a little line like calling me beautiful." I shoot him condescending wink. He eyes me a beat before his head falls back on a laugh. I stare at him as he chuckles. If I wasn't so angry right now, I would probably enjoy his attention.

Dancing In Sin

His eyes meet mine as his tongue traces his full bottom lip. My eyes dart to the movement, watching as he wets the perfect plump flesh. "Pessimism doesn't suit such a beautiful face." I groan as the bartender hands us our drinks – the green-eyed stranger sliding him some bills across the bar in return. He turns with a sigh. "Look, we obviously got off on the wrong foot. You probably get hit all the time and by the look on your face, it is the last thing you want. So, let's cut the shit and start over. I'm Nate." He thrusts his hand out for me to take. "I can leave you be, if that's what you really want? I just don't want to sit alone. And as much as you probably don't think you want it; something tells me you could use the company. What's your name, Blondie?"

A smile tugs at my lips. He is right. I was used to being hit on. Half the male population at my school in Seattle had hit on me to no avail. The boys I went to school with, they were immature, their sole purpose in life was to see how many girls they could sleep with by graduation. I wasn't going to be another notch on some boy's bedpost, so I steered clear, earning me the nickname 'Pruden'—a mix of prudish and Eden. They thought they were clever. I didn't care. When they eventually realized they wouldn't get anywhere with me they stayed away.

I take a sip of my drink before taking Nate's hand with a smile. "Eden. I apologize for being a bitch. It's been a bad day." He grins with a nod of his head.

"I know that feeling," His jaw ticks, a dark look in his eyes. "I just found out my ex of six years is engaged to the guy she cheated on me with." My mouth gapes in disbelief that anyone would want to cheat on him, before I let out a low whistle

"And I thought I was having a bad day. You definitely win."

He shrugs, waving me off. "Yeah, it was a shock for sure. But they are welcome to each other." He dismisses it like it isn't a big deal, but I don't miss the anger flashing in his eyes. "So, what happened to you? Boyfriend? Ex-boyfriend?" He licks his lips as his eyes rake over me, his gaze scorching my skin in ways I didn't know could happen. "Nah, not an ex. I can't imagine any guy lucky enough to have you would ever leave you. And if he did, he is an idiot." A laugh bubbles out of me and I shake my head in amusement.

"You can't help yourself, can you?"

He chuckles. "Not when there is a gorgeous lady involved. Sorry." He smiles sheepishly. "So, what is it, then? What is so bad?"

I eye him, debating what to tell this man. I can't say too much about my situation because it will give away my age. And since I am underage...with a fake ID...drinking in a bar, I don't need trouble, so I keep it simple. "It's just family stuff. Asshole fathers." I grumble.

Nate searches my face, over the top of his beer. Obviously noticing a shift in my mood, the tension in my body, he smiles. "How about we leave the deep stuff?"

I chuckle, feeling my body relax. "That's the best thing you have said since you walked in here."

He shifts his whole body to face me, caging me in with his muscular legs. His green eyes lock onto my blues as he leans into me. My pulse speeds up, breath hitching at his nearness. His throat bobs as he swallows his beer, my eyes track the movement. I want to run my tongue up and down his strong throat, taste him. As if sensing my thoughts, he smirks knowingly. I give my head an almost imperceptible shake, needing to gain some self-control.

"Tell me about yourself Eden? What do you do? How old are you?" he asks.

Again, I need to keep the answer simple, I will never see this guy again; he doesn't need to know I am repeating my senior year at high school, that I am only eighteen, in here with a fake ID. "I graduated in June. Twenty-one. What about you?"

An emotion flashes in his eyes, but before I get a chance to decipher it, he smiles, but this time it doesn't quite reach his eyes. "Twenty-eight and I'm an app and software developer." I freeze, not at his age but his job. What are the chances? He is in the same line of work as Declan. I'm not about to talk about *him* though so instead, I blurt.

"You are way too hot to be a techy guy."

He laughs, heartily before gently nudging my shoulder. "Now look who's flirting."

I shrug. "I doubt you are unaware of how attractive you are. Your ego is so big, I'm surprised you could get through the entrance." I jerk my head towards said entrance.

He chuckles harder. "I like you, Eden. Straight to the point, real, don't apologize for who you are. It's rare in people nowadays. Especially for people in Orange County." I bite my bottom lip; his eyes narrow in on the movement. Warmth spreads through my body, my stomach swirling in excitement. This reaction is foreign to me. I have never felt like this with a guy before. Ever.

Nate shifts his stool closer. I take a deep breath, his masculine scent invading all my senses, making me feel dizzy. "Do you live round here, Eden?"

"I do. For now," I croak out. He moves in closer - leaving hardly anything between us -his big body dwarfing mine. His hand drops to my bare thigh, my skin prickles when he draws small circles on my skin.

"Are you cold, Eden?" He asks huskily, his hot, minty breath fanning across my face. I swallow, shaking my head. He smiles. "You know. I've never done this sort of thing before," My brows furrow in confusion. "Never hit on a woman, I mean. I've never had too. I know I sound egotistical but it's the truth. They usually come to me," He shrugs, "But you? There is something about you, you're different."

I roll my eyes, even though his words are doing things to me. Mainly soaking my panties. "Another one of your pickup lines, Nate?"

"Nope. Just the truth. You can't tell me you don't feel this connection between us? Its electric." I search his face, only finding truth in his words. My gaze drops to my lap. He is right, there is a pull between us. I startle when his thick fingers grip my chin, lifting till I meet his eyes. The intensity in his has my breath hitching. "I want to see your gorgeous face." He slowly moves closer, so close his lips ghost mine. "I know you don't know me, and I don't know you. But I think you're really fucking sexy. I have never wanted to kiss anyone as bad as I want to kiss you. And as much as you think you don't want this..." His hand on my thigh moves higher, "I can tell you do. Your body gives you away. I can smell your arousal from here." He growls.

I pull my chin out of his grip, as my eyes widen in embarrassment. Can he smell my wet panties? Jesus, right now I wish I hadn't been a Pruden. I wish I were more experienced to deal with a guy like him. He raises a brow, daring me to deny what we both know to be the truth. He is turning me on. He knows it. I know it. I stare at him, neither confirming nor denying his accusation so he continues. "I can tell by your erratic breathing. The way goosebumps coat your soft skin. You're not cold, Eden. Your turned on," He winks smugly. "I have a talent for reading women." I clench my thighs at his words, my panties getting even wetter. I don't even want to think about the puddle I will be leaving on this stool.

I have kissed boys before, but they were just that. Boys. Nate is all man. I'm not experienced like other girls my age. I am still a virgin at eighteen. But somehow, I have gone from not wanting him to hit on me to wanting to do very naughty things with him. A stranger. I want his hand to travel higher, I want him to feel my wet panties. Hell, at this point I am about ready to let him take my virginity on this bar. I inwardly chuckle at the situation. Maybe I should do something for me. To be irresponsible. To fuck someone, I have only just met.

My tongue darts out to wet my dry lips. Nate's eyes follow the movement. I lean in, my lips resting against his. I can taste the beer. Taste the man. "And maybe I have a talent for reading assholes." I pull back, smirking with a wink.

He barks out a laugh, the sound going straight between my legs, "Touché, Eden. But don't kid yourself, you could cut the sexual tension with a knife right now." I snicker. He is right, you can. It would be so easy to lose myself in him right now. Maybe I should? I do want to forget, after all and something tells me Nate could make me forget everything.

My cell buzzes breaking me from my thoughts. I snatch it off the bar, groaning at the name on the screen. A message from Declan, demanding I get home now. I furiously type a message back before pulling up my Uber app.

"Everything okay?" Nate asks. I click on my ride and push my cell into my shorts pocket before turning to Nate.

"Yeah, I gotta get back. Family stuff." I shrug. Pushing to a stand, I get ready to make my exit. "Thanks for the drink Nate." I don't give him a chance to respond, turning on my heel, I make my way to the door. Just as I step outside, a big hand wraps around my elbow. I turn, jaw clenched - ready to shout at whoever dared to touch me - when my eyes lock with emerald ones that have somehow become familiar.

"At least let me wait with you. It's getting dark, you don't know what weirdos are about," Nate rasps.

I cock a brow. "You mean apart from you?"

He chuckles, shaking his head as he leads me to the sidewalk. After a long beat of silence, Nate speaks. "I know I said I wouldn't hit on you, but can I at least get your number?" I look up at him with a smirk.

"Your tenacity is admirable Nate."

He smiles, something that looks a lot like determination flashes in his eyes. Grabbing my hand, he pulls me towards the alley at the side of the building. I should be afraid. Should scream for help. But I don't do any of that as excitement course through me. "Where are we going?" He doesn't answer but flashes me a smile. Coming to an abrupt stop, he backs me up until my back hits the wall, his big arms caging me in.

"Tell me to stop if you don't want me to kiss you?" he whispers, searching my face. My head spins, this is all happening so fast. But as I look at him, I know I don't want him to stop. I want him to kiss me.

Before I can stop myself; I wrap my arms around his neck, yanking his head down to me. His lips crash on mine, taking my breath away. In this moment, with his mouth on mine, my whole-body sparks alive in a way it has never before. Nothing has ever felt so freeing as his mouth on mine. I never want it to stop. Nate devours my mouth like a starved man, finally having a meal. His tongue darts out, seeking entrance to my mouth. I give it him, moaning when his hot tongue meets mine. His hands move down my legs, wrapping round my thighs as he lifts me like I weigh nothing.

My eyes fly open as I feel his dick harden. It only takes seconds before I am grinding against the hard length, losing all my inhibitions. Who am I right now? This isn't me. I moan, at the feel of him and briefly wonder how he would feel inside me. I internally roll my eyes; I might be acting completely different to usual but it's not like I'm actually going to fuck him against this wall. He groans as his hand snakes between us. Through the fabric of my denim shorts he rubs my swollen clit. The feel of his hand there and the material rubbing against me has me gasping. Shit, if he keeps this up maybe I am going to fuck him against this wall.

Shaking the thoughts away. I push into his hand, chasing the friction I desperately need. He chuckles against my mouth, the sound vibrating through my body, shooting straight to my pussy. My orgasm builds, taking me higher and higher only to disappear when Nate pulls his hand and lips away. Frustration courses through me as I pant, trying to catch my breath, He smirks before his lips move to my neck, kissing and nibbling the sensitive flesh.

"You are so fucking sexy, Eden," he murmurs thickly, causing me to shiver. His hand comes up, unhooking my arms. Never breaking eye contact, he guides my hand down to the hardness in his pants. "Look what you have done to me. I'm so fucking hard for you." My eyes widen, he isn't lying. He is rock hard, and big. Very fucking big.

Dropping my hand, I slide down his body, a moan escapes as I graze his hard cock. I clear my throat. "My ride will be here," I chew on my lip, realization setting in at what I have just done. His eyes search mine.

"At least let me get your number?" he rasps; his tone almost pleading.

I smile, I shouldn't give it to him, but I want to. "Sure, why not?"

He grins, pulling his cell out of his pocket. He hands it to me, my thumbs race across the screen as I input my number before handing it back. Seconds later my cell buzzes in my pocket. I fish it out, frowning when a number a don't recognize flashes on the screen. I look to Nate who smirks back at me.

"Just making sure you didn't give me a random number." I roll my eyes before starting back to the main sidewalk. Feeling confident, I spin.

"I would never do that to someone who kisses as good as you." I wink.

An arrogant smirk spreads across his face, "If you think that was good, just you wait till I get you in my bed." The confidence in his voice has my cheeks heating. I have no doubt this man, knows how to please a woman. "Don't worry, Eden. I assure you will enjoy every second of it." I shake my head before spinning on my heel and rushing to my Uber which is now waiting. Jumping in the back seat, I pull the door only to find it won't move. My gaze snaps up to find Nate holding it. He crouches so he is eye level with me. My pulse races up as he moves in and kisses my cheek. I squeeze my eyes shut as my skin tingles from his touch.

"'Night, Eden." he whispers seductively.

"Night, Nate." I croak in a voice I don't recognize. His eyes flash triumphantly. Like he knows something I don't. Pushing to a stand, he gently closes the door. The car peels away, I fall against the seat, releasing a harsh breath. I know full well nothing good can come from seeing him again. I lied to him. About my age. About college. I should block his number. But even as the thought passes, I know I won't. I want him. And I have never wanted a man.

I don't need the distraction, but if I am going to have one, Nate will be the perfect one.

Printed in Great Britain
by Amazon